D1250461

Black
Lab Press

Chalet *on* Cliffside Drive

AN *Emerald Cove* NOVEL

LILLY MIRREN

WELCOME TO EMERALD COVE

Read the series in order...

CHAPTER 1

BEN

*W*ith a backward glance over his shoulder, Ben Silver pushed his bicycle forward and began to pedal. He tucked his head down against the coastal breeze and let the bike glide down the hill to the main road. Squinting behind his sunglasses, he studied the road for traffic, then pulled onto it with a sharp turn and pumped his legs hard, the bike flying as he headed for the beach.

It'd become a favourite part of his daily routine, swimming laps in the ocean. Only, they weren't laps in the typical fashion, since all he did was swim from one end of the bay to the other and back again to where he left his bike propped up against the log fence that guarded the dunes.

It'd been four months since he moved to Emerald Cove, and he was finally feeling settled. He still hadn't met a lot of new people, but that wasn't the fault of the

Cove's friendly residents. More the fact that he was a natural introvert and he worked from home. The IT company he worked for allowed him to travel to their head office in Brisbane once per week for the team meeting, but otherwise he lived and worked in the tiny beachside hamlet—which meant that he only went out into the community to shop, something which wasn't a favourite pastime of his, or to swim solitary laps in the town's picturesque cove.

The last time he'd spoken to his elderly parents on the phone, they'd encouraged him to join some community groups, to get out and mingle. But the thought set nerves jingling in his belly. He wasn't exactly sure how to socialise without it being forced and awkward and about a hundred other nerve-wracking things that meant he still hadn't done it and wasn't likely to anytime soon.

He was good at living in his own world, doing the routine things that made up each day. He wasn't good at stepping out of his comfort zone and meeting new people. Thankfully, he'd gotten to know his biological parents, Diana and Andy, reasonably well in the time he'd lived in the Cove. As well as his cousin, Emily, who'd gone out of her way to make sure he visited her bed and breakfast once per week for morning tea. He was grateful for the effort his family members had made to spend time with him, but after four months he knew it was time he put himself out there, network with some people he wasn't related to—perhaps even single women. Although he couldn't imagine there were many his age in Emerald Cove.

The tiny beachside village stretched out before him as he rounded the corner onto the main drag, past the regal old tree with the timber still raw where half of it had tumbled to the ground, crushing the front of the Food Store in the recent cyclone. Workers on ladders with paint brushes in hand put finishing touches on the new white and red entryway to the shop. He looked forward to its reopening—driving to Tweed Heads for groceries every week was putting everyone in a temper, especially since they had to deal with the traffic. As Marg reminded him every time she ran into him, as she leaned on her crutches with a pained expression, one of the reasons she'd moved back to the Cove after uni in the first place was so she could get away from that darned traffic.

He pulled his bike onto the footpath, slowing to a stop before he reached the sand. Then, leaned it in its usual spot against the railing and removed his helmet as he studied the ocean. The angry froth and peaks of the cyclone had been replaced by the Cove's usual sparkling azure waters and lazy, curling waves. The debris that'd been scattered across the sand was mostly gone now, after a community wide working bee a couple of weeks earlier. The golden sand sparkled beneath the warm, afternoon sunshine.

The sun was lower in the sky than he would've liked. Usually, he swam laps in the morning before work, but today he'd had an early video conference, so had postponed it until the afternoon. Although, he hadn't realised how late it'd gotten. He'd be lucky if he managed to get back before dusk, with the way things were going. A few families still played on the beach. Children ran and squealed at the edge of the surf. Joggers trundled along the hard-packed sand with rhythmic steps. And two Surf Life Savers slowly packed away the flags and other equipment they'd used to monitor the beachgoers throughout the day. He'd have to hurry —it was getting late.

He changed into his wetsuit under a towel wrapped tight around his waist as quickly as he could manage, then settled his sunglasses inside the bike helmet and hung it by the chin strap around the handlebars. As he jogged through the sand towards the water, he prepared his body mentally for the jolt of cold. It was still something he hadn't quite adjusted to, after living in the warmer northern Queensland for so many years —that sudden dive into the crisp water, the gasp that tried to push its way from his mouth with bubbles that climbed to the surface above him as he kicked through a wave.

"Hey, Ben!" called a voice.

He turned to find Mick McIntosh striding towards him, wetsuit peeled to his waist, surfboard hung beneath one tanned, muscular arm.

"I thought that was you." Mick grinned, holding out a hand for Ben to shake.

"How's it going?" asked Ben, shaking Mick's hand.

"Good. Just coming in from a surf. The waves are a bit slack today."

"Nice for swimming, not so great for surfing, I guess." Ben chuckled.

He'd met Mick through Diana—at one of the regular dinner parties she'd attended and dragged him along to, at her friend Cindy Flannigan's house. There were so many people at those things, all connected somehow through marriage, blood, or friendship, he found it hard to keep track of them all. Mick was married to one of his half-sisters, Sarah.

The family ties were complicated and made his head spin. So far, he hadn't had much of a chance to get to know Sarah. He was still reeling over the idea that he had siblings after having grown up as an only child, adopted late in life by two wonderful parents. He'd always wanted a brother. He remembered crying over it when he was young and couldn't push his bike up the hill to the small, brick house where he'd lived. If only he'd had a brother, he'd sobbed to himself while regarding the blood on his gravel-grazed knees, they'd be able to push the thing up the hill together.

Still, he'd been content enough once he understood it would never happen. And now, in a strange twist of fate, it had. Not only did he have a brother, but two sisters as well. He wasn't exactly sure how to act, what to say or do. So, he waited for their lead in the matter, since they were the ones practiced in sibling relationships.

"Have a good evening, maybe I'll see you later..." he said.

Mick waved and jogged towards the end of the beach where an outcropping of black rocks lay scattered along the sand and out into the waves. A small parking lot nestled behind it, surrounded by wispy bushes and pandanus. Only a few cars remained on the lot; Ben could see Mick's truck with a ladder protruding from its bed.

Ben waded into the water, the cool of it causing him to suck in a quick breath. Then he dived beneath a wave, and emerged on the other side, energy already surging into his limbs, his body ready for the task ahead.

He swam parallel to the beach, hands slicing through the water. His body rose and fell with the passing waves, not yet broken but surging towards the sandy shore. He wore goggles to see better, without the saltwater stinging his eyes, so when a shadow rippled across the deep water beneath him, he startled and paused, his head emerging from the water. He looked around, then ducked his head beneath the surface, spinning in a circle. It was difficult to see more than a metre in front of himself, with the swirling sand filling and bubbles rising to the surface from nearby waves.

Then, something grabbed his leg. The impact shuttled him through the water, taking his breath away.

He shouted, reached out for his leg, feeling for what was there. Then he kicked with his free leg and encountered something hard. He spun about, jostled by the attacker, gasping for breath, and saw the fin, even as he kicked again, his foot impacting on a stout, slick body. The pressure on his leg released, but there was blood in the water. His blood. The pain came then, in a wave that shocked him.

He cried out again, as loudly as he could manage, "Help! Shark!"

Faint screams from the beach reached his ears.

Thoughts lay sodden in the recesses of his mind. His breathing came in quick bursts. He couldn't think of anything but getting to shore. He had to get back to the beach. The pain in his leg grew worse by the second. He pulled himself through the water with his hands, gulping in mouthfuls of water as the waves grew choppier closer to shore.

People on the beach watched him, standing still. A few ran in his direction. One leapt through the shallows with his knees pumping high.

It was Mick. Mick was coming.

He opened his mouth to speak again, but no words came out. Instead, he continued pulling, each stroke bringing him closer to shore. Salt water filled his mouth, making him cough.

Then, Mick was there, curling an arm around him.

"I'm here, mate. It's gonna be okay. Hold on, I've got you."

CHAPTER 2

VICKY

*T*he pain in her head reverberated around her skull in a dull kind of way. Vicky Hawkins knew it'd get worse if she didn't take care of herself. One of the many joys of living with lupus—something she was still growing accustomed to. She hadn't understood her symptoms for a long time, but the diagnosis helped her be more in tune with her body, giving her the warning signs she needed to prepare for a coming flare-up.

Beneath her, the palomino mare trotted with an easy gait. She broke into a canter and Vicky leaned back in the saddle to enjoy the ride, relaxing into her seat the way she'd learned during the riding lessons she'd been taking for the past few months.

"Looking good!" called Debbie, from the back of a bay gelding who cantered alongside her.

Vicky grinned, joy bringing a lump to her throat, the headache momentarily forgotten.

Riding had always been a dream of hers. As a girl growing up in a suburban brick house in Emerald Cove, she'd watched television shows and read books about girls who owned horses, attended pony club, and basically had a dream life from her perspective. But beg as she might, her parents never bought her a horse, something she understood better now she was an adult. Horses were expensive, and the land they grazed even more so. But she was a veterinarian, and an adult with very few expenses to pay for. She could afford lessons now and had bought Mindy, her mare, last week, after a month of trawling through every horse website and advertisement she could find.

Green grasses waved in the cool breeze. Storm clouds gathered behind them, darkening the landscape. The paddock undulated towards the horizon, then dipped in the distance down to the lowlands that were covered in squat shrubs, coastal gums and ended in the long, golden beaches that graced the northern New South Wales coastline and separated the land from the deep, blue Pacific Ocean. The waters sparkled beneath the burning sun, like jewels scattered across a blue silk blanket oblivious to the darkness gathering in the west.

They slowed to a trot together, then a walk. Vicky let Mindy's reins hang loose, the horse pulled on the bit, relaxed her neck, and plodded along the cattle trail they were following.

"How was that?" asked Debbie.

Vicky offered her a wide smile. "It was amazing. I'm feeling so much better in the saddle. My teeth aren't rattling out of my head…at least, not all the time anyway."

"That's great—you're looking much more comfortable."

They rode for a while along the track. Birds twittered in the trees nearby, darting and diving to catch insects as the sun inched down the sky towards the horizon. The breeze from the ocean was cool, although sweat still soaked the length of her back from the day's work outside. She'd helped a cow give birth to a calf when it got stuck in the birth canal, then she'd rescued a dog stuck in barbed wire and stitched up his torn leg. There'd been several immunisations for various animals, and the day had ended with having to put down a much beloved, twenty-year-old cat. Her least favourite part of the job.

The emotional toll of helping so many people through the loss of their pets drained her at times. Horse riding after work had helped her release some of the tension that built up as an ache in her neck and shoulders. These days it also gave her the strength she needed to better manage her lupus flare-ups—reduced her stress levels, relaxed her body, and tamed her thoughts, which all contributed to better health.

She'd use every advantage she could get. Having lupus had changed her life, made her think about things like her health, strength, and nutrition in a way she never had before. When she was sick, it made everything more difficult. The nausea, fevers, body aches and pains, not to mention the headaches. Sometimes she even had a rash. She'd honestly believed she was dying of some horrible illness until she'd gotten the results back from the doctor.

Her relief had been quickly tempered when she

realised it was an illness she'd have to live with for the rest of her days.

Still, it could be worse.

The phrase drifted through her head as the two riders turned their horses for home. She smiled to herself. That was one of her mother's favourite sayings. Going through something horrible? Never mind. It could always be worse.

She'd wondered at the time how that saying could help anyone who was in the middle of pain or hardship, but now found herself relying on it to keep her spirits up—no doubt, in the same way her mother did when she'd been sick.

"So, do you have a hot date tonight?" asked Debbie, her hazel eyes sparkling.

Vicky huffed. "Hardly. I'm probably going to fall asleep on the couch with my neighbour's cat — she visits sometimes, eats my food, then leaves."

Debbie chuckled. "Sounds about the same as my plans, only with the dog. And, of course, my husband snoring in the armchair beside me."

"Do you miss having the kids at home?" asked Vicky.

Debbie shrugged. "Yes, and no. It's nice to have our own space again. And I'm tired…" She grunted. "I'm joking… kind of."

Vicky laughed. "You've raised four children, anyone would be tired."

Debbie pushed her short brown hair back from her forehead, tucking it beneath the black helmet she wore. "I'm sure that's true. Although, if I'm being completely honest, raising kids is the best thing I've done in my life. They're expensive, and difficult, and argue far too much with me...but I love them to pieces. Do you think you'll have children?"

The question prompted a rush of panic down Vicky's spine. She'd grown accustomed to the feeling. It'd begun the day she turned thirty. From then on, whenever anyone talked about babies or children, asked her about who she was dating, if she'd ever get married or have children, the nerves down her back jangled.

"Um...of course, I'd love to. But I suppose I have to face the possibility that I might not. I mean, I'm thirty-four this year, and I don't even have a boyfriend."

Debbie smiled but stayed quiet.

Vicky understood. No one liked to talk about it. Whenever she opened up, was honest or vulnerable on the subject, everyone around her clammed up.

"The problem is, I never meet any single men. None who aren't tourists." She chuckled and shook her head.

"You're probably living in the wrong town for meeting men," offered Debbie.

"True. But I do love it here. I finally feel as though I've put down some roots, made some good friends, set up the kind of life I want...but perhaps I should think about change. My dad wants me to move to Ballina. He's got a small hobby farm just outside of town there. He's worried about me, living on my own. Which is silly really because he's on his own too. Although my sister lives nearby, so they see a lot of each other. And I am lonely sometimes..." The admission brought a lump to her throat.

"I thought you were an Emerald Cove girl?" Debbie's eyebrows furrowed.

"I am...through and through. But Dad moved to

Ballina after I left to go to university in Sydney. I was in Sydney for a few years after graduation, then came back to the Cove."

"Ah okay, that makes more sense. It must've been strange for you to come back, with your parents gone."

Vicky nodded. It'd taken her some getting used to. Every now and then she still cruised by her old childhood home by the beach to take a look. The last time she'd done it, she saw small children toddling around the yard. It'd been repainted in a light-yellow colour, instead of the horrid peach tint it'd had throughout her childhood years.

"Yeah, I wasn't too happy about them moving. But Dad got a job in Ballina, and he sold up and moved in the space of about two months. So, I really didn't get a say in the matter—besides, as he pointed out to me at the time, it's his life." She shrugged. "I'm used to it now. It's nice to be able to visit him and my sister in Ballina, but not have them living in my pocket all the time."

"So, would you consider moving so close to him?"

Vicky couldn't imagine it, but maybe she should try. Having loved ones nearby would give her a safety net. But the relationship with her dad had been strained in recent years—would moving closer help that, or only make things worse? And the source of that tension, her sister, was in Ballina too.

"I'm not sure. It could be good I suppose. Although maybe we'd clash."

"Well, it's something to think about," replied Debbie.

They rode back to the yards together and dismounted. Then they chatted about other things while they brushed the horses, hung up the tack in the tack shed and cleaned up. By the time she was done, fat raindrops fell from the sky. She ran for the car, then sat behind the steering while her vehicle was pummelled by the thundering rain.

She'd wait out the worst of it before driving back to town. While she waited, Vicky's mind stayed hung up on their earlier conversation. Her father had been pushing her to make a decision about whether to move back home, but she'd bucked against the suggestion so far. Perhaps he was right. Debbie seemed to think it was an idea worth considering. And if she never met someone to spend her life with, she should be close to family. It seemed like the best option—still, she considered the friendships she'd built in the Cove something of a family. Sarah, Meg—her two closest friends were the ones who kept her going, filled her days with fun and laughter. But they were both busier now than they'd ever been, and their trips to restaurants or the beach together had been fewer in recent months.

She hated to be alone. Had always been that way. Although, over the years she'd learned to manage the sadness that crept in whenever she felt isolated for more than a few days at a time. Animals helped, of course. Being around them brought her joy. But lately even that hadn't been enough to fill the void.

CHAPTER 3

CINDY

*H*er feet ached. Her back spasmed somewhere near the base of her spine, making her sciatic nerve twitch. And she could do with a nice, long nap. Cindy Flannigan sighed and sat in the nearest chair, pressing both hands to the small of her back. As much as she loved the Emerald Cafe, the business bequeathed to her by her parents when they died, and where she'd worked even as a girl behind the counter, or as a hostess guiding people to their tables, she knew it was time to hang up her apron.

The one thing she didn't know, was when or how she'd manage it. She didn't want the cafe to close, but that meant finding a buyer. She'd had a few offers over the years but had always turned them down since at the time she'd had the energy and needed the money to raise her family and pay the bills. Adele was in town, staying at the house for now to recover from a broken heart. She'd been an amazing help at the cafe since she got home. But it was her day off, and Cindy felt the strain.

She was in the process of downsizing her life. If she sold the cafe, the money from the sale would make a nice little nest egg for her to retire on. If she didn't sell, she supposed she could offer it to someone else to manage and live off the income the cafe produced. The nice thing was, after selling the house and downsizing, she could manage even without selling the cafe. She wouldn't be flush, but she'd have enough to get by on.

Either way, she didn't want to continue working in the cafe, spending hours every day on her feet, serving people, carrying heavy dishes, washing plates and bowls whenever kitchen staff called in sick. She was only sixty-one years old, could still handle the exertion, but she didn't have the drive to do it any longer. She wanted other things for her life—wanted to have some fun. Running the cafe for so many years along with raising her children, had meant very little time off to travel, see the world, do all the things she'd watched others doing from afar. It was her turn to have some fun.

"You okay, Cindy?" asked Crystal Waters, a young waitress who'd become an unlikely friend to Cindy in recent years.

Cindy sighed. "Just getting old and tired, my dear."

"Can I get you a drink or something?" Crystal's long black hair swung over her shoulders, a single pink streak ran from her forehead to the tips of her hair, highlighting her dark, almond-shaped eyes.

"A glass of water would be lovely, thanks."

Crystal brought her the water, then took a seat

beside her. The morning rush was over, there would be a lull in customers for about half an hour until the lunch crowd arrived. It was a routine Cindy was intimately familiar with, and both women knew now was the time to put their feet up and rest a few minutes before they began lunch preparations. It was quieter than usual, since the main beach had remained closed after the shark attack. As a result, most beach goers had stayed home. That and the weather.

Rain fell like thunder on the roof. Behind them in the kitchen, the sounds of the kitchen staff echoed through the small, tiled space—slicing, dicing, the clinking of silverware being washed, laughter over a murmured joke. Sounds almost drowned out by the rain. Cindy loved every one of those sounds. She'd miss this part of the job when she finally retired, if she was ever able to manage it.

She offered Crystal a smile before taking a sip of water. "Thanks, honey. I don't know what I'd do without you."

"You're welcome."

"How's your studies going? I haven't asked you for a while. Everything still on track?"

Crystal shrugged. "I've cut back to one subject this semester."

"Oh?"

"I'm not sure I want to be an accountant now. I don't know…part of me really wants to be a professional musician. Is that crazy?" Her Thai accent was soft—diluted from three years living in Emerald Cove and attending a nearby university in Coolangatta.

"It's not crazy at all. This is the time in your life to take risks, to follow your dreams. Once you have a family, all that gets much harder. I wish I'd taken more chances, tried different things and been a bit irresponsible when I was your age. But I got married young, I was in love I suppose, and I wanted to build a life around family—so I made all the responsible, sensible choices instead of the crazy ones." She chuckled. "I'm certainly not going to tell you to be sensible...I mean look at me, I did everything right and I'm single in my sixties, and still working in a cafe."

Crystal smiled. "Yeah, but it's your cafe. That's something."

"True, and I love it here. I don't regret keeping this place...it was the only thing my parents gave me before they died, and it's carried me through some hard times. Still...I do wonder what might've been if I was more impulsive..."

"So, you think I should do it?"

Cindy nodded. "You're already a professional musician in Emerald Cove—this place is packed out whenever you play. Everyone loves you."

"That's true, I suppose..." Her cheeks rounded as she smiled, and she ducked her head. "But people here are so kind."

Cindy placed a hand on Crystal's arm. "I don't know what the future holds, no one does. But let me give you some life advice, honey. You'll never regret taking chances, following your dreams, or going on adventures...but you will regret not doing those things. If you fail, at least you'll know you gave it your all and there wasn't anything else you could've done. And you'll have plenty of fun along the way. Besides, you can always go back to accounting if needs be."

Crystal's eyes glistened with unshed tears. She blinked. "Thanks Cindy. I don't have family here in Australia, no one to talk to about these things. My friends don't understand, they think life's one big party—but I want more than that." She shook her head, black hair cascading down her tanned arms. "How's your new house going, by the way?"

Cindy chuckled. "I haven't moved in yet. Two weeks to go until we settle and it's all mine. I'm a little nervous about it all. I haven't received an offer on my house yet, so I'm not really sure what I'm going to do. I can't afford to keep both places...besides that, I haven't told everyone in the family I'm selling up and moving yet. Sarah knows, but no one else." She grimaced, a stab of fear making her gut clench. She hated to think what Andy, Ethan, and Adele would say when they discovered she was selling the family home. She'd suggested it once or twice, and they'd been adamant about wanting her to stay there. Still, it wasn't up to them—as Athol had reminded her more than once, it was her life, not theirs, to live.

"Why haven't you told them?" asked Crystal.

"I don't know... I'm afraid of upsetting them, I guess. It's funny, even when your kids grow up, you still want to do everything you can to protect them, make them happy. Of course, that's not my responsibility anymore, they're adults and it's up to them. But I worry about them. Adele's been a bit down lately, I don't want this to make things worse for her... It's complicated, I suppose. Especially with everything that's happened between Andy and me—him running off with Keisha, our divorce, the debts he left me saddled with. The kids really struggled with it all..."

Crystal stood, pushing fisted hands over her head with a yawn as she stretched. "Well, you can't hide it forever. They'll find out sooner or later, and it's probably best they hear it from you."

She walked away and Cindy watched her go, amazed at the way Crystal could seem like a small, lost girl one minute, then dish out mature wisdom the next. She chuckled and pushed herself to her feet, then groaned as her sciatic nerve twinged.

At her request, the real estate agent hadn't hung a sign in front of the house yet. She didn't want to alert her children or the neighbours to the fact that she was moving. After all, Ethan had only recently moved out, and Adele had moved back in. It wasn't a permanent arrangement, as much as she'd love it to be. She knew Adele would be back to her old self in no time and would soon head back to Darwin and her job as a pilot. Her adventurous spirit could never be held down for long.

Right now, Cindy didn't want to rock the boat. She was afraid to tell Adele she was selling the house after she'd convinced her daughter to move back to the Cove and live with her. What if it contributed to her depression? But surely her strong, capable daughter could handle it. Cindy shouldn't molly-coddle her. Should she?

Perhaps it was time—how would the house sell if no one knew it was up for sale? And Adele could always move into the chalet with her. She sighed and shuffled off to the small office that jutted from one side of the cafe's kitchen. She'd call the agent now and get them to put together a sign for the property. The new house on Cliffside Drive was exactly what she'd been looking for and she didn't want to miss the opportunity to make it her home if she could help it.

Perhaps she'd gather them all together for a family dinner at the house. One last big get together to bookend all their happy memories before she moved out. Yes, that's what she'd do. That way, she could tell them all at once and hide away in the kitchen making mimosas or something while they hashed it out. Then, she'd have to get packing, or she'd never manage the move in time.

Good plan.

CHAPTER 4

VICKY

*V*icky awoke to the sound of her mobile phone ringing. She'd been sleeping so soundly that at first, she thought she was riding a train to the university in Sydney where she'd studied to become a veterinarian. The train jolted, and an alarm bell sounded. Her heart thundered against her ribcage and she searched frantically for a way out of the carriage. Suddenly she was alone, the rest of the commuters having managed to find the exit she couldn't locate. She felt her way along one wall, panic levels rising, until finally her eyes flicked open and she found herself in her bedroom staring at the white ceiling above her, sweat cooling her forehead.

She felt around on the bedside table for her phone, yanked it free of the charging cable and answered in a croaky voice. "Hello?"

"Is this Vicky Hawkins?" asked the caller.

"Sorry…yes, this is Vicky. How can I help?"

"Great, hi Vicky. It's Mick, do you have a moment to talk?"

Vicky sat up in bed, rubbing her eyes with her fingertips and willing the blurriness away. "Oh, hi Mick. Yeah, of course. What's up?"

"We've had a shark attack in the Cove."

"What?" Her eyes widened, and her thoughts were suddenly lucid. "Who?"

"It's Sarah's new half-brother, actually. Not sure if you've met him…Ben Silver?"

Vicky's heart dropped. "Of course, I met him at Cindy's. Oh no! Is he okay?" She dreaded the answer. About one third of shark attacks were fatal.

"He's fine. We got him to hospital in time. A nasty bite to the leg, unfortunately. He lost a lot of blood, but he's recovering. At least, that's what the doctor told Diana earlier this morning…she called Cindy… anyway, I'm sure you know how that goes."

She'd been in the Cove long enough to understand that news travelled quickly, especially whenever Diana Jones was involved. And this time it was Diana's son that was the subject of the news, so it was likely the news was traveling through the town at the speed of light.

"I'm glad to hear it." She sighed, pressing a hand to her hammering heart. "I know Sarah must've been worried to death."

"Yeah, she hasn't really had a chance to get to know him yet, so she was pretty upset. I was there, pulled him out of the surf. There was so much blood…I wasn't sure…" He cleared his throat. "Ahem, anyway. There's a reason for the call—a few of us are going out to see if we can find this darned shark before it attacks someone else. And we were hoping you might come with us."

Her brow furrowed. "What? Me...really?"

He chuckled. "You're the only vet in town...we need someone on the boat with us to make sure we catch the right shark. None of us really knows much about them."

"Oh, but I'm not a marine biologist, Mick. I don't specialise in ocean life..."

"You're more qualified than any of us. It's up to you, Vicky, but I'd really hate to start some kind of shark killing spree in the area because of the attack. The local fishermen are chaffing at the bit to get out there and find it, the surfers are egging them on...you can imagine how it might go."

She could, and the thought of it made her stomach churn. If the community was afraid of the shark, they might end up culling a large number of sharks just in case one of them was the shark who'd attacked Ben, and they still might not find the right one. That was the last thing she wanted to see happen—even though she hadn't studied marine science, she had a great love for ocean creatures. There was something so majestic about sharks—she hated to see them killed for no reason.

"Okay, well I take your point. I can't promise anything because I'm not an expert. But if there's no one else to help you—"

"There isn't," he interrupted.

"Fine, I suppose I can do my best to identify the shark type. Do we have photographs of the wound?"

"Yep, got them on my phone," he replied.

They set up a time and place to meet down at the small marina on the outskirts of town, and Vicky hung up the phone. With another yawn she climbed out of bed and padded into the bathroom to take a shower. Her unit was on the top floor of a small complex two streets back from the beach. It was a spacious two bedroom, with white walls and ceilings, pale cream carpet and with a view of a park where children played in the mornings or after school, their squeals and laughter sifting through the screen sliding door that led out onto her cozy, private balcony.

When she moved to the Cove three years earlier, she'd bought the unit—her first real estate purchase and the first time she'd ever lived alone in her entire life. She'd moved from her family home in Emerald Cove, to the dormitory at university in Sydney, then into a shared house with two other friends after graduation. She wasn't sure at the time how she'd feel about living alone, and for the first few nights it was awfully quiet. But now, she couldn't imagine living any other way. The freedom, the feeling of sanctuary when she walked in the door after a hard day at work, it was just what she'd needed to be able to grow into the person she'd become in that time. Instead of the meek, insecure girl of the past, now she felt strong, confident, and ready to face the kinds of the challenges that her former self would've run from.

Living alone, away from her university friends and her family, had been hard at first. But over time it'd given her the space to discover who she was as a person. Given her the opportunity to fail, pick herself up and try again.

Would moving to Ballina change all that? She didn't want to go backwards, to become the anxious, quiet girl she'd been. Spending time with her dad often felt like a trip back in time to her teenage years where she'd push against his restrictive rules and judgemental attitudes to everything she did. Not to mention the conflict between her and her sister that heightened tensions whenever they were together.

She dressed in a pair of bike shorts, a long T-shirt, and sandals then picked out a wide-brimmed hat, slathered sun cream on any exposed skin and packed a bag with food and water. When she arrived at the marina, Mick and his friends were already there, loading things onto a decent-sized fishing boat. Nerves flickered in her stomach. She'd never been out of sight of the shoreline on a boat before—the idea of being stranded or shipwrecked in the deep, dark Pacific Ocean turned her stomach into a bevy of knots. That was probably why she'd decided on veterinary medicine rather than marine biology when flipping through career brochures in high school.

"There you are," said Mick, throwing a coiled rope onto the boat.

He reached out a hand to shake hers. "I hope I can help."

"Let's get going, then," he replied.

* * *

THE WATER WAS A DARK, greenish blue with waves that chopped and frothed as the fishing boat sliced its way out to sea. Vicky held onto the railing that surrounded the deck with one hand, clinging to her fluorescent orange life jacket with the other. Bile rose up her throat. She swallowed hard, then swallowed again, willing herself not to lose her breakfast in front of the fishermen who acted as though they were on a stroll through the park.

With flared nostrils she spun to face the ocean, squeezing her eyes shut, and breathing long deep breaths of the salty air.

"You okay?" shouted Mick, coming up alongside her. His blond hair whipped about his head as the wind buffeted the boat.

She nodded and offered him a tight smile. "Fine. Not a big fan of the whole up and down..." Another swallow.

He chuckled. "It can take a bit of getting used to."

"You fish a lot?"

"Sometimes. I have a little tinny of my own, take it out in the Cove whenever I can. But I don't get out this far very often."

"You seem fine. I'm fairly certain I've turned green!"

He grinned, dimples flashing. "Well, if you have to be sick, make sure it's over the side of the boat."

She shook her head. "Thanks for the sympathy."

He slapped her on the back. "No worries. Hey, you think you're up for taking a look at the photos of the wounds now?"

She wasn't sure anything could make her feel worse than she did. Her stomach roiled every time the boat lurched over a wave. "I guess so."

He pulled his phone out of his back pocket and flipped through photos until he found the ones he'd taken of Ben's leg. "Here you go."

She took the phone in her hands and stared at the screen. The bite wasn't a big one—thankfully. Although there was plenty of blood. The image was of a leg, with sand and the shallows of a wave beneath it. Blood lay pooled below the wound, drifting away on the remnants of the wave.

"From the size, I'm going to suggest it was a juvenile or smaller species of shark." She studied it a little longer, trying to remember what she'd read about sharks over the years. She may not be a marine biologist, but her interest in animal health extended to sea life too—she was fascinated by all types of creatures and read widely on the subject.

"Any idea what size or species we're looking for?"

"Give me a few minutes."

He nodded, wandering off to talk to the other men in the boat.

She pulled her own phone out of her pocket and did a google search for bites, shark species and anything else she could find that might help her narrow the search. She hated to think how many sharks might die needlessly if she got it wrong, or worse still, didn't help the men to focus their search. She had to hurry, since she wasn't sure how much longer she'd have phone signal.

When she waved Mick over, she felt confident she knew what size and type of shark had wounded Ben. She only wished she could command her stomach to hold still. Looking at two phone screens hadn't helped the matter. She knew she wouldn't be able to keep things under control for much longer, so the words rushed out.

"It's a tiger shark. Maybe one point five or two metres long. The bite marks seem to have been made by a shark with a wide jaw, and they've sawed back and forth a little bit...see here?"

Mick nodded, rubbing his stubbled chin with one hand. "Yeah."

"Tiger sharks do that. Plus, the top and bottom of

the bite looks like cutting wounds, rather than teeth marks...that's a tiger shark signature too."

He nodded. "Thanks, that helps a lot. We're looking for a small tiger shark—narrows things down for us."

She handed him his phone, he set off to tell the other men her findings, and she promptly spun on her heel and hurled up her breakfast over the side of the boat.

* * *

THEY SPENT the day navigating the ocean in the Cove, around the headlands and out in the deeper waters offshore. After several bouts of sickness, Vicky was certain she didn't have anything more to lose and joined in the search. They used a fish finder to pinpoint larger fish, then bait and chum to lure them closer and check them out.

By three o'clock in the afternoon, they'd only found a pod of dolphins, a school of tuna and a few flying fish, one of which had whacked onto the deck at Vicky's feet when it leapt from the water. She deftly scooped it up and threw it back into the water before she'd even had a chance to think about what she was doing.

"Aww that could've been bait," complained one of the men.

"Sorry." She shrugged. She was a vet, she saved lives, didn't turn them into bait. It was an instinct she couldn't repress.

"Hey, I think we've found something!" called Mick from the other side of the boat.

She hurried to join him. He leaned over the side, the boat idling and rocking with the movement of the dark ocean. Holding the railing, she peered into the water, reddened by chum.

"Where?"

He pointed. Soon she saw it, a dark shadow cruising beneath the surface. A fin broke through, and several of the men cried out in celebration.

It was a shark.

"Let's hook it in!" called the captain as he turned the boat about to follow the fin that sliced through the water's surface.

Vicky stayed out of the way while they worked. Half an hour later, they hauled the shark onto the deck. While they set about restraining it, she hurried over to examine the creature. It looked to be a juvenile, approximately the right size. But something was off—juvenile tiger sharks had stripes on their sides. This shark didn't. It had a white belly with slate-grey covering the rest of its body. It writhed back and forth, tail whipping in the struggle to get back into the water. The hook hung from the side of its mouth, a great big piece of steel.

"It's not the shark!" she cried. "This is a juvenile great white, we're after a tiger shark."

Mick tipped his hat back, scratching his head. "Are you sure?"

"I'm sure." She knew what it meant. They'd spent the day looking for the shark, and if they threw this one back it might all be in vain. They'd have to head home soon and tell the community they hadn't found it—it was still out there. Still, she couldn't pretend it was something it wasn't—she'd been certain the bite came from a tiger shark. If she was correct, this wasn't the animal they were looking for.

With plenty of grumbling beneath their breath, the

men tossed the shark back into the ocean. Vicky leaned over the side to watch it swim away, her heart in her throat. She knew what the men must be saying about her, but she felt good to know the shark could return to its life, perhaps grow into an adult. Most great white sharks would never encounter a human in their lives, she sent up a quick prayer that it never would again.

Before long, the boat turned back for shore. The swell had quieted, and the ride back was smoother than it'd been on the way out. Her stomach, still sore, didn't give her any further trouble. She was able to hold onto the railing, the wind in her hair, and enjoy the sights and sounds, the taste of salt in the air.

"Thanks for coming." Mick leaned against the railing beside her and crossed his arms over his thick chest.

Her nose wrinkled. "I don't think the others are very grateful."

"They'll be fine. It's hard to volunteer for an entire day, give up work and your pay check, then not find anything."

"I know…I understand."

"You did the right thing," he replied.

She smiled. "Thanks."

He sighed. "But this means the shark is still swimming around, possibly near the Cove. We have no way of knowing if it'll attack again."

"Let's hope it doesn't."

He grinned. "Yeah, let's hope."

CHAPTER 5

BEN

*H*is first blink was blurred. Ben squinted, blinked again. Something came into focus. A face?

He tried to speak but his throat was dry.

"Ha…"

He couldn't emit anything more than a rasp no matter how he tried.

"Ben, oh you're awake dear!"

Diana's voice startled him. What was she doing in his bedroom?

He tried to sit up, but her firm hand pushed him back into place. "No, no…don't move. I'll get you some water. I'm so happy to see you waking up, it took longer than we'd thought and I was beginning to worry." Deep brown eyes peered down at him with the eyebrows drawn low in worry like two slopes of a mountain coming together. Eyes so much like his own.

What was she talking about? His head was fuzzy, his thoughts swirled—he tried to grasp one, examine it, figure out what was going on, but they spun by just out of reach.

He blinked again. This time the room drew into focus when his eyes flickered open. It was all white. A hospital room.

That was when it all came back in a rush of memories. The ocean. Swimming. Something hard against his leg.

He'd been attacked by a shark.

His heart rate accelerated, and he attempted to rise from the bed again. Then his head swam, and he sank back on the mountain of soft pillows behind him.

"Shark!" he whispered.

Diana offered him a warm smile and a cup with a straw protruding from the top. Her dark bob was pushed behind her ears. "Yes, my dear. You were attacked by a shark. You've just come out of surgery and everything's going to be just fine."

He remembered it then. The trip in the ambulance, with Mick reassuring him. He'd blacked out for part of the way, coming to every now and then to the sound of wailing sirens.

After a sip of water, he handed Diana back the cup. "My leg?" His voice was stronger now—clearer.

"Your leg is coming along nicely, according to the surgeon. You lost a lot of blood, but the damage wasn't too bad, considering. You'll have a scar, but I think we can agree that's the last thing to be concerned about at this particular moment." She slipped into a chair beside his bed, reached for his hand and squeezed it. "Your parents are on their way here from Brisbane."

She cleared her throat. "They should arrive at any moment."

His eyes drifted shut. "Good. Thank you, Diana."

"Of course, I'm happy to do anything I can to help. Only…they haven't met me yet, so if you'd rather I left before they get here…I don't want things to be awkward."

He shook his head slowly where it rested on the pillow. "No, please stay. I know they'd love to meet you."

She sighed and squeezed his hand again. "Then, I'll stay."

The fight they'd had before the tropical cyclone Zelda three months earlier was behind them now. They'd talked about the past and the way Diana had given him up for adoption. She'd felt as though she had no other option, she was young, and she'd been adamant about her regret over missing his childhood as well as her gratitude that he'd been raised by loving parents. He'd forgiven her for it all—knowing there was nothing that could be done now except to move on and build a relationship based on mutual affection and a desire to know each other better. She'd forgiven him for the heated words, saying there was nothing at all to forgive.

And he was grateful.

He felt peace about it all now —as though he could move forward without the ache of abandonment eating away at him on the inside. It was still there, a dull remnant of it, but nothing like the sharp emotional pain he'd felt in the past whenever he'd wondered or dreamed about his birth parents, where they might live and what they might be doing. Or why they'd given him up in the first place.

He wriggled in place, shifting a little higher on the mound of pillows, blinking again. "Why doesn't it hurt?"

"You're on quite a bit of pain relief, I do believe." She chuckled. "Enjoy it, because I'm sure the pain will come roaring back before too much longer."

He grimaced. "Something to look forward to."

There was a knock on the door, and it swung open a little. His mother's face appeared at the opening.

"Mum," he rasped.

Her blue eyes filled with tears at the sight of him and she rushed into the room, arms outstretched. "Oh, honey, I can't believe…" She kissed his cheeks one at a time, then did her best to hug him gently, her arthritic hands shaking slightly as she did. "Does it hurt?"

He shook his head. "No, I feel okay right now."

His father stood behind her, hands linked together in front of him. His mother stepped aside, and Dad moved forward, rested a fist on Ben's shoulder. "Son… I…I'm glad you're okay." His voice broke, as he bent to kiss Ben's forehead, wisps of grey hair falling forward as he did.

Ben's throat tightened. "Thanks, Dad."

They chattered about what'd happened and Ben filled them in on the parts he recalled. They lifted the sheet on his bed to examine his leg, which was encased in an assortment of bandages. It still didn't hurt, but he winced at the sight of it. He remembered how it'd looked on the beach, when he lay on the sand waiting for the paramedics to arrive. He'd been certain he would die, had run through all his regrets while he lay there. The things he'd never done, the words of love he'd never spoken to the people he cared about.

"Mum…Dad…I want you to know, I love you," he

said suddenly.

They both startled. He'd never told them that before. They were an affectionate family, but the words didn't come to any of them so easily.

His mother reached for his hand, then held it to her cheek, her eyes glistening. "We love you too, honey."

His father nodded, the words seeming to get lodged in his throat.

Ben turned to Diana. "Mum, Dad...this is my birth mother, Diana Jones."

They both faced Diana, seeming surprised to see her standing in the corner of the room. She'd retreated there, out of the way, the moment they'd shown up at the door. She stepped forward now.

"It's so nice to meet you both."

"Diana, this is Gary and Jan Silver, my parents."

They hesitated a moment. Then Mum threw her arms around Diana in an embrace. Dad shook her hand.

"I'm so glad to meet you," said Mum, wiping her eyes with her fingertips. "I've wanted to for so long, you know. You're the reason we got to raise this darling boy."

Diana nodded mutely.

"We're so grateful to you," added Dad, his voice gruff with emotion.

"I...well..." Diana shuffled from side to side then met Ben's gaze. "I'm going to tell Mick and Sarah you're okay. They've been in the waiting room all this time."

He nodded. "They didn't have to do that. Thank them for me, will you?" His voice strengthened with each word he spoke. His head was clearer too, his thoughts less foggy.

"I will. Gary and Jan, we'll talk more later. I'll give you a chance to catch up with Ben."

She left with a backward glance in his direction, pulling the door shut behind her.

Mum kissed his cheek once Diana was gone. "Oh, darling...we were so worried about you. The drive down was torture. We didn't know...Diana called us a couple of times. Thank goodness she was here with you."

Tears built in his throat. "I'm sorry...I'm so sorry." They slid down his cheeks. "It was stupid, I shouldn't have been out there at that time of day."

Dad cleared his throat. "None of that. It wasn't your fault. We're just glad you're on the mend. Aren't we Jan?"

"Yes, of course we are." Her hair had been auburn when she was younger, now it was a dark grey. It suited her, but the lines on her face made him realise suddenly just how old his parents were. They'd adopted him when they were in their forties after trying for a family of their own for a long time. He'd grown up with friends thinking they were his grand-parents. It'd bothered him at times, then he'd grown used to it. But now...the realisation dawned that he wouldn't have them around forever. They were in their eighties, after all. What would he do without them?

He pulled Mum to him for another hug, this time holding her as tightly as he could manage. "Thanks for coming," he said, his voice muffled against her neck. "I don't know what I'd do without the two of you."

She sniffled and pulled away to find a tissue in the purse that hung from her shoulder. "Well, you don't have to worry about that—because we're right here."

CHAPTER 6

SARAH

*T*he shushing of waves at the base of the cliffs calmed Sarah McIntosh's nerves as she sat at the small round table on her back deck. The cottage was silent, but for the gentle wind rustling in the nearby trees and the sighing ocean. She stared into the distance, the blue sky empty of clouds—an emptiness that went on and on into oblivion, taking her thoughts with it.

At her feet, Oscar rolled over with a grunt, his black back landing on her feet. He growled in his sleep, his feet moving restlessly as though running through a field. The sensation brought her back to the moment all in a rush. She leaned down to ruffle his fur with one hand, he wakened, glanced up at her, then lowered his head back to the floor. She returned her attention to the laptop in front of her.

She'd written eighty thousand words of her debut

historical fiction novel, but for some reason couldn't find the words to make the last line sing.

Why was it so difficult?

All she had to do was write a line that drew together the overarching themes of the book, wasn't corny, yet had a happy ring to it. That wasn't so much to ask, was it?

With a groan, she slumped down in her chair and flung both arms up over her face.

Once again, Oscar brought her to her senses, this time with a soft snore that made her smile.

"Okay, come on," she said to herself. "One last line. I've got to get it done before Mick gets home because once he's here I won't be able to concentrate at all. He'll make absolutely certain of that."

She loved her husband, but if there was one thing she'd learned about him in their short marriage it was this: when he came home from work, he wanted to tell her all about his day, what was going on with his contractors, anything he'd learned around town, and generally have her entire attention fixed on him for the rest of the evening. There was no way she'd be able to invent a pithy finishing line for her book with him around. And she wanted it to be done—couldn't bear the thought of getting up again tomorrow with the novel incomplete. The first draft of it, anyway.

It'd been six months since she'd quit her job at the publishing house in Sydney. Six months, but it felt like one. The time had flown by. Her dream was to write a book, then look for another job. That was, if she couldn't find a publisher. Perhaps she'd still have to find another job anyway, since it could be a long time until her book was in print, even if she was successful. Still, she'd loved being home, writing when the inspiration hit, trying out new recipes, taking walks along the beach with Oscar. She'd even tried painting with acrylics and had a few small canvases to hang on the cottage's freshly painted walls.

It'd been absolute bliss.

But it couldn't last forever. She only had to finish this last line, and the arduous process of looking for an agent and a publisher would begin. Her heart thudded against her ribcage and nerves built in her stomach.

She couldn't think about that now. How was she expected to be creative when she was stressing over whether anyone would like her work?

With a deep intake of breath, she let her eyes drift shut and focused her attention back on the story. With fingertips pressed to the keyboard, she wrote one final sentence, pressed save, then pushed the laptop shut.

It was done.

She'd finished her book. Her eyes widened, and her mouth fell open. She'd done it!

The sound of Mick's truck in the driveway brought her to her feet. She skipped inside, set the laptop on the dining table, then ran out through the front door to greet him. He stepped from his truck, lunch box in hand. When she reached him, she threw her arms around his neck, and kissed him passionately.

He fell back a step, then set the lunchbox on the bonnet of the truck and curled his arms around her waist to deepen the kiss. When he pulled away, his eyes were hooded.

"Well, hello wife—what a nice welcome."

She laughed. "I'm really glad to see you."

"Me too." With a quick movement, he slipped one arm beneath her legs and lifted her easily into his arms, making his way for the front door. "I'm anxious for another one of those kisses."

She chuckled, tracing a line over his chest where a sprig of hair peeped above his collar. "There are plenty more where that came from. Only, I want to talk to you about something first."

He set her down on the couch, kissed the tip of her nose. In the kitchen, he set the kettle to boil, then joined her on the couch.

"I'm dirty, in need of a shower and a good cup of tea. But first tell me what's going on, and then I'll jump in the shower."

Sarah could hardly sit still. "I finished writing my book!"

"That's amazing!" He wrapped her up in his arms and kissed her. "I'm so proud of you."

"Thank you."

The kettle finished boiling, and Mick stepped into the kitchen to pour two cups of tea. When they were ready, he carried them out to the deck. Sarah followed him and they sat side by side on the deck, listening to the sounds of the ocean.

"How does it feel?" he asked.

She shrugged. "Strange. I've really struggled with the last few chapters and thought it was never going to end. Of course, I still have to do edits and rewrites, but the first draft is done."

"So, what next?" Mick took a sip of tea.

"I suppose I'll reach out to some of my publishing contacts and see if I can get a few people to read it. I mean, it might be horrible. I honestly don't know. I'm too close to it."

"I'm sure it's not horrible," he replied.

Her nose wrinkled. "It could be. I've read a lot of manuscripts, I've critiqued them, I've edited and published them, but I still have no idea if mine is any good. It's the strangest thing. I can't be objective, I guess. The best thing I can say about it, is it seems to be okay."

He laughed. "You're too hard on yourself."

"No, I'm realistic."

"Well, I suppose we'll see about that. It could be in print this time next year. Then, I'll get to say I told you so."

"That's if I get a publisher to take it on," she replied with a groan. "There's no guarantee, even with my contacts in the industry."

He stood and leaned over to kiss her forehead. "Regardless of the outcome, I'm proud of you for taking the risk and accomplishing something so many people say they'll do, but never get around to doing. You wrote a book. That's something to celebrate. In fact, as soon as I have a shower and get dressed, I'm taking you out to dinner to do just that."

WAVES HUSHED TO SHORE. The moon glowed bright in the sky, hanging above the ocean like a sentinel pushing back at the darkness. In the Emerald Cafe, Mick and Sarah sat across from each other at a small round table. Between them, a bottle of red wine and a basket of breadsticks. Twinkle lights sparkled, woven in between the climbing vines that decorated the walls of the outdoor seating area.

Mick poured wine into two wide glasses, then raised one towards Sarah. "Let's drink to you finishing your book. It's a major accomplishment and you should be proud of yourself for doing it."

They ordered two plates of carbonara, then sat to wait for the food to arrive. Mick told her about his day, she filled him in on what Oscar had done when a snake slithered through the yard — he'd barked for a full ten minutes until it was gone, disappearing down the cliffs towards the beach.

When the carbonara arrived, Sarah couldn't wait to eat it. Her stomach growled at the sight of it and she realised she'd forgotten to eat lunch; she'd been so engrossed in her writing.

It was creamy and tasty, and she squeezed her eyes shut as the flavours hit her tongue.

"Mmm…this is so good."

Mick smiled. "I love the food here. Even if it wasn't your mum's cafe, and I wasn't biased, I'd still say that."

"Me too. It's one of my favourite places in the world."

She took a sip of wine.

"What are some of your other favourites?" asked Mick, with a wink.

She laughed. "In your arms is top of the list, of course," she replied.

He nodded his approval. "Glad to hear it."

"Then, the cottage, with Oscar sleeping at my feet. Mum's house, of course —it's still strange to me that it's hers, and not 'Mum and Dad's'." She shook her head. "And after that, I'd have to say, Casciano."

Mick stopped chewing. "What? Where's that?"

She sighed. "It's this little village in Italy—Tuscany actually. It's perched on the edge of a hill, overlooking Tuscany. The streets are cobblestone, and the buildings are stone too. It's beautiful, and tiny, and walking down the street feels like a trip back in time."

He smiled. "Sounds amazing. When did you go there?"

"I spent a few weeks in Italy after I graduated from university. I went with a group of friends and we camped around Tuscany and a few other places. It was amazing. But that village always stuck in my mind—I thought it would be so romantic to go back there someday with my husband."

"Then, we'll have to go. I'd love to see it. I've always wanted to go to Italy," replied Mick, twirling carbonara noodles around his fork. "I mean, the food's great. And if it's one of your favourite places in the world, then I'll have to see it with you. Right?"

"Right," she agreed.

"Let's go for an anniversary. You know, before we have kids."

Her heart leapt into her throat. They hadn't had the conversation yet. Sure, they'd both said they wanted a family before they agreed to marry each other. But since then, neither one of them had raised the subject.

"Yeah, we should go before that. Everyone says you should travel before you have babies—apparently they make it harder somehow." Sarah arched an eyebrow. "Although, I'm sure we could manage traveling with a baby if we wanted to do that. We're both pretty capable."

"How hard could it be, really? I mean, they're so small. And they just eat and sleep."

She shrugged. "Exactly. But if we *can* go to Italy before we have a family, that's probably for the best."

He nodded, chewing. "Yeah, I agree."

"So..." nerves fluttered in her gut. "When do you think that might be?"

"Um what? Italy?"

"Babies." She swallowed. It shouldn't make her nervous to talk to her husband about having children, but it did. Probably something to do with the fact that just over a year earlier she'd never have considered she'd be living in Emerald Cove, married to a local contractor, thinking about having a family. And she definitely wouldn't have imagined she'd have quit her lucrative career in publishing to become a novelist.

Her entire life had changed so much in the space of about fifteen months. The idea of becoming a mother too made her head spin.

"Oh." Mick set down his fork. "We haven't really talked about that. Have we?"

"No."

"What do you think?" he asked.

"I don't know exactly. I mean, we haven't been married long."

"True. I suppose we don't have to rush." Mick rubbed his chin with one hand.

"We don't *have* to."

He nodded. "I know, I'd love to have kids right away. But you're doing this whole book thing. I don't want you to give that up."

The idea took shape in her mind. Why not? It didn't have to impact her career. Writing gave her plenty of flexibility. She'd always wanted a family and assumed it would happen sometime. She was in her thirties, if they were going to have children—now was the time. "I could keep writing with a baby."

He grinned. "Yeah?"

"It's early in our marriage, but I think the timing is

pretty perfect. I'm at home writing, you're doing well with your business. We've finished renovating the cottage. It's big enough for three…just."

He reached for her hand, cupped it with his. "I think the timing is perfect too."

"So, we're going to try to get pregnant?" she asked, her throat tightening with tears. "We'll have to postpone Italy…"

"We can wait to travel — Italy would be perfect for our ten-year anniversary," he replied.

She nodded. "I love that idea."

He beamed. "I'm so excited to start our family together. You're the only one in the world I'd want to share this with. It's going to be amazing." He winked. "And of course, I can't wait to try—and I think we should try a lot."

CHAPTER 7

REBECCA

*W*ith a shiver, Rebecca Russell rolled onto her side, tucked her knees up to her chest and wrapped her arms around herself to fend off the morning chill. Her eyes flickered open, her mind grasping for coherent thoughts—birdsong and streaks of sunshine piercing through gaps in the blinds. It was morning, but still early since her alarm hadn't sounded yet.

She reached for the blankets, searching around her legs, her feet. There was nothing there. With one eye open, she glanced around the bed. Franklin lay on his side, facing her, the blankets tucked around his athletic frame, his dark hair standing up all over his head.

She sat up; her eyes narrowed. Goosebumps extended across her entire body. Her teeth chattered together. She shook her head. He'd taken all the bed covers. Again.

Before she could grab them and pull them over herself, her alarm clock erupted into a series of sounds that were supposed to be soothing. Birdcall, waterfalls, the noise of the rainforest. Only right now, it irritated her—reminding her that she couldn't curl up beneath the blankets and fall into a warm slumber. Instead, she had to climb out of bed and head to the boxing gym while her husband continued to sleep peacefully, with no understanding of what he'd done.

With one last glare at her husband, still sound asleep in his toasty cocoon, she clambered out of bed and pulled on her workout gear. Rain fell loud and steady on the roof, beckoning her back into bed where she could pull the covers over her head. But she pushed the feeling aside and headed out.

By the time she'd finished her boxing session and driven home for breakfast, she expected to see Franklin in the kitchen, showered and dressed, ready for work. Instead, the house was dark and quiet, the curtains in the living room and kitchen still drawn.

With a frown, she padded into the bedroom to find her husband in much the same position as she'd left him over an hour earlier. She shook her head. In all the time she'd known and worked with him, she'd had no idea he was such a late sleeper. In the four weeks they'd been married, she'd found he liked to sleep until the very last moment, rush through a shower, grab coffee and a piece of toast and head out the door completely unprepared for the day ahead.

In contrast, she'd worked out, showered, dressed, meditated and had a leisurely breakfast while reading a chapter from the latest self-help book she'd picked up from the local library. By the time she got to work, she felt ready to face whatever challenges came her way, while Franklin still had half-lidded eyes and toast crumbs on his shirt.

She was determined to change his unhealthy morning routine.

The shower was hot and refreshing. She had to admit, she didn't miss the single bedroom unit over the fish and chip shop. In comparison, Franklin's house was spacious, warm and homely. The decor was a little dated, but otherwise, it was a wonderful three-bedroom home. A place she could imagine raising a family in. Although, maybe they'd need a little extra room if they were going to have more than one child. The thought brought a smile to her face.

She dried off and dressed in her police uniform, pulling her long, brown hair back into a ponytail. When she passed through the bedroom again, Franklin was awake, lying with his arms folded behind his head.

He reached for her as she walked by, grabbed her and pulled her onto the bed on top of him. She yelped, then burst into laughter as he tickled her ribs.

"Just going to walk past without saying good morning, were you?"

"No, I thought you were asleep." She blurted the words through her laughter.

He released her, then reached up to cup her cheeks and pulled her close for a kiss. "Good morning."

"Good morning, husband." She curled up beside him, fully dressed, nestling her head beneath his chin.

"I hate that you're always gone when I wake up." He pouted, making her smile.

"Sorry, but I like to get things done in the morning."

"I've noticed." He sighed.

She poked him in the side with one finger.

"Speaking of which, it's time to get moving. Or we're gonna be late for work."

He groaned. "Come back to bed."

She climbed out of bed, ducking away from his reaching arms. "No. You're gonna make me late every single day, the way things are going. I have a reputation to maintain, mister."

"No one cares," he complained. "Besides, I'm the boss, and I think you should go in late to work this morning."

She shook her head, her ponytail bouncing. "You don't mean that. We have plenty of work to do. Besides, as you're always saying, if we're late, then the nightshift has to stay late, which isn't fair to them."

"Ugh!" He pulled a pillow over his head, burying his face in it. "Fine." His voice was muffled.

In the kitchen, she made them both scrambled eggs and toast. She heard the shower turn on, then off again a few minutes later. By the time she'd buttered the toast and made two cups of tea, Franklin emerged from the bedroom, dressed in slacks and a blue buttoned shirt, his hair still wet.

"You look nice," she said.

He stood behind her at the bench, his arms wrapping around her. She turned in his arms and reached up to kiss him. "Breakfast is ready."

"You know, this whole being married thing is pretty great," he whispered against her lips. "A beautiful woman to kiss, and a hot breakfast. What did I do to deserve such bliss?"

She laughed. "You must've been very good."

He took his plate to the table, sat down and ate a bite of eggs. "No one told me marriage would be this good. Really—I should've asked you to marry me months ago."

Her heart felt full at his words. He'd always been such a grouch at work that she'd been surprised by how loving and kind he'd been since their wedding— he encouraged her daily.

She sat across from him and took a bite of toast. "I definitely can't complain. Although I'm pretty sure if you'd asked me to marry you any earlier, I would've said no."

He grunted. "And then I would've given up, I suppose. So, I take it back, I'm glad we waited."

"I think our timing was perfect." She laughed. "Now I just have to train you into a better routine."

One eyebrow arched. "What, like a dog? My routine is fine. It's a champion routine, in fact. It keeps me in fighting form - it honed this magnificent specimen you see before you." He waved a hand up and down the length of his torso.

She laughed. "Yes, but you waste so much of the day. You stay up late watching junk on television, then you sleep the morning away and rush to work."

He winked. "See—it's perfect."

"But I feel like I hardly see you, since I go to bed early and get up early."

He nodded. "I agree. You should definitely stay up later. We can sit on the couch and watch documentaries together."

"Ugh. I can't think of anything I'd worse to watch."

He huffed. "Well, if you put it that way."

"I didn't mean I don't want to spend that time with you. Of course, I do. Only, if I stay up late, I won't be able to go to boxing in the mornings. And all this..." She copied his gesture, waving one hand in front of herself. "… requires a lot of upkeep, let me just tell you. If I don't exercise regularly, I'll lose all the muscle tone I've worked so hard to build and go back to being the skinny, helpless creature I was on the first day I met you."

He laughed. "Fair point. Look, I understand what you're saying. I'll try to change my routine, but I'm really not much of a morning person."

"Don't worry," she sighed. "We'll figure it out. But there was one other thing I wanted to talk to you about."

"Shoot," he replied, finishing off his tea.

"How do you think the team is taking it?"

"Taking what?" he asked, brow furrowed.

"Us being married, working together. Do you think they're okay with it?"

He shrugged. "I guess. No one's said anything to me. Why wouldn't they be okay with it?"

"I don't know. I worry they're uncomfortable. I hope they know you're not going to give me any special treatment, that everything's going to continue the same way it always has. Nothing has to change."

"Well—some things will change."

"Like what?" she asked.

"Like…well, we're married. I'll probably want to kiss you. Things like that."

"Not at the station," she replied.

He frowned. "What? We can't kiss at the station?"

How did he not understand this? "No, of course not. We're professionals."

"Okay, well I'm glad we talked about this. Because I didn't know kissing would be off limits. Anything else?"

"While we're talking about it, we really shouldn't hug at the station either."

His nostrils flared. "No hugging or kissing. Great. Can I *talk* to you?"

She laughed. "Of course, you can."

"Wonderful. Any other rules I should know, about how I'm allowed or not allowed to interact with my wife?"

"I'll keep you posted," she replied, carrying her plate to the sink.

* * *

THEY DROVE to the station together in Franklin's cruiser. Since she was his junior partner, she didn't have her own cruiser yet, so it worked out well for them to share. They'd stopped at the cafe to get take-away coffees for the rest of the crew. Franklin climbed out of the car and rushed at the station doors. He tripped up the stairs, almost landing on his face, but managed to keep a hold of the coffee tray. As soon as he'd righted himself, he ran headlong into the glass sliding doors.

Watching from behind, Rebecca stifled a burst of laughter. She'd seen him do it before, but witnessing it as his wife, after the hurried way he'd gotten ready for work and sped to the office, she finally understood—it was all part of him, part of what made him who he was, the man she'd fallen in love with. God help her.

"You okay honey?" she called.

Franklin swore beneath his breath, then waved back to her. "Fine. The coffee didn't spill, so that's something. These darned doors…"

She offered him a thumbs up, then followed him up the stairs and into the reception area.

Steph sat at the reception desk, her red curls tamed by two buns on either side of her head. She buzzed the two of them in and Rebecca sat beside her with a grunt. They both sipped the coffee Franklin had brought in. Rebecca watched him head into the office, laughter still bubbling up her throat.

"What's so funny?" asked Steph.

"He ran into the doors again."

Steph let out a snort. "You'd think he'd learn."

"He's a mess—I had no idea how much of a mess he really is."

"That's the beauty of marriage. You get to find out all the bizarre, annoying and quirky things about the man you love. It can take a while."

"How long?" asked Rebecca.

"Let's see…" Steph counted on her fingers. "I've been married eight years, so I guess it must be longer than that."

"Really? You don't know everything about him after eight years?"

Steph shook her head. "Nope. Like this week I found out he has a secret toothpaste that he keeps in a drawer to use when I'm not looking, because he doesn't like the way I squeeze the other one. But he didn't want to say anything, because it might hurt my feelings."

Rebecca threw back her head to laugh. "That's so strange."

"Tell me about it."

"Franklin likes to sleep until fifteen minutes before we're due at work."

Steph's eyebrows curved high. "Well, that explains the hair."

Rebecca laughed again.

"So, are you going to keep working together?" asked Steph. "You know, now that you're married?"

Rebecca's stomach clenched. It was the sort of question she'd been dreading. One she didn't have an answer for. "Um yeah, I guess so. I mean, we're partners."

"Isn't that going to be awkward though? I mean, he's your boss, your partner and your husband?"

"I don't know. Honestly, I wondered about it myself, but Franklin doesn't seem to want to talk about it."

Steph shrugged. "Maybe I'm wrong. But what will he do if there's a situation that places you in danger—will he be able to separate his feelings as a husband from what the the police officer in charge should do in that situation?"

Rebecca took a sip of coffee and stared at the desk in front of her, Steph's words echoing in her thoughts. Steph was right—these were the kinds of questions they needed to ask themselves. But Franklin didn't want to think about it, and Rebecca couldn't figure out the answer on her own. She'd worked so hard for this job and was finally happy in a career that brought her so much satisfaction and joy. She couldn't walk away now. And Franklin had been in his role for so long, she couldn't ask him to give it up either. It was his whole life.

She'd have to think it through on her own, figure out how they'd handle things. Maybe they could make it work. Surely, there was a way.

CHAPTER 8

BEN

*H*is bed was soft and comfortable—a complete relief after the hard mattress in the hospital. Besides that, the hospital was always busy. There was so much noise, Ben had hardly gotten a moment of sleep ever since the pain medication wore off. So, being back in his quiet house, in his comfortable bed, brought him more relief than he'd ever imagined was possible.

It was like letting out a big sigh, but all over his body.

A quiver of contentment ran through him as his eyes flicked shut.

The bedroom door banged open and Dad shuffled in. "Sorry to disturb you, son, but there's a story on the news about the shark attack."

Ben sat up in bed, blinking back sleep, as his dad

turned on the television set that sat on his dresser drawers.

"Oh? I wonder what they're reporting now. I thought they'd forgotten all about it."

They found the channel. A reporter was questioning a young woman with mousy blonde hair blowing about her face, down at the marina.

"So, Miss Hawkins, you're saying you didn't find the shark today?"

The woman shook her head. "No, unfortunately we didn't. But I am pleased to say we saw a wonderful variety of sea life. It was a very pleasant…if somewhat bumpy, day out on the water."

The reporter nodded, faced the camera. "So, there you have it. According to local veterinarian, Vicky Hawkins, the shark that attacked Ben Silver right here in Emerald Cove, is still out there. If you're planning to go swimming, be careful and stay safe folks!"

The report ended and Dad turned off the television set, setting the remote back on top of it.

"They're trying to catch that darned shark," said Dad, his eyes wide.

"Wow, I didn't realise they were doing that. I can't imagine how they could possibly find the same one that bit me."

"I guess they've got their ways."

"That woman—the local veterinarian. I'm pretty sure I know her. I've met her at one of Cindy or Diana's get togethers, I'm sure of it."

Dad nodded. "It's a bit strange to have a vet involved."

"I suppose they couldn't find anyone else locally," replied Ben.

"She's pretty. I wonder if she's single," said Dad with a smile.

"She's very attractive. Of course, she's much too young for me if that's what you were thinking."

Dad shrugged. "Maybe. Maybe not."

Ben shook his head. "I don't know Dad, I'm forty-four, perhaps it's time for you and Mum to finally give up on the idea of me ever getting married. I have."

Mum walked in at that moment; her eyes widened. "Benjamin Silver, don't you say such a thing. You can't give up."

Ben sighed. "I'm happy with my life the way it is."

"Are you telling me, you wouldn't like to share your life with someone?"

He hesitated. That wasn't it at all. There was a time when he'd hoped for it. But that was so long ago. Since then, he'd had several failed relationships. Each one had broken his heart to some extent, although the first had stung the most. Every time things ended, it'd brought him closer to the point where he was now—content as a single man, with no great desire to change things for fear of getting hurt all over again. Although the shark attack had shifted something deep inside — regret. He didn't want to die with regrets, and the solitude he cultivated was his biggest regret, if he was honest with himself.

Still, peace was better than turmoil, in his experience.

"I'd love to share my life with someone, but maybe we should accept that it isn't going to happen for me."

"He thought that vet on the TV was pretty," piped up Dad.

Mum's eyebrows arched. "Really? Hmmm, I

63

thought so too. Very pretty. Seemed nice and smart too."

"Mum, come on."

"And he knows her," added Dad.

"Dad you're not helping things."

Mum pressed her hands to her hips. "Ben, there's something you need to think about. Your father and I aren't getting any younger. One of these days, you won't have us around. It kills me to think of you being all alone." Her eyes filled with tears.

Ben bit down on his lip. "Mum, please don't cry."

"I'm not crying," she said with a sniffle. "Only, don't give up on finding someone. Not yet."

He smiled. "Okay, Mum. Come here and give me a hug."

She waddled over to him, then leaned down to embrace him.

"Is your hip playing up?" he asked.

"Yeah, it's always causing trouble."

"What did the doctor say?"

She sniffed. "He wants to replace it. But that means surgery, and I have no intention of going into surgery at my age. I've never been cut open before, and I'm not about to start now."

Dad shuffled from the room. Mum sat on the bed beside him. "Do you have everything you need?"

Ben nodded. "I do. Thanks for all your help, Mum. You and Dad should go back to Brisbane. You're both tired, and I'm fine. I can manage on my own."

She sighed. "I don't want to leave you alone. You're still in pain. And I don't understand why you won't just come on back to Brisbane with us. There's no reason for you to stay here. You said yourself that you can do your work anywhere."

"We talked about this, Mum. I want to be close to Diana and Andy. I know it's hard for you, but I've got to take this chance to get to know them."

She sniffled again, reached for a handkerchief she had tucked in her sleeve and wiped her nose with it. "Fine, I suppose that makes sense. Although you already have a family."

He squeezed her arm gently. "Yes, I do. You and Dad are all the family I need. But I really want to get to know my biological family too. It doesn't make sense, I get that. But it's something I have to do."

CHAPTER 9

CINDY

*T*he smoke from the BBQ floated across the deck. Cindy basted the prawns with a little more garlic butter sauce, then glanced up as Athol stepped outside. She slipped out of her apron and went to greet him with a kiss.

They'd been dating for a few months now, but she still found every kiss exciting. Like embarking on a brand-new adventure, starting a whole new life. She'd known Athol most of her life, but their friendship hadn't involved romantic feelings until Andy walked out on her after almost forty years of marriage.

Now it seemed, the more time she spent with him the more she liked it. She hadn't felt this way about anyone since she was a newlywed in her twenties. It was different, of course. Less infatuation, more warm affection. But the passion she felt for him was building, slowly growing into something special that made her heart jitter inside her chest.

"It smells delicious," he said, wrapping an arm around her waist. "Can I take over? Everyone's arriving and I know you'll want to greet them."

She nodded, kissing him again. "Thank you, darling. That would be wonderful."

She handed him the apron, then headed inside. She'd been looking forward to the evening and dreading it in equal parts. She'd already had the discussion about selling the house with Sarah back when she'd found the chalet, and with Adele, earlier that afternoon. Since Adele lived with her and currently worked at the cafe, she didn't think it would be fair to spring the news about selling the house and the cafe in front of everyone.

Knowing her youngest daughter as well as she did, Adele would need time to process the information. And in true form, she'd given Cindy a hug, told her it'd all be fine, and retreated to her bedroom for the rest of the day. Cindy hadn't seen her since, other than poking her head through the door to offer a cup of tea which Adele had declined. She hated seeing her daughter that way—sitting on the window seat, staring out at the yard as though her thoughts had taken her a million miles away. Her face reflected a sadness that was like a punch to Cindy's gut.

She'd hoped the move to the Cove would help Adele regain her footing. And in some ways, it had. She'd caught her smiling and laughing more, but then there were those moments: the ones she interrupted, when it was clear there were still things on Adele's mind. Things she didn't want to talk about. Which frustrated Cindy, and worried her, all at the same time.

Sarah and Mick were already in the kitchen, pouring themselves a glass each of the punch she'd mixed earlier. She greeted them both, just as Ethan and Emily arrived, carrying a bottle of wine.

"It's so good to see you, neighbours!" she joked.

Emily lived at the Seaside Manor Bed & Breakfast next door. Ethan had a unit downtown and the two of them had been dating for almost a year. Cindy loved seeing them together. Emily brought a calm and peace to her son's life that he'd never really exhibited before. And the two of them ran the Manor together, with Ethan also working as an engineer in Murwillumbah.

"We had such a long way to travel to get here," quipped Ethan, kissing her cheek, his light brown eyes twinkling.

She made certain everyone had a drink, then ushered them all out onto the back deck. She was about to step outside when Andy walked in, without knocking. He held up a dessert in the air.

"Lemon meringue pie?"

She smiled. "That's perfect. Come on in. Everyone's here."

She'd invited Andy and his girlfriend Keisha, but he'd come alone. Perhaps he wasn't ready for everyone to see him with Keisha at a family dinner yet, or maybe she hadn't wanted to come. Either way, Cindy was a little disappointed. She'd hoped the two of them would be able to put the past behind them after she'd rescued Keisha during the cyclone a few months earlier.

"Keisha couldn't come?" she asked.

He shrugged. "She had a headache."

"Well, tell her we hope she feels better soon."

He nodded. "You're always so kind, Cindy. Thank you."

He looked a little ragged around the edges. His hair had more grey in it, and he'd lost another inch or so around his waist so that his pants sagged, held up by a thin, brown belt.

They walked outside together, and Cindy made her way over to the BBQ while Andy said his hellos. Athol arched an eyebrow.

"Now, I'm not sure if I've done something wrong, but these lobster tails were looking like they were done, so I took them off the heat. Is that okay?"

She cried out, slapping a hand to her forehead. "Oh my, I should've said something. Yes, you did the right thing. Thank you. They'd have been overcooked for sure if you left them on the grill."

Athol smiled. "I think the first course is ready, then."

They all sat down at the table to eat together. It was one of Cindy's favourite things to do—to have her family and friends gathered around the enormous oak table on her deck. It was long enough to house every-one, although it was difficult to hear the conversations at either end.

While everyone was loading their plates with seafood and salad, she stood to her feet in the centre of the table and held up a glass.

"I hope everyone has a drink handy, because I'd like to raise a toast," she said.

The conversations at the table fell silent and the entire family looked her way. Each person lifted a glass in one hand.

"What are we toasting, Mum?" asked Ethan.

She inhaled a deep breath. Hesitated. "We're toasting new beginnings. I wanted you to be here, so I could tell you all at once. I've decided to sell the house and cafe, and downsize my life."

* * *

THE AFTERMATH of her announcement was as loud and dramatic as she'd thought it would be. Cindy spooned creamy lemon pie with crisp meringue into bowls, then topped it off with a scoop of vanilla ice cream. Perhaps with enough sugar in their mouths they'd take a break from the in-depth analysis of why she was selling up, what they'd done wrong, and how they could change her mind.

"Can I help?" asked Sarah, coming in from the deck.

Cindy offered a tight smile. "Only if you're not going to attack me."

Sarah huffed. "We weren't attacking you, Mum. It's a big change, it'll take us a little while to get used to it. I've had more time than the others have to think it through. But I'm still processing. And because of that, we might have some questions."

"Questions are fine—but there are a lot of you, so it can feel like an attack if you launch them all at me at the same time." She handed two bowls to Sarah.

They carried the desserts out to the deck and set them down on the table, before returning inside to collect more.

"That's a fair point. Fine—I promise to wait my turn to ask questions, and I'll try to get the others to do the same."

"Thank you," replied Cindy, her throat tight.

She'd known this would be difficult. Athol had held her hand as soon as she'd said her piece and taken a

71

seat beside him at the dinner table. He really was her rock. Still, as he'd mentioned to her before the others arrived, it wasn't his place to get involved. So, he hadn't said much, instead listening, nodding, and squeezing her hand whenever things got heated.

When everyone had their dessert, she returned to her seat, and took a bite of pie. It was delicious. Still, she only nibbled around the edges, her appetite gone. It wasn't as though their reactions were unexpected, or over the top. They were a lively bunch, always had been. She knew them inside and out, knew what they'd think, and how they'd express it. But it was hard for her to make the change. Selling the only home she'd known in her adult life, the place she'd raised her family, was difficult. The cafe had been given to her by her parents before they died. It was a precious part of her heritage that she'd held onto ever since.

So many times, she'd changed her mind, almost backtracked, and told the agent to remove the listing. But then, she'd considered the alternative—she couldn't continue to live in such a big house all alone with only Petal, her dog, for company. Besides the fact that it took her the entire day every Saturday to clean, from top to bottom. She was exhausted by the time she was done and could only collapse on the couch. Not to mention the enormous gardens that were being over-taken by weeds, try as she might to keep them at bay.

Between the house and the cafe, she couldn't keep up with it all. And for the first time in her life, she didn't want to. She had Athol now, and the new beginning for her love life had given her the inspiration to start again in other areas of her life too.

"So, what will you do with the cafe?" asked Andy, spoon poised above his bowl.

She sighed. "I'm going to sell it. I've had a few buyers make offers over the years, and I contacted them recently. One of them is still interested."

"You might've talked to me about it first," muttered Andy, staring into his bowl.

Athol shifted in his seat beside her.

"Sorry?" asked Cindy.

"I'm just saying—this house was ours and we ran the cafe together for a long time. A heads-up would've been nice."

Athol grunted. "That's enough from you, Andy."

"Please, let's all stay civil," pleaded Cindy.

"No, let him talk." Andy glared at Athol. "After all, he was my best friend for such a long time but moved in on my wife without so much as a second thought, so I'd love to hear what he has to say on this topic."

"Andy!" cried Cindy.

Athol stood to his feet, threw his napkin down on the table, his face red. "That's not what happened, and I can't believe you'd bring that up in front of the family."

"They're my family!" stated Andy, pushing himself up from the table.

Athol's nostrils flared. "And now they're mine too."

Andy fairly growled at that. "You just couldn't help yourself could you? Jealous all those years, and now you're taking my place."

"Andy please…" Cindy wrung her hands together, standing between the two of them. "Both of you, this isn't the right time."

"It never is," replied Andy.

"Taking your place? You left. You abandoned them. That's not my fault."

Andy shook his head. "No, nothing ever is. Is it, Doctor?"

Athol stormed into the house, letting the backdoor slam shut behind him.

Andy chuckled. "Can you believe that guy?"

Cindy shook her head. "Andy, was that really necessary?"

He shrugged. "Ask the backstabber."

"Dad, come on," said Sarah. "Don't talk about him like that."

Andy raised both hands in surrender. "Fine, I'll drop it."

"Thank you," said Cindy, her stomach in knots. "I had no idea my talking about downsizing would impact you so much, Andy."

He shook his head. "You're moving on, I get it. Doesn't make it any easier for me."

"It's definitely happening," said Adele, a weak smile on her pale face. "So, we should all get on board."

Cindy nodded. "Yes."

"But you love the cafe," added Sarah.

"You're right, I do love it there. But I can't physically keep up the pace I've been running at any longer. I'm tired." She offered them a weak smile as if to prove the point.

"I get it," replied Sarah. "It makes sense. But how will you afford to live?"

"All good questions," replied Cindy. "But perhaps we can talk about it all another time."

"Sure, Mum—that's fine with me," replied Sarah.

"Well, I support whatever you decide," piped up Ethan.

Sarah rolled her eyes skyward.

He shrugged. "What?"

"Always the perfect son," laughed Adele.

He smirked. "I can't help it. It's just who I am."

The entire table burst into laughter. Cindy joined them; glad the tension was broken. Ethan winked at her, bringing tears to her eyes. He'd known exactly what he was doing. In her opinion, he'd been the perfect son from the moment he was born.

CHAPTER 10

VICKY

*T*he coffee scorched Vicky's tongue. She set the mug down on the saucer with a grimace. Seagulls hovered nearby, waiting for someone to leave their plate of hot chips unattended. Sarah waved them off with one hand.

"Ouch. The coffee's hot."

Sarah arched an eyebrow. "Oh no, did you burn yourself?"

Vicky could only nod as she took a gulp of cold water.

"So, since it's Saturday and I'm assuming you're not working…"

"No, not working. My first Saturday off this month. I plan on doing a whole lot of nothing. Well, besides meeting you for coffee, of course." She smiled, her tongue feeling better after the cold water.

"Good, glad to hear it. You deserve a rest. But

before you go home and get all settled on your couch for the day, I was hoping you might come with me to visit Ben."

"Your half-brother, Ben? Is that the Ben you're talking about?"

Sarah grinned. "That's the one. He's at home recovering after his surgery, and I promised Diana I'd stop in and check on him. It's bound to be completely awkward, since we're related but I hardly know the guy. So, I thought you could come along, make it less uncomfortable for all of us."

Vicky's lips pursed. "For all of us, or for you?"

"Well, for me. Look, you don't have to come. But I'd really like you to."

"No worries, I'm happy to do it. In fact, I've been wondering how he's doing after everything that happened. It's such a miracle that Mick happened to be there and was able to drag him out of the water."

Sarah nodded, pressing her hands to her forehead. "I know. I told him afterwards that I was glad he did it, but just once I'd like him to think about his own life before he risks it for someone else. Of course, the someone else happened to be my half-brother, so I'm grateful. It's all very complicated," she finished with a groan.

"I get it—and I'm glad they're both okay."

"Me too."

They finished up their coffees, told Cindy goodbye, and left the Emerald Cafe in Sarah's car to head to Ben's house. His house was close to the water. It was a nice two-story modern home, set on a small block of land at the base of a hill. Sarah parked in front of a white garage door, and the two of them climbed out.

"I hope he doesn't mind me tagging along," said Vicky.

"It'll be fine."

Sarah knocked on the door, waited, then knocked again. There was a pane of glass beside the front door; she cupped her hands to it and peered through.

"Sarah!" admonished Vicky.

"What?"

"He's not expecting us. What if he's in his underwear and scurrying past to get dressed?"

Sarah laughed. "Is that what you do?"

Vicky's cheeks warmed. "Well…"

"Really? You sprint for clothing when someone knocks on the front door?"

She laughed. "Yes, I do. And I used to have a glass panel just like this one when I lived with my parents. I hated it when people peered through and saw me dashing by with one hand across my bra. You don't do that too?"

"No, I'm usually dressed."

"How uncomfortable."

The door opened and Ben Silver looked out at them, leaning on a pair of crutches. One leg was encased in bandages. His dark brown hair flopped over his forehead and deep brown eyes met hers. There was something intense about his eyes that made Vicky feel as though he knew her deep down, could see into her very soul.

"Hi," he said.

Sarah waved awkwardly. "Hi Ben. I hope you remember me—your sister, Sarah Flannigan."

He smiled. "Of course, come on in. It's good to see you."

They walked inside. He shut the door behind them,

and Vicky held out a hand. "I'm Vicky, by the way. We met at Cindy's I believe. But you met a lot of people that day, so you may not recall."

He took her hand. His was large and warm as he shook hers. "I remember."

His words were few, but his touch sent a shiver of anticipation through her body that unnerved her. He was handsome, that much was true, but it was more than that. He seemed grounded, mature, at ease in his own skin in a way that was very attractive to her. She felt herself drawn to him, wishing she could spend time with him and hear his story. She knew he was adopted, everyone in town knew that, but what had his life looked like? Suddenly she longed to know.

"Come into the living room and grab a seat. I was about to make a pot of tea. Would you like a cup?"

"Yes, please," replied Sarah.

They both sat on the couch. There were a few boxes pushed up against the living room wall. The furnishings were sparse, practical. There was only one piece of art on the wall, an abstract painting in bold colours with various shapes and lines.

Vicky stood suddenly. "I'm going to help." She followed Ben into the kitchen. "I thought you could use a hand. You can't carry anything with those crutches."

He smiled. "Thanks. I was wondering how I'd manage it."

He put the kettle on to boil, and Vicky searched cupboards until she found cups and saucers.

"I saw you on the news," said Ben.

Vicky leaned against the bench, crossed her arms over her chest. "You did?"

"Yeah, you were out shark hunting, right? Mick gave me a call afterwards to let me know how it went."

She nodded. "We didn't find the shark that bit you though. Sorry."

He shrugged. "You don't have to apologise to me. I hope they forget about it. Doesn't make the shark culpable—I mean, I was in the water at dusk. That's my fault. Not the shark's."

She smiled. "Good perspective." Perhaps they had more in common than she'd realised. Anyone who cared about a shark that'd almost killed them earned a lot of brownie points in her estimation. He was growing more attractive by the moment.

"I'm glad you were with them, I'd have hated to see a whole lot of dead sharks coming back into the cove on that boat."

"Thanks, I'm glad too. I have to say, I'm surprised you're siding with the shark considering it tried to eat you."

He chuckled. "Nah, it wasn't trying to eat me. Just had a little nibble. I think it was testing me out to see if I was tasty."

"You must've tasted pretty bad," she quipped.

He laughed. "I'm still here, aren't I?"

Once the water was ready, Vicky carried the teapot and cups back into the living room on a tray with Ben hopping along on his crutches behind her.

CHAPTER 11

BEN

*T*he chess board sat in a sliver of sunlight on the side table between two armchairs in his living room. Ben studied the board, one hand cupping his chin as he leaned forward on the side of the chair.

"Check," he said.

Andy blanched, stared at the board, then stood up to look at it from another angle. "What? How did you...?"

Ben smiled. "Sorry. I thought you saw that one coming a mile off."

Andy's eyes narrowed. "Nope. Well, I have no idea how I'm going to get out of this one."

He sat again with a grunt and moved a pawn. His move made no difference to the outcome of the game. It was clear he hadn't played often, not that Ben was an expert. He appreciated that Andy had brought the chess set over to play with him—it showed his birth father was trying to get to know him. The gift was a thoughtful one, and Ben was grateful for the gesture.

Still, he'd have been happy to do something Andy was more comfortable with. "You know, next time we can do something you enjoy, if you like," he said, as he shifted his bishop into a checkmate position. "Checkmate."

"Ugh!" exclaimed Andy, standing up and pacing into the kitchen.

He returned in a moment with two glasses of water and handed one to Ben.

"No, it's fine. I like this—gives us a chance to get to know each other."

"Okay, that sounds good to me."

"Besides, you're not really ready to throw a football in the park or anything right now. So, we'll do indoorsy things."

"You're right about that," replied Ben, shooting a dismayed look at his bandaged leg. "Hopefully it won't be too much longer before I can get the dressing removed. But it'll be a while before I can run and jump, so catch is probably out of the question for now."

Andy chuckled. "So, apart from the shark attack—how's the move gone for you, so far?" He sat on the couch opposite Ben and crossed one leg over the other.

Ben shrugged. "Okay. Nothing much to complain about. It takes time to feel settled in a new place—so I'm trying to be patient."

Andy nodded. "I know what you mean. Keisha and I wanted a new start somewhere else, but in the end, I had to move back to the Cove. It was too hard—no one knew who we were, no one cared."

"You like the small-town vibe. I get it," replied Ben with a nod.

Andy grinned. "Can't help it—I grew up in this town, it's home to me. And Keisha's lived here a long time too. Although, she doesn't seem to mind where we live. And by that, I mean, she can't stand it anywhere, so we might as well live here." He laughed heartily.

By the time Andy left, Ben was ready to take a nap. He'd been taking more naps since the attack and had gotten into something of a habit. In the past he'd make a cup of coffee when the inevitable two o'clock slump hit, but since his hospital stay, he'd been heading to bed for an hour instead.

He cleaned up the kitchen as best he could, hopping on one foot. He left the crutches leaned up against the dining table—didn't really need them anymore. He could manage fine without them. Putting weight on his injured leg no longer hurt. And the crutches only got in the way. He was about to make the short trek down the hallway to his bedroom when the doorbell rang. He frowned and hesitated. He could simply ignore whoever it was. Most likely it was a delivery person, although he didn't recall ordering anything.

With a sigh, he made his way to the front door.

"Diana, I wasn't expecting you," he said.

She smiled at him, her face a little paler than usual. She wore a red pantsuit with gold buttons down the front, and her dark hair seemed to have developed more grey streaks, although it might've been the way the afternoon sunlight bathed her. She had her own set of crutches and a therapeutic boot on one foot.

"I thought you might like some dinner. I know it's a

bit early, but I didn't want you to have to worry about cooking anything. So, I made apricot chicken. It's in the car—I couldn't figure out how to carry it inside. My neighbour helped me stow it in the car. But once I got here, I realised I was stuck. And of course, you're injured too. So…"

He smiled. "We're a couple of invalids, aren't we?"

She laughed. "Pathetic really. I can't believe I still have to wear this thing. After all, it's been three months since my roof collapsed on me during the cyclone. But the doctor says I can get it off next week — the bones weren't healing the way they'd hoped they would. I'm crossing my fingers!"

"Never mind, I can get the dish for you. I don't need my crutches anymore and I can walk okay—only a little bit of a limp to hold me back."

He carried the dish from the car, held the door open for Diana, and soon they were both seated in the living room with the meal safely put away in the fridge.

"It's nice to see you again," he said.

"You too, my dear. Before we go any further, I have to tell you something," began Diana.

"Okay. What's up?"

She offered a nervous smile. "I got you a gift."

"You didn't have to do that. What's it for?"

"Well, you can think of it as a housewarming gift."

He wasn't sure he'd ever received a housewarming gift before. It was usually the kind of thing people gifted to couples, and since he'd never been married —

"It's not here. Obviously." She smiled. "But it's coming."

"Oh?"

"Any minute now."

His eyes narrowed. "Um. Okay."

A car pulled into the driveway outside, its tyres crackling on the gravel. Ben stood, shuffled to the front door. Another car parked behind Diana's. The woman in the driver's seat looked like Vicky Hawkins.

"Vicky's here," he stated.

Diana stood too, moving her crutches back into place beneath her arms. "Oh good. She's right on time."

His brows pulled together. "She is?"

"She has your gift."

"Oh?" It didn't make any sense to him. Why did Diana need Vicky to bring him a gift?

Diana hobbled through the front door just as Vicky climbed out of her car. She walked around to the back door, carrying a short rope, pulled it open and reached inside. Then, she spun to face them, a small reddish-brown ball of fur in her arms, the rope dangling.

She grinned. "Hi Ben!" The smile lit up her face. Her blue eyes sparkled, dark blonde hair glowing under the fading afternoon light. The sight of her made his heart race. He had no idea why she was there, but he was glad to see her.

"Hey Vicky, how are you?"

She strode up the footpath to the front door, still cradling the fur ball. "I'm great. And this is for you." She held out the fur ball in his direction.

He frowned. "Huh? What?"

Diana placed a hand on his forearm. "I got you a puppy. Isn't he cute?"

Ben glanced at Diana, gaping. "You bought me a dog? That's the gift?"

Diana's face fell. "Yes, I thought —"

"Oh wow, well that's so thoughtful of you." He didn't want to seem ungrateful, and obviously Diana had put a lot of thought into it. So, he took the dog from Vicky and held it in an awkward kind of fireman's grip. "Wow, so cute."

He'd never owned a pet in his life, unless you counted the bird his parents kept in a cage in their backyard for part of his childhood. Although he'd had very little to do with the creature, and in the end it hadn't survived long. He loved animals, though generally from a distance. Although he supposed he could give it a try—after all, what did he have to lose?

The satisfied grin returned to Diana's face. "I knew you'd love him. He's absolutely perfect. Now you won't be alone, he'll be right here with you all the time."

He swallowed. "Uh, thanks."

When he met Vicky's gaze, he found concern in her eyes.

"I didn't realise the puppy was going to be a surprise, Di," she said, her brow furrowed. "It's not usually a good idea to spring a pet on someone."

"Oh no, Ben's a great animal lover. Aren't you, Ben?" Diana hobbled back into the house, leaving the two of them behind.

"Are you a great animal lover?" asked Vicky with a chuckle, hands pressed to her hips.

He quirked an eyebrow. "Apparently."

She shook her head. "I should take him back."

He held the dog a little closer, attempting to wrap an arm around the creature's middle as it wriggled to get free. "No, that's fine. I mean, I don't want to upset Diana. She's trying to do a nice thing. And I do love animals, she's right about that."

"But a dog is a big commitment. You need to think about it before you take that kind of leap. So many people end up giving them away when they're fully grown, and by then it's hard to find them a permanent home." Her gaze fixed on the dog and she reached out to stroke its back.

"I'll keep that in mind," he said. "What kind of dog is it…I mean, he? What kind of dog is he?" Ben gave up the fight and set the dog on its paws in the entryway, then shut the front door behind them.

"He's a kelpie pup. He'll need a lot of exercise and plenty of attention. I highly recommend you take him to some classes to learn how to train him properly, or you're likely to have a bit of trouble with him."

Vicky walked with him to the kitchen where they found Diana setting biscuits on a plate.

"I thought I'd make us a nice pot of tea, and you can tell us all about how to care for a brand-new puppy, Vicky," said Diana.

Ben and Vicky exchanged a glance. It was starting to feel a bit like a set up to him. He'd told Diana how Vicky had visited with Sarah and how much he'd enjoyed it. Perhaps she'd read more into it than was there. Or maybe she'd spoken to his parents. After all, Vicky must be in her twenties—Ben was far too old for any kind of relationship with her. Even if she was as old as thirty, she wouldn't be interested in an old bachelor like him. Still, he was glad she'd come. He could enjoy her company even if it'd never be anything more than that between them.

* * *

AFTER A CUP of tea and two chocolate biscuits, Vicky excused herself and left. Ben found himself missing her smile, her lively conversation and positive outlook as soon as she stepped through the door.

89

Diana set her cup on the coffee table with a sigh. "Such a lovely girl."

"Yes, she is."

Ben carried the dirty cups and the plate back to the kitchen, Diana shuffled after him. At her feet, the puppy trotted along, almost as though trying to trip her. Ben scooped up the dog before it sent Diana sprawling. This time he managed to get a better hold on the dog, and it reached up a pink nose to bump his cheek, then licked him.

He laughed, patted the dog's head.

"What will you call him?" asked Diana, her eyes gleaming.

"I don't know. He's such an amazing reddish colour —perhaps he should be Rusty."

"A perfect name," replied Diana.

Ben smiled, setting the dog back on the floor. The animal scampered off.

"You should probably let him out in the backyard before too much longer," suggested Diana. "The mess they can make—brings back memories."

"You've had dogs before?" he asked.

She nodded, vigorously. "Oh yes. We used to own cocker spaniels and would let them roam around the gardens at the Manor. But they were Rupert's really— so when it got so that walking them was too much for him, we didn't replace old Missy. She died about five years ago and I miss her still." The smile faded from her face but was soon replaced with a forced cheer. "Nevertheless, I think you're going to love being a dog owner. It's really quite wonderful."

"Maybe, although I'm not sure I'm the type."

"Of course, you are. You told me how much you love animals."

"Wildlife," he corrected her. "Out in nature—I enjoy seeing them when I go mountain biking or four wheeling."

She waved a hand. "Wildlife, animals, they're the same thing. This'll be perfect for you. I worry about you, living all alone. You need some company."

"I've lived alone for half my life, Diana," he replied with a chuckle.

"And now you don't have to."

He shook his head. There was no way he'd win this argument. He might as well resign himself to the fact that he now owned a dog. The last thing he wanted to do was to upset Diana when their relationship was already in a precarious position. He'd moved here to get to know her and Andy, and if owning a dog was part of that, then he'd willingly go along with it just to please her.

"Thank you," he said. And he left it at that, because he wasn't sure what else he could say.

CHAPTER 12

SARAH

*T*he tall, spindly Norfolk Pines that lined the beach front were bursting with birdlife. Rainbow lorikeets ducked and wove through the branches, then settled in for their night's rest, their screeches filled the air with a cacophony of song.

Sarah covered her ears with her hands as she and Mick wandered along the footpath that wound beneath the trees.

She shouted to be heard over the birds. "They're so loud!"

Mick laughed, resting a hand on the small of her back as they crossed the street. "Don't you love it?"

She had to admit, there was something special about the way the birds returned to the same trees every night and took their time settling onto perches. But the volume of their bedtime conversations made her eardrums ache.

They strolled along the other side of the street, peering through the pine trees to the beach beyond. The sun ducked behind the tall buildings to their left, throwing long shadows across the dunes and the sandy shore. The ocean lapped black against the shore, ominous in the fading light. Small waves rose and fell, in a hypnotic rhythm.

Dozens of small restaurants lined the left side of the street. They settled on a Mexican eatery decorated with brightly coloured rugs and woven hats. She and Mick sat at a small round table, out of the wind, and ordered a pitcher of water, chips, and salsa to start.

"Do you want sangria?" asked Mick, as the waitress left to get their drinks.

Sarah shook her head and gritted her teeth. She'd felt sick for days. At first, she'd wondered if she'd caught a stomach bug, now she thought it might be something more serious. It was an odd kind of illness, it settled in her gut like motion sickness, but she couldn't figure out what'd caused it.

Unless she was pregnant.

She shook off the thought with a quick intake of breath.

No, she couldn't be pregnant. They'd only spoken about it a few weeks ago, and they hadn't really decided what they were going to do yet. Sure, they'd both agreed they wanted to try, but they hadn't spoken of it since. Tonight would be a good time to continue the conversation.

"What's wrong?" Mick asked, reaching for her hand, and cupping it between his.

She grimaced. "I don't know. I'm not feeling well."

"Do you want to go home?" he asked. "Or is it more urgent—like find a bathroom, fast?"

She laughed. "I'm okay, I think. It's a low-grade nausea. But maybe it's hunger too. I'm really not sure. Only, I've felt this way for a few days now. So, perhaps I've caught something."

His eyes narrowed. "That's not good. Maybe we should take a rain check on date night."

"No, I've been looking forward to this dinner all week. You're working so hard at the moment, and I've fallen asleep early every night—so I feel like we've hardly seen each other."

He sighed, released her hand, and leaned back. "I know what you mean."

The waitress brought their waters and chips. Sarah reached for a handful of chips and stuffed them into her mouth, savouring the flavour and not bothering with the salsa.

"Mmmm," she murmured.

Mick watched her with a hint of a smile teasing the corners of his mouth. "Good chips, huh?"

She nodded, took another handful. "The best."

"How do you feel now?"

"Better already," she replied.

"Maybe you were only hungry."

She nodded, but her stomach did a flip. There was another possible explanation.

"Or it could be —" She chewed and swallowed, her heart racing.

"What?"

"I might be pregnant," she replied.

His eyes flew wide. "Really? Do you think so?"

"I don't know. I've been feeling unwell and I'm late, plus eating really seems to help with the whole nausea thing—so I don't think it could be a stomach bug."

He combed fingers through his hair with a grunt. "Wow, that was fast."

"We don't know anything for sure yet. But if I am pregnant, that would be —"

"Amazing!"

He finished her sentence for her, and relief flooded through her body.

"Yes, amazing." She grinned. "But I suppose we'll have to wait to find out."

He shook his head. "I can't wait. There's a grocery shop inside The Strand. Let's get a pregnancy test after dinner."

She laughed. "Okay, let's do it."

* * *

THEY TOOK their time with dinner. Sarah enjoyed every bite of the chicken quesadillas with guacamole, followed by a serving of churros with melted chocolate. Excitement buzzed in her chest throughout the meal. It was hard for her to think about anything else other than the possibility that there was a baby growing inside of her.

What would everyone say?

It was fast—that much was true. They'd eloped and now might be pregnant too. It could seem as though they were in a rush, to someone on the outside. But from where she stood, their entire relationship was unfolding in a wonderful and completely natural way. She was ready. As much as she hadn't thought she was only a year earlier, she'd embraced every step they'd taken since then.

"What about the cottage?" asked Mick as he licked the last of the chocolate from his fingertips.

"What about it?"

"It's a bit small to raise children. Not to mention the dangerous cliffs on three sides. We tore down that old broken fence when we did the renovations, so there's nothing to stop little people from investigating the cliffs for themselves."

Sarah stopped chewing, her throat constricting. Of course, the cottage wasn't the right place to raise a family. She'd never intended it for that. It'd been her getaway from the world, her refuge. She hadn't considered the possibility that she might marry her contractor and bring children into that world—returning to Emerald Cove had been an escape from a bad engagement. She'd seen it as a rejection of marriage, but now knew it was more a rejection of her former fiancé than anything else.

"You're right. I hadn't thought of that. We can't raise our child there. It's a deathtrap!"

He chuckled. "I'm not sure I'd use that word, but I agree that it's probably not suitable. Of course, we could build a fence, but that would ruin the aesthetic of the place—the beauty of the cottage is the wild, untamed feel of it, and the outlook over the ocean. A fence would partially block that view."

"No, we can't build a fence," agreed Sarah. "We're going to have to move."

"But where would we move to?"

Her fingernails tapped out a rhythm on the table. "Somewhere in town, I suppose. It would be nice to be closer to everyone."

"I agree. Plus, it would be handy to have the shops nearby, in case we needed something for the baby."

Sarah had a sudden thought. "What about Mum's house?"

"Yes? But she's moving, remember."

"I know, that's what I'm talking about. We could buy it from her. It could be our house."

Mick's eyebrows arched high; he cleared his throat. "I don't know, it's probably out of our price range, honey."

"Maybe," she agreed. "But we should at least find out."

"I agree—it would be the perfect place to raise a family. Plus, you love that house."

She grinned. "Yes, I do—I really do."

AFTER DINNER, Sarah slipped her hand into Mick's and they strolled into The Strand shopping centre. She purchased a pregnancy test, then Mick waited outside the Ladies. She finished up and washed her hands, then carried the test in a wadded-up paper towel out to where he stood, leaning up against the wall.

When he glanced up to see her walking his way, her heart skipped a beat at the look of pure love and vulnerability in his wide green eyes. His expression asked the question on his mind.

She smiled. "I don't know yet, we have to wait."

They sat together on a bench seat, side by side. She set the pregnancy test on one knee and stared at it, willing the minutes to pass more quickly.

"What are we looking for?" asked Mick.

"Two lines for yes," she replied.

And gradually they appeared. Two pink lines. She studied them a moment. Was it really two lines? One was fainter than the other. Perhaps she was imagining things. No, there were definitely two lines.

"So…does that mean…" asked Mick.

She leapt to her feet, the test in her hand. "I'm pregnant. It means I'm definitely pregnant."

He jumped up beside her with a hoot, took her in his arms, and kissed her softly on the mouth. Then, he spun her in a circle, her arms wrapped tight around his neck.

"We're having a baby," he whispered against her ear. "I'm so happy."

"Me too."

He kissed her again, then set her feet on the ground. "Let's go home, Mrs McIntosh."

She laughed. "I'd love to, Mr McIntosh. But first, I want to go and see Mum and make certain she hasn't sold her house to anyone else."

"Tonight?"

She laughed. "Yes, tonight. Because I want it— desperately. There's nowhere else I'd rather raise this baby than in my childhood home, and with you by my side. And I don't want anyone else to get the chance to buy it, so we have to do it tonight."

They drove from Coolangatta back to Emerald Cove, chattering together about how their lives would change with a baby, and what it meant to them to begin this new phase of their lives together. All the while, Sarah couldn't stop thinking about what it would mean for her. How it would change everything in her own life, her work, her day to day. She'd seen what it'd done to Meg—had visited Meg a few times since baby Amari came home from the hospital. Meg's entire day revolved around that sweet tiny baby, and her nights too. How would Sarah manage a writing career as well as motherhood? Not to mention her surfing, running, social life, and everything else she did that made her life so full. Still, she didn't want to raise the subject with Mick—not now, when the two of them were so excited about the pregnancy. Her fears and insecurities could wait to be aired another day.

When she knocked on the large timber front door of the house where she'd spent so many wonderful years, she feared for a moment that her mother had already gone to bed. But within seconds the porch light came on, then Mum was there, opening the door with a smile. Petal barked once, then whined a welcome as she turned a circle at Sarah's feet. She bent to pat the small, white dog, then followed Mum into the kitchen.

"Well, this is pleasant surprise. I'll put the kettle on, shall I?"

Sarah and Mick sat on bar stools at the kitchen bench while Mum buzzed around the kitchen, pouring tea and cutting slices of banana cake. Sarah didn't have the heart to tell her they'd already eaten dessert.

"I don't think I could eat another bite," whispered Mick, beneath his hand while Mum prattled on about her trip to the hairdresser that morning.

Sarah grinned. "Come on Mick. I mean, is there such a thing as too much dessert? Really? I'm sure you'll manage."

"What's that?" asked Mum.

"Oh, nothing," replied Sarah. "Actually, Mum we came over here to tell you something and to talk to you about the house."

Mum's eyes widened. "Well, in that case, let's get settled on the back deck. It's a beautiful evening."

The moon was nothing but an arc of chalk on a blackboard sky. A few stars hung glittering, but the night was otherwise dark. The air was cool on the deck with a light breeze that blew strands of Sarah's long, brown hair across her face. She pushed them back behind her ears and sat at the table. Fatigue washed over her, making her eyelids heavy. It was a new kind of tired that felt as though she were being pushed down beneath a thick blanket of sleepiness.

She yawned, covering it with one hand, then reached for a cup of tea from the tray her mother had set on the table in between them.

"The suspense is killing me, so go on then you two —tell me whatever it is you came here to say." Mum smiled and took a bite of banana cake.

Sarah exchanged a glance with Mick, who gave her an encouraging smile.

"Have you sold the house yet?" asked Sarah.

Mum shook her head. "No, they're putting the sign up tomorrow. I wanted to wait to talk to the whole family first. So now, it's full steam ahead."

Sarah inhaled deeply. "I'm glad, because Mick and I would like to buy it."

Mick cleared his throat. "She means, we'd like to talk about it."

"Really? Well, that's fantastic news. I think it's a wonderful idea. But what brought this on so suddenly?"

Sarah grinned. "We're having a baby."

A hand flew to Mum's throat, she hurried around to Sarah's side of the table and threw her arms around her daughter. "Oh, darling, that's wonderful news. I'm so happy for both of you."

She hugged Mick, then dabbed her teary eyes with the back of her sleeve.

Sarah stood and rested a hand on her mother's arm. "So, that's why we need a bigger house. And I thought if Mick and I buy it, then we can keep it in the family. Besides, I had such a wonderful childhood here, I know my children will love it too."

Mum sniffled. "It's perfect. I can't tell you how much this has lifted the weight from my shoulders. I hated to sell this old place—it means as much to me as it does to you. Keeping it in the family will make me very, very happy. But even more than that, a baby! Oh, how wonderful! This is the best news in the world."

CHAPTER 13

REBECCA

*T*he line-up of cars stretched for a kilometre over a rise and down to the bridge. Rebecca glanced at Franklin in the cruiser's driver's seat beside her.

He shook his head and offered her a smile. "This should be fun."

He parked the car on the verge, and they both climbed out. As they marched down to the bridge, slipping and sliding on the muddy ground, they fielded questions from drivers and passengers.

"Hey Sarge, what's going on?"

"Is this going to clear up anytime soon, or should I turn around?"

"Is the bridge really falling into a sink hole?"

Franklin brushed them off as Rebecca studied the bridge. From what she could see it was bent in the middle, with both ends at a slightly odd angle.

"What do you think happened?" she whispered to Franklin, as they scrambled over a rocky outcropping.

"I don't know. It might be all the rain we've had. The ground's very soft, and they've had a lot of water travel through this creek."

"The structure looks pretty old," added Rebecca.

"At least a hundred years," agreed Franklin.

They reached the bridge and stopped. A third of the way down the bridge, a minivan and a station wagon had swiped each other. The accident didn't look bad, in fact, the passengers were all either milling about on the bridge or staring out over the rushing waters, arms resting on the railings.

"So, what's the plan?" asked Rebecca.

"Let's see if anyone's hurt, then we'll have to get them off the bridge. I'm not sure they realise how damaged it is, or they wouldn't still be standing there. The main thing is not to panic anyone."

"Right, got it," she replied.

Franklin stood on the end of the bridge, eying the structure warily. "Hey folks, how's it going?"

One of the drivers, a woman in her forties, ambled their way. "There you are. Am I glad to see you, officer. This maniac side-swiped me in the middle of the bridge."

Andy Flannigan crossed his arms over his chest. "I did not. The bridge moved. It wasn't my fault."

"Hi, Andy," said Franklin. "Tell me what happened…?"

"The bridge moved? Do you hear how ridiculous you sound?" continued the woman.

"Now, now, let's take a breath. There's no need to be upset, we're going to get to the bottom of everything, I promise you. But first I have a few questions. Is anyone hurt?" called Rebecca.

"We're fine," replied the woman, waving a hand at two children who were studying a pile of small stones on the edge of the bridge, picking them up and heaving them into the water. Below the bridge, the swollen creek waters rushed by. They gurgled and bubbled around the structure's pylons, frothing, and swirling as they went.

"I'm okay," agreed Andy.

"Are your cars still operational?"

Both drivers confirmed that they were.

"Great. I'm going to need all of you to get into your vehicles and drive off the bridge."

"But don't you have to study the crime scene or something?" asked the woman with her brow furrowed.

"Normally I would, but the bridge isn't safe."

"What? Why not?" the woman's eyes narrowed, and her gaze swept back and forth over the bridge.

"I told you it moved!" piped up Andy with an exasperated shake of his head. The cap on his head was set back and he wore a pair of shorts and a T-shirt.

The woman huffed. "Well, it sounded insane. Is it true, officer—did the bridge move?"

"It looks that way. So, please get back in your vehicles and drive over here, to where I'm standing."

With a few grumbles, both adults climbed into their vehicles. The station wagon was in front, so Andy straightened the wheel and drove it off the bridge. Behind him, the minivan revved but didn't move. It seemed stuck in place.

"You deal with him," said Franklin, stabbing a finger in the direction of the station wagon. "I'm going to see what's wrong with the minivan. Then, we'll have to call the council, get an engineer down here to check the bridge."

Rebecca dipped her head in acknowledgement and turned to talk to Andy. He told her his version of events; she took notes in her notepad. Behind her, the minivan continued to growl, wheels spinning in place.

She called in via the radio to ask Steph to get an engineer out to look at the bridge, and to send a tow truck. If they couldn't move the minivan, then they'd need someone to pull it free. Finally, she asked Andy to wait in his vehicle and turned her attention back to the bridge.

Just then, the bridge shifted. There was a loud cracking sound, and a grinding, followed by the entire structure shifting downstream at the far end.

Rebecca sprinted to the near end of the bridge. "Franklin, get out of there, the bridge is failing!"

Her heart thundered against her ribcage as she watched it moving. Slowly it ground sideways caught by the flood waters below.

Franklin stood, knees bent, as though trying to gain his balance. He shouted something to the woman in the minivan, then strode to the back of the van and bent to push it. Rebecca bit down on her lip. He should get out of there, tell them all to climb out and run for it.

"Franklin!" she shouted, but her voice was lost beneath the noise of the gunning engine and rushing water.

He heaved again, and the van's tyres caught on the gravel and the van lurched forward. Tyres squealing, the van sped towards Rebecca. She jumped out of the way, just as the van plunged from the bridge onto the verge, bouncing over the muddy ground.

Gasping for breath, Rebecca headed onto the bridge. "Franklin, come on!"

He ran towards her, along the tarmac, arms pumping. Then, the bridge shifted sideways again, with the high-pitched squeal of metal on metal. The ground buckled in front of him. He tripped on it and fell, sprawled out on its black, gravelled surface.

He raised his head then shook it. What was he doing? Was he hurt? He was taking too long. The bridge was bending and cracking all around him. The other end of the structure had moved away from the road and had begun falling in pieces to the bank below.

"Franklin!" she cried with her hands cupped around her mouth.

Without waiting another moment longer, she launched herself onto the bridge, running as fast as she could towards where Franklin sat on hands and knees, still shaking his head. The ground gave way beneath his legs and he fell.

"No!" she screamed, still running.

Her breathing was laboured, her heart pounding. This couldn't be happening. They'd only been married for such a short amount of time. She couldn't lose him now. All the little things she'd complained of beneath her breath seemed ludicrous in the stark light of loss. She'd do whatever it took, give up anything to keep him safe.

When she reached the broken section of the bridge, she found him hanging there, hands grasping one edge of the tarmac, his body swinging in the gap between the middle section of the bridge and the end still attached to the road.

She fell to her knees and reached out for him. "Franklin, I'm here. Give me your hand."

There was a gash on his forehead, blood oozed like a slash of red paint. "Bec, you'll get hurt. I'm too heavy for you. Go back!"

"No, I'm not leaving you. Give me your hand."

He reached up a hand and she took it in both of hers, stood and pulled. The bridge moved again, and she lost her footing, almost plunging headfirst through the gap. But she caught herself, not letting go of Franklin, and righted herself with a grunt.

"Bec!" cried Franklin.

"I'm fine, I'm okay. Come on, help me get you up here."

They worked together, and in a few moments, Franklin lay on his back on the pavement beside her. They were both breathing hard but didn't have time to waste.

"Let's go," said Franklin as he hauled himself to his feet.

They sprinted side-by-side from the bridge, just as the entire structure gave way and collapsed. Metal screeched and the centre of the bridge fell into the water, which frothed and rolled over it. Both ends of the bridge crumbled to the creek banks, scattering the mud and grass with chunks of concrete and tarmac.

Franklin and Rebecca turned, puffing hard, to watch. Rebecca raised both hands to her forehead in disbelief. A minute longer and they'd both have been in the water or crushed by falling concrete.

Franklin looped an arm around her shoulders. "That was close."

She nodded mutely.

"You shouldn't have done that. You could've been killed," he continued.

She glared at him, not believing what she was hearing. "If I hadn't come out there, you'd be dead right now."

He nodded. "Thank you."

She offered him a half-smile. "You're welcome."

* * *

IT TOOK hours to clean up the mess at the bridge. Franklin was taken away in an ambulance, leaving Rebecca to deal with the traffic, the distraught commuters, and the tow-truck driver who wouldn't be paid, since there was nothing to tow.

Meanwhile, an engineer arrived from the Murwillumbah Council and stood with his hands on his hips, gaping at the destruction.

Finally, another cruiser arrived, giving Rebecca a chance to leave. She called Franklin, who'd already made it home, and told him she'd be there in thirty minutes. He said he didn't have a concussion, just a few stitches in his forehead. He was fine—a headache, nothing more. A couple of Panadol would do the trick.

Darkness fell as she drove. Clouds obscured the sky, although she knew the moon would be nothing more than a sliver even if she could see it. The temperature dropped, although the humidity level didn't change and sweat made her uniform cling to every part of her body. She'd sweat through it hours ago, now it felt cool and damp in the air-conditioned cruiser. The landscape flashed by—a winding country road, green fields, and clumps of shadowy trees.

She hadn't had a chance to think about what'd happened. It'd all passed so quickly, then she'd been caught up in answering questions, organising, and managing things. As she drove, she began to shake. Her hands on the steering wheel shook so badly, she decided to turn up the radio to see if she could distract herself with loud music.

It didn't help. There wasn't anything that could pull her mind away from focusing on one thing—she'd almost lost her husband today. He could've been killed, or at the very least, badly injured. For days she'd been focusing on the little things about him that bothered her: he was a late riser, he didn't have a routine, he was clumsy and rushed about madly to get things done. She'd wondered why he couldn't be more organised, more patient, and add a little discipline into his life. But now, all she felt was shame. She loved him; he was everything to her. What did it matter if he liked to wear the same pair of socks two days in a row, or that he was always running five minutes late, and arrived dishevelled?

By the time she reached their house, tears blurred her vision. She parked the car and hurried inside, ready to beg his forgiveness.

The house was dark. Had he gone to bed?

She flicked on the kitchen light. There was a sound in the living room. She found Franklin there, seated in an armchair in the dark.

"Honey, what are you doing? Have you eaten anything?" she asked.

His hands were steepled in front of his chest. He spun the armchair to face her, his lips drawn into a straight, thin line. "Listen, Bec I've been thinking about something."

She frowned and sat on the coffee table beside him.

"I don't think we should be partners anymore."

Her breath caught in her throat as it constricted with the tears she'd held in for the entire drive home.

"What? Why not?"

He leaned forward, cupped her face between his hands. The wound on his forehead was dressed—it glowed white in the dim light. "You could've been killed today because of me. You didn't think clearly, you saw I was in trouble and you jumped to action. You saved my life, I know that, and I'm grateful. Don't think I'm not grateful. But I don't want you to get hurt because of me."

"That's what it means to be partners. Doesn't it?" she asked, doing her best to choke back tears. She didn't want him to have another excuse to bail on their partnership. Would he say she was too weak if she cried?

A muscle in his jaw clenched. He lurched to his feet and paced across the room. "Yes, that's what it means. Which is why we can't be partners anymore. I can't see you get hurt. I can't lose you."

She followed him, reaching out to him, her voice pleading. "But we're both cops. That's what it means— what the job entails. You knew that when you married me. It's not a surprise."

He ran both hands through his hair, sighed. "Of course, you're right. I knew it, but I couldn't help it—I fell in love with you."

She slipped her arms around his waist. "And I fell in love with you."

He groaned. "But that's exactly why we can't work so closely. I can't think clearly when you're there. All I know is that I want you to be safe, and I'm so focused on that I don't know what else to do."

She pressed her hands to her hips. "But this is my job. The only other option I have is to work night shift. Is that what you want—for me to be on the night crew? Or maybe I should join the Tweed Heads station?"

He grunted. "I don't know. Perhaps."

She stifled a scream of frustration. "Franklin! This is crazy. We're so good together. You saw what happened today, I was there for you. If I hadn't been there—"

"I know. I get it. But I can't shake the feeling that things could've gone very badly. I wanted you out of harm's way. What if you'd listened to me? What if you didn't listen and you'd fallen?"

Tears slipped from her eyes. "I was worried about you too. But the fact is, we're going to be in dangerous situations sometimes. You've got to come to terms with it, honey. How are you going to feel when I'm pregnant with our child and working the job?"

He blinked. "If you're pregnant, you'll quit."

Her nostrils flared. "What?"

"Of course, you will. I didn't think that'd be something up for discussion. If you're pregnant, you can't be out roaming around town, bringing down drug dealers and chasing home invaders."

She huffed. "We get maybe one or two of those every year. It's hardly a daily occurrence, Franklin. And no, it's not a given that I'll quit. I've never even considered doing that. I'm a cop, I love being a cop, it's what I want to do with my life."

"Even when we've got children?" His eyes widened.

She couldn't believe what she was hearing. Maybe

they'd rushed into marriage too quickly. They weren't on the same page over her work, over children—what else didn't she know about the man she'd vowed to spend the rest of her life with?

"I don't know, honey. I haven't really thought that far ahead. Maybe we should take a beat and draw a breath. It's been a rough day. We're both shaken up."

He nodded slowly. "You're right. We're not making any sense, either one of us. We're both going to fight, no matter what's said because we're in shock."

"Come on, I'll make us some dinner and we can talk about other things—safe things, like the weather, surfing, or going fishing this weekend."

He followed her into the kitchen, his stockinged feet padding softly on the hardwood floors. "So, you still want to go fishing this weekend?"

"I think it's a good idea. We need a break. We should do something relaxing and fun together. All we seem to do is work. We still haven't even had our honeymoon, so maybe we can talk about that. Where should we go."

He sat at the table and cradled his head in his hands.

"Does it hurt?" she asked.

He offered her a wan smile. "Only when I breathe."

"Did you take anything?"

"Right before you got home," he said.

He stood and walked to her, then pulled her into his arms. Her cheek was cushioned against his chest, her entire being connected to him by his warmth, his love.

"I'm sorry," he said.

She reached up to kiss him, then pulled away to make dinner. Every now and then she glanced at him, seated at the table again. He was so strong and yet so vulnerable, concerned about her safety to the point of despair, and all she could do was yell at him over it. She wasn't comfortable with being married yet, especially to a man who fought with his words instead of his fists. It felt as though she was always on the alert, bracing for when the argument would climb to the next level and she'd feel the brunt of it in her ribcage or on her face. But Franklin wasn't like that. He argued, then the storm calmed, and he showered her with affection.

She didn't know what the future held, or how they'd tackle it. But one thing was certain—with him by her side, she wouldn't have to face it alone.

CHAPTER 14

VICKY

*T*he poodle tugged at its leash. Its owner frowned and flashed Vicky a despairing look.

"It's okay, she won't feel a thing. I promise you."

The owner inhaled a quick breath and tightened her hold on the leash. Vicky offered the dog a treat as she slipped the injection into the dog's woolly coat. It barely noticed, still busily crunching on the treat as Vicky rubbed the place where the needle had pierced the skin.

She'd been so nervous about giving injections during her first year on the job, but now it was second nature to her. Thousands of needles over almost a decade of working as a veterinarian had inoculated her to the fear that'd gripped her so long ago.

Still, sometimes it was difficult, especially when an

animal wouldn't cooperate—and certainly when they were the larger breeds, like the Hereford bull last week who hadn't wanted her to come within a metre of him, let alone stick a large needle through his thick hide.

"All done," she said. "If you head on out to reception, they'll fix up the bill for you."

Vicky patted the dog, offering another treat as its tail wagged vigorously.

The woman holding the leash shook her head. "You're amazing—its why I always come back to see you Dr Hawkins, you've got such a gentle way with animals. Thank you so much!"

Vicky waved goodbye, then set the room in order again so it'd be ready for the next day. The poodle was her last patient, and she was very ready to go home. Her head ached, more of a throbbing really rather than an ache, her eyes stung as though she'd been caught in smoke drifting from a bonfire, and her stomach growled with hunger. She should've eaten lunch but hadn't been able to take the time to find something to eat. Now she was paying the price. If she didn't take better care of herself, the lupus would flare up and she'd have to take time off work to recover.

On the drive home, she couldn't get Ben Silver out of her mind. The radio station played a love song and an image of his deep brown eyes and warm smile flitted across her thoughts. She shook her head and changed the channel, only to find a talk show host answering people's relationship questions. She wondered if he was in a relationship. Of course, he'd only recently moved to the Cove and he lived alone. But there might be someone in his life—someone who planned to follow him to his new home when she was able to get away. Or perhaps he'd had a recent breakup. Either way, she kept thinking about Ben, when all she wanted to do was go home, relax in a bubble bath, and not think about anything or anyone at all.

Then there was the puppy.

She sighed. Ben hadn't known he was getting a dog and didn't appear to be much of a dog person. What if the poor creature was driving him crazy? What if neither one of them was coping well with their new living arrangements?

With pursed lips she changed course and drove towards the beach where Ben lived. She should check on them, if only for the puppy's sake. Make sure the animal was at least being fed. And if she spent a little time with Ben too, then that would be a bonus.

When she arrived at his house, she knocked on the front door three times and didn't get a response. She peered over the fence on the side of the house and saw a chew toy and straggly grass that hadn't been mowed in a while, but nothing more. With a frown, she scratched her head. Ben's car was parked in the driveway and he had an injured leg, so he wasn't likely to have ridden anywhere on his bike.

She tried the front door again. "Hello?" If he was hurt, she wondered if anyone would know—he hadn't been in town long. Perhaps he'd fallen, tripped on his injured leg, and couldn't get up. She couldn't leave the house without knowing he was okay.

She tugged her mobile phone from her pocket and searched for his number, then dialled.

"Hello," answered a gruff voice.

"Ben, it's Vicky Hawkins here."

"Oh, hi, Vicky, how are you?"

She smiled to herself. He sounded fine; she'd been worried for nothing. "I'm at your house, I came to check on you and the puppy. To see how you're going. But you're not here."

There was a bang and Ben grunted. "Ah, oh sorry. I'm home, I didn't hear the front door. Wait a minute and I'll be right there."

The phone went dead. Vicky stared at it a moment, then put it back in her pocket and chewed on her bottom lip while she waited.

When the front door flew open, Ben stood in front of her in a pair of shorts and a tightly fitting T-shirt that accentuated his lithe, muscular frame. He held the puppy in one arm. His injured leg was bandage-free and had a set of red scars down the length of his shin and calf.

He grinned, his brown hair flopping across his forehead the way it always seemed to. It gave him a boyish charm she found irresistible. "Hi, come on in. Sorry, the place is a bit of a disaster."

She nodded. "No worries. I'm glad to see the two of you are fine."

He grunted again. "Uh, yeah. We're surviving, I suppose you could say."

When Ben stopped walking, Vicky almost ran into his back.

"Oh come on!" he exclaimed. "Rusty, this is not acceptable."

Vicky peered around Ben and saw a small pile of dog poop on the tiled floor in front of him.

"He left you a little pressie," she said with a giggle.

"It's not the first time. This is getting ridiculous." With a shake of his head, he manoeuvred around the pile and led her into the kitchen, then set the dog on the floor. "What can I get you to drink—tea, coffee, water?"

She slid into a chair at the small round dining table. "I'd love a cup of tea."

He washed his hands, flicked on the kettle and searched for cups and tea bags. "I hope you're having a better week than I am."

She arched an eyebrow. "Oh? What's going on? I thought you were on the mend."

He chuckled. "I am. I shouldn't complain since I'm here and in one piece. But this dog...ugh."

She bit down on her lower lip to keep from making a sound. Not everyone loved animals as much as she did. But she was surprised to hear that Ben wasn't enjoying Rusty. She was usually good at reading people and she'd thought he was an animal lover after his comments about the shark.

"Not a dog person?" she asked.

He shook his head. "It's not that. I don't know if I am or if I'm not—I've literally never owned a pet in my life before. I love animals, but usually they're in the wild and I'm simply watching them. I'm at a complete loss with this puppy. Maybe there's something wrong with him—are some dogs defective?"

He looked up at her, waiting for her response.

She wasn't sure whether to laugh or bite her lip. "Um, well I'm not sure defective is the right word."

"Sorry," he replied. "You must think I'm awful. You spend your life taking care of hundreds of animals, and I'm not even capable of looking after one little puppy."

Rusty trotted around Ben's feet, as though trying to

trip him up. The little auburn tinted dog looked up at him, watching his every move.

"Don't be so hard on yourself," replied Vicky, walking to him and picking up Rusty. "Puppies can be tricky. Especially one as smart as this little fella."

Ben carried a teapot and two cups over to the table. He had a slight limp but otherwise seemed fine.

"He's smart, huh?"

She stroked Rusty's head and he wriggled hard to get to her face with his little pink tongue. "Very. He's extremely trainable too. And he'll be eager to please. Kelpies are a loyal breed. They're descended from the border collie and rumour has it they've got a bit of dingo in them too. Did you know that?"

He frowned. "Really? Wow, that's pretty cool."

"They're an amazing dog. Nothing else like them. But they're not always suited to the suburban life. They're great on properties though, where they can round up cattle or sheep and work hard." She loved Kelpies and had grown up with them. They were loyal to a fault, high energy, smart, and keen to please. They could be ferocious to anyone threatening their pack, which included their humans. Besides that, they were a lot of fun.

He set the teapot on the table and poured two cups of tea, then sat down, waving a hand to invite Vicky to sit too. She put Rusty down and washed her hands at the sink before joining him.

"Well, I'm glad to hear he's smart. A little concerned about the high energy part though, since I do have a fairly small yard."

She shrugged. "Yes, but you're very active. I think Rusty suits you and your lifestyle perfectly. He'll tag along with you on all your adventures, and he'll love it."

Ben grinned. "I like the sound of that." He sighed. "Although right now I think I'm failing in the parenting department. He cries all night long—neither one of us is getting any sleep. And I don't know why, but every time I take him outside, he only plays. Then he comes inside and goes to the loo on one of my rugs." He combed fingers through his dark hair, making it stand on end.

She took a sip of tea. "Well, he's crying at night because he thinks he's been left behind by his family. It's natural for him to alert his mother to the fact that he's alone. So, I'd suggest buying a crate for him to sleep in and putting something of yours, that smells like you, in with him—since you're his family now. Also, if you can have the crate close by, so he feels less alone, that might help."

He nodded thoughtfully, cupping the tea between his hands. "Okay, I can do that. Thanks."

"And the toilet training—I can help you with that too. He's clever, so he'll catch on quickly. In fact, why don't we start now?"

* * *

TWO HOURS LATER, Vicky and Ben were seated on the floor next to the coffee table, across from each other, deeply engrossed a game of twenty-one.

"That's twenty," said Vicky with a smug grin, splaying out her cards in a fan shape on the table.

Ben groaned, laying his cards down. "Eighteen."

"Yes!" she shouted. She pumped one arm in the air, then stood to her feet and danced in place.

Ben threw his head back and laughed. "Okay, that's it. I give up. You're the twenty-one champion." He stacked the cards together and pushed them into the centre of the table, then stood with a groan.

"I'm getting too old to sit on the floor for so long."

She stretched her arms over her head. "Me too."

"Oh please," he objected. "You can't be more than twenty-five years old."

"Thirty," she replied.

His eyes widened. "Really? See, I'm so old I can't even tell the difference between someone who's twenty-five and someone who's thirty. All you kids look the same to me."

"Kids?" she blurted. "Hardly. You act as though you're eighty years old. I'm sure you're only a few years older than me."

"I'm forty-four," he replied, and the way he looked at her it seemed he was waiting for her reaction.

She smiled. "Forty-four isn't old."

"It's fourteen years older than you are. I was a teenager when you were born."

"So?" She shrugged. "It mattered then, I suppose. But it doesn't now." Why were they arguing about this? She hated the idea that he thought himself too old for her, but what did it matter? Surely, he wasn't interested in her in that way. And she was making it far too obvious she found him attractive with her determination to prove their age difference didn't matter.

Her cheeks flamed with heat and she sought desperately for a new topic of conversation. "How's your leg, by the way?"

He studied her a moment, his dark eyes half-lidded. "It's much better, thanks. Hey, should we order some dinner? It's pretty late and I'm starving."

She glanced at the window—it was pitch dark outside. She'd overstayed. What must he think of her? That she was desperate, for one. And that she had an enormous crush on him.

"Thanks, but I should get home. It's been a long day."

He nodded. Did he seem disappointed? Or perhaps he was simply tired too.

As she walked out to her car, she glanced over her shoulder at the house. The curtains in the front room were drawn, the light glimmering out around the edges. There was a warmth to the place that was inviting. Spending time with Ben left her dreading her own quiet, dark unit.

She'd thought him handsome but quiet. Now, after playing cards together and working on Rusty's potty training routine for the afternoon, she'd learned that he was also fun, witty, and kind. There hadn't been a single lull in their conversation—they'd had plenty to talk about. She'd been surprised by how talkative he was, given her first impression.

She'd never dated a man so much older than her, but he didn't seem older—in fact, they had more in common than any man she knew her own age. And after she'd shown him how to help Rusty toilet outside, he'd been so gentle with the dog. She was certain he'd make a good pet owner—an essential characteristic for anyone she dated.

Why was she thinking of dating? He hadn't given her any indication he liked her. Although he had asked if she wanted to stay for dinner—most likely that was because he was starving, and she'd stayed too long. She hoped she hadn't annoyed him. Although he seemed to be having as much fun as she was. Ugh, she really should stop following the spiralling, anxiety-driven thought process that always derailed her love life.

Whatever he was thinking didn't matter—she liked him and enjoyed his company. She hoped to spend more time with him in the future. It was enough for now.

CHAPTER 15

SARAH

*T*he hallway at Mum's house had a tall, arched ceiling. It was one of the things Sarah loved most about the place. That and the spacious bedrooms. The master bedroom had its own sitting room overlooking the extensive gardens, as well as an enormous bathroom with a claw-foot tub. She'd never used the tub in that room, but remembered Mum taking long, soaking baths with candles dotting the bathroom when she was a little kid. She'd wander in there, dragging her teddy bear or doll behind her, thumb in mouth, wondering why her mother seemed to enjoy her bath time almost as much as she did herself.

Mum's house.

It'd be her house soon. The thought sent a pang of anxiety through her chest. It was so big with so much to take care of. The mortgage alone would be a burden to she and Mick. They'd talked numbers with Mum a few days after their visit to her that night and had decided they could swing it—with a hefty loan from the bank. A trip to their local bank the next day had affirmed the matter—they were approved for a loan and it wouldn't be long before the house was theirs.

Mum seemed overjoyed about the house staying in the family. Still, Sarah hadn't spoken to Ethan or Adele yet and wondered what they might have to say on the subject. No doubt they'd let her know if they had an issue with her and Mick buying their childhood home. Adele had often been jealous of Sarah over the years; would this be another reason for her to believe Sarah was favoured?

She strode up the stairs and found her mother in one of the guest rooms, kneeling on the floor beside an open box.

"Mum, there you are."

She kissed the top of her mother's head and set her purse on the floor.

"Hello darling. I'm so glad you came. I could really use the help."

"I can see that," replied Sarah, scanning the room. She'd loved this room as a child—it'd been a great hiding place during one of their epic games of hide and seek. The four-poster bed had a long bedspread that brushed the hardwood floor, giving little girls a wonderful place to squeeze into where they couldn't be seen unless the fabric was lifted. Now, boxes lay strewn around the room. The large closet doors hung open, shelves were stacked with linens, knickknacks, books and more—half had been packed already and the rest were scattered askew.

"You have so much stuff," complained Sarah, reaching for an empty box.

"Too much!" agreed Mum. "I should've gotten rid of most of it years ago. But I've been a bit busy."

"That's true. Anyway, I can't help you to go back in time. So, instead I'll help you sort through it all now. Deal?"

Mum chuckled. "Deal."

Sarah marched to the closet and began putting things into piles—one for donations, another for rubbish and the last to pack.

"You don't need these sheets, do you Mum?"

Mum grimaced. "Need? Probably not. But still, I hate to part with them."

"Mum, you're going to have to be a bit more callous. The chalet isn't going to be big enough to hold it all."

"I know," Mum whined. "But still, they're good sheets."

"I'll tell you what—I'll pack the best ones, but I won't tell you which. It'll be my little surprise. That way, you won't have to feel badly about it."

Mum shook her head. "Okay."

"Great. So, how much is there left to do?"

"I packed up the office months ago. But then I kind of got sidetracked with other things. So, I've got pretty much the entire house left to go. Adele is doing her room and she's started on the living room. So, I thought we could focus on the upstairs."

"Perfect. Is Adele okay? Wouldn't she rather be up here packing with us?"

Mum sighed. "I don't know. I think she's better than she was, but I'm still worried about her. She doesn't open up much, though, so it's hard to say.

Right now, she's working at the cafe. She really seems to like it there. And she's made some great changes to the layout and the menu already—she's got a good knack for it. Reminds me a bit of myself at her age."

"I'm so glad. I've been concerned about her too. But she doesn't seem to want to talk to me about anything. She did mention a horrible boyfriend who broke her heart, but that's all she'll tell me."

With pursed lips, Mum shook her head. "I know, it's so difficult to get through to her. But we'll simply keep trying. So, for now it's just you and me, babe."

"Sounds good," replied Sarah.

She reached for her purse and pulled out a chocolate bar, peeled back the wrapper, and took a large bite.

"Mmm...that's better." She squeezed her eyes shut to enjoy the flavour and waited for the nausea to pass.

"You're not usually one to eat chocolate bars. You've always been such a health food fanatic," said Mum, one eyebrow quirked.

"I know, it's this pregnancy. I can't get enough chocolate."

"Oh dear. Does it help?"

Sarah nodded, still chewing. "It does. For some reason, even one bite helps with the morning sickness."

"Well, enjoy it, my darling. This is such a special time in your life. And I can't believe I'm going to be a grandmother—it's all I can think about."

Mum's blue eyes crinkled at the corners and her mouth widened into a grin. "I'm going to be such a young, hip grandmother. You wait and see." She winked.

Sarah laughed. "Ah Mum, you almost had me convinced until you used the word 'hip'."

They both giggled together as they packed, and Sarah wondered how she'd ever managed to live so far away from her family for such a long time. She felt whole again being back and home, spending time with her mum and siblings. The Cove was where she belonged.

* * *

BEN

The truck's tyres squeaked on the tarmac. Ben reversed the vehicle into a parking spot, then hurried around the other side to help Diana out. He retrieved her crutches from the back, then walked with her into the doctor's office.

"So, they're checking to see how your leg is healing?" he asked.

She nodded, her brown bob brushing the shoulders of her green pantsuit. "Yes, they want to make sure the bones are coming together well. I'm hoping they'll say I can take it off. Finally."

"That'd be good."

"I shouldn't complain. It could've been worse." She offered him a wry smile. "If you hadn't shown up when you did."

They found seats in the waiting room. Diana shifted about in hers with a grimace.

"Everything okay?"

"These seats are so hard. I haven't been taking my walks along the beach because of my leg, so my entire body is twitchy for lack of exercise. I can't seem to get comfortable at all these days."

"I'm sorry. Thankfully, it won't last forever."

"Yes, that's true. I'm hoping when I get this cast off maybe I can start swimming laps with you."

"You'll find me at the local swimming pool," he said with a chuckle.

"I should hope so," she replied, her brown eyes sparkling. "I thought it was nice that Vicky offered to bring the puppy over the other day."

He noticed the not-so-delicate segue but decided not to draw attention to it. "That was very kind of her."

"She's a lovely woman."

"I think so."

"And she's single, I believe." Diana examined her fingernails as she spoke.

"Is that so?"

"Hmmm."

"Are you making a point?" asked Ben.

She glanced his way, her mouth turning up at the corners. "Not really. Only, you could ask her out on a date. It's really the only polite thing to do after she helped us so sweetly."

He chuckled. "Really? The polite thing to do. Well, in that case —"

"So, you'll call her?"

Ben sighed. "She's far too young for me, Diana."

"Pshaw! You're young and sprightly."

"Not so young anymore, I'm afraid," he replied.

"I worry about you, that's all."

He offered her a smile, patted her arm. "Don't—I'm fine. Really, I came to the Cove to get to know you and the rest of my birth family better. I'm not looking for a romantic relationship."

She sighed. "Well, I suppose that's fine. But please don't miss out on life's little opportunities. When you get to my age, you realise that chances don't come along very often. If you don't take them when they do, you may not see them ever again, and you'll live to regret it."

As she shuffled into the doctor's office, Ben considered her words. He'd had no intention of calling Vicky or bothering her in any way. She was young, fun, and full of energy. He couldn't imagine that he was her type. Still, Diana did have a point—it'd been years since he'd met a woman like Vicky. Someone he was attracted to, who was also fun to spend time with, and considerate of others' needs. Perhaps he should think about it a little more before making a decision. He'd never felt lonelier in his life than he had since moving to Emerald Cove. Even if Vicky didn't see him in a romantic light, spending time with her might drive away the emptiness. At least for a little while.

CHAPTER 16

CINDY

"*How's* the packing coming?" asked Athol, manoeuvring his way around a tussock of seagrass.

Breathing hard, Cindy set her hands on her hips, and stopped to take in the view. "It's coming. I really hate moving—I suppose that's why I haven't done it in so long. Still, I'm excited about the new place, just wish I didn't have to pack up everything I own. I had no idea how much useless stuff I'd accumulated and shoved into cupboards, nooks, and crannies all over the house."

She puffed between words, gasping for breath.

The headland rose high above the ocean, black rocks topped with waving clusters of grasses and shrubs. The wind whistled as it met the rocky cliffs and found its way around them. On either side of the headland, long white beaches stretched to the horizon, with impossibly blue waves seeming to lap at the sand.

From where they stood, the waves were small. A few people jogged or walked along the beaches; surfers straddled surfboards beyond the break. Each seemed tiny from their vantage point—like miniature dolls in a make-believe world.

"I know what you mean," replied Athol.

His grey hair had been whipped this way and that, and now stood almost straight up on top of his head—its natural waves making it thick and full. Brown eyes full of warmth met hers, his smile crinkling their edges.

"Do we really have to climb all the way to the top of this thing?" asked Cindy with a grunt. "It's so steep."

He chuckled. "Come on, you can do it. I promise it'll be worth it. The view from the lookout is spectacular."

"The view from here is pretty amazing," she countered.

He took her hand, tugged her forward up the winding, dirt path. "Let's go, my darling."

She loved it when he called her that. Andy hadn't used words of endearment. Said it was too corny. But corny was exactly what she was looking for at her age. Cliched, corny—she'd take all of it. A man who adored her, a simple and drama-free life with a white picket fence—yes please, sign her up. She didn't need the excitement of wondering whether her husband loved her, if he was seeing someone else, or if he'd put a mortgage on their house without telling her. What she wanted was a stable, sensible life and the love of a man with no secrets.

And that was who Athol was. She'd known him

forever, and she'd never seen him act in an under-handed, secretive, or selfish way. He'd been a good husband to his wife—had adored her for all the years of their marriage until she passed. But she'd been gone a long time, and now he loved Cindy. He told her so every time they saw each other—another thing in his plus column. In fact, at this stage in their relationship, she couldn't think of a single negative when it came to Athol Miller. And she was kicking herself for only realising how wonderful he was so late in both their lives. But as he'd told her the night before when she'd expressed as much to him while they sat on his back deck beneath the stars, hands entwined—better late than never.

And the timing was right.

If things had developed between them any sooner than they did, it wouldn't have worked out. She was married until a year ago; Athol had been her husband's best friend. No, it was for the best. Instead of looking back with regret, she should simply embrace what she had in this moment—the love of a good man, her family all back in the Cove together, and a chance for a new beginning in a cute little chalet by the beach.

"Have you spoken to Andy lately?" she asked.

Athol didn't reply right away. He leaned forward, arms and legs pumping as he climbed the steep trail. "No. Not since the dinner."

"He came to see me yesterday." Athol didn't respond. So, she continued. "He was on that bridge that was swept away two days ago. Did you know that?"

"What? Really?"

She nodded, puffing hard and watching his stiff back as he made his way up the trail ahead of her. "He's fine, but he says he almost ended up in the swollen creek." She swallowed as a rush of panic swept over her at the thought. "I don't know, I think it's made him more aware of what he could've lost—perhaps he'll be more appreciative now. At least I hope so. But regardless, it prompted me to think about what my life might be like without him—and I realised that I care about him despite everything he's done."

"Okay."

With pursed lips, she considered his response. He was a man of few words, but even for him, a one-word response was unusual.

"Do you think you'll get a chance to talk soon?"

He stopped, spun to face her, his breathing heavy. "I don't know. Do you want me to talk to him?"

"I suppose I do. I've made peace with him and with Keisha. He's the father of my children, so we're bound to see them around. We were married for such a long time, we're family even if he is my ex-husband. In fact, I'll probably invite them to family events at times, and I'd prefer if you were on good terms with them both."

His eyes narrowed. "I know you've forgiven them, but it's hard for me. The way he hurt you, it makes my blood boil. I don't know why I didn't see it coming—I mean, I knew him so well. But he understood what marriage meant to me, so I suppose that's why he hid things the way he did."

"He hid things from everyone. He's still doing it—I mean, he came to see me without telling Keisha about it."

Athol nodded. "He still hasn't learned."

"And he probably never will. He hates confrontation, so he tries to avoid it by lying. But the good thing about all this is it's no longer our problem—you and I have moved on. We can forgive him, include him in our lives to some extent, but how he lives isn't going to impact us anymore. His choices are his own from this point forward, they have nothing to do with me, or with you."

Athol reached for her hands and took them in his own, squeezing them. "You're very wise." He winked. "I haven't spoken to him because I suppose I feel like he betrayed me too. He didn't say anything, just ran off with Keisha. Not a word. And he was supposed to be my friend."

Cindy reached up a hand to cup Athol's cheek. "He *was* your friend."

"So, I should forgive him and mend fences?" he asked.

She nodded. "If you're ready. It would mean a lot to me—I don't want you holding a grudge for my sake."

"We'll never be friends again like we were, but since you've asked me to, I'm happy to have a conversation with him and put the past behind us."

She sighed. "Thank you."

They finished climbing the headland. At the top, the wind buffeted them as they walked to the lookout —a small, rectangular outcropping of concrete surrounded by a metal fence. A large set of pay-per-view binoculars stood in the centre of the lookout. Beyond it, seagulls soared on the wings of the wind, gliding up and down on its currents above a turgid ocean.

Side by side, they stood leaning against the railing, looking out across the white peaks and rolling crests of unbroken waves.

"You were right, this is magnificent," said Cindy.

Athol smiled, looping an arm around her shoulders. She nestled into his warmth, enjoying the feeling of safety, love, and hope that filled her heart as they stood together.

After a while, Athol turned to face her, letting his arms drop to his sides. "I'm so glad I have you in my life."

She grinned, her throat tightening. Hearing his love for her spoken out in different ways would never grow tiresome. She didn't take it for granted as she might've done in her younger years—to have a good man love her and for him to express it every chance he got was a treasure she'd keep with her always.

"So am I. I can't tell you how much I've appreciated you being here with me, every step of the way, through all the good and bad in recent months."

He nodded and pushed his hands deep into his pockets. His eyes glimmered with unshed tears. "I know it's been hard on you, but selfishly I'm glad—because everything that happened brought us together."

She laughed, tears forming a lump in her throat. "I'm glad too. I couldn't imagine still being in that same place now. If Andy hadn't taken the leap and run off with his mistress, I'd still be married to him, still be unhappy. I would never have left him, it wasn't in me to do that, to break my vows and tear apart my family. But now that I have you, I can see how miserable I was, and I'm grateful things have changed even if the process was gut-wrenching."

"That's all behind you now. And I know what it's like, I've gone through my own share of gut-wrenching pain."

She nodded, her vision blurring with tears.

"And I want to tell you that the pain fades, then it

138

leaves, and you have happy memories to keep with you forever. But I also know that time passes swiftly and missed opportunities can bring their own share of pain with them. The pain of regret."

She frowned, wondering where he was going with this. Did he regret spending time with her?

"Regret?"

He swallowed, his cheeks colouring. "Yes, I don't want that for us. Don't want us to regret not seizing the opportunity to be together, to be happy."

"I don't want that either," she replied.

He pulled his hands out of his pockets and held up a ring. A simple gold band with a bouquet of small diamonds clustered together in a circle around a pearl in the centre. She gasped.

"That's why I brought you here this evening. To seize the moment. To take a chance."

He reached for her hand, and held it with his free one, then struggled onto his knees on the concrete.

She shook her head. "Oh no, please don't kneel. You may not get up again!"

He laughed. "I'm not that old, my love. And I'm going to do this right."

She pressed a hand to her mouth, tears streaking her cheeks.

"Cindy, my darling, will you do me the honour of spending the rest of your life as my wife?"

She hadn't expected it. They'd been doing so well lately, spending a lot of time together. Every moment with him was precious, and she'd come to know that more and more each day they shared. Still, she hadn't seen this coming. There was a part of her that'd vowed deep down never to remarry. But she knew she couldn't honour that vow. She loved him and the only way they could truly give their lives to each other was through marriage—she wasn't willing to compromise on her values to live any other way.

The commitment would bring a level of hope and love, confidence and trust into their relationship—she understood that with sudden clarity. And she knew in that moment what her answer would be.

"Yes!" she cried. "I will marry you."

CHAPTER 17

VICKY

*C*louds rolled across the sky, turning the blue-sky grey in short order. Vicky strode alongside Sarah and Meg. Meg pushed a pram and held onto Walton's leash as she walked. Sarah held Oscar's leash, but the dog kept straining at it in an attempt to sniff a rock or pee on a bush just out of reach. Rebecca, the newest member of the group who Vicky had run into at the gym during a boxing class, strode along on her other side.

"You're multi-tasking very well there, Meg," said Vicky between breaths.

They were power walking. Vicky had suggested they stroll instead, but Meg was determined to get back into pre-pregnancy shape. She'd used the word "snap," but Vicky wasn't sure snapping back into shape was the most realistic thing to aim for after everything her body had been through. Of course, she'd never say as much, she only hoped Meg would be kind to herself.

"Thankfully, Walton does as he's told, otherwise this might not work. Also, he weighs almost nothing. I'm not sure how Sarah manages to keep Oscar in check, he's so strong and determined."

All four of them laughed as Oscar made a lunge for a tree almost tripping Sarah over. She grimaced. "I don't think I'll be able to walk him and push a pram at the same time, that's for sure. The baby would be upside down in no time."

The footpath beside the beach wound along the coastline. The sun drifted towards the horizon behind them, casting a reddish glow over the sky. The humidity had dropped and a fresh breeze riffled Vicky's hair as she walked.

"How are you feeling, Vicky?" asked Rebecca. "Last time we spoke at the gym, you were a bit under the weather."

"I'm good today. I feel well, strong too. Which is nice. I definitely don't take it for granted the way I used to."

She'd made sure to get to bed early the night before and had eaten well all day.

"I think I'd eaten eggplant parmigiana the last time we spoke. I'm still learning about what might trigger an episode, but so far it seems to me that tomatoes and eggplants are both foods I'm sensitive to. So, I'm starting a list of things to avoid."

"I think that's a great idea," said Meg.

"The shame of it is, I love eggplant parmigiana—it's one of my favourite go-to recipes for when I forget to take meat out of the freezer."

"Ugh, that stinks," replied Sarah with a shake of the

head. "I love it too. I think you made it for me one time when I had a cold and was stuck in bed. I wanted to dive into it and swim around it was so delicious—all that cheese!"

Vicky laughed. "I probably add too much cheese to my Italian dishes, but I love the stuff. Mozzarella, cheddar and parmesan—I use all three in the parmigiana."

"And it really works!" replied Sarah, licking her lips.

"Then, I'll have to make it for you—but unfortunately I think I'm going to have to steer clear of it myself. Wow, having lupus really sucks."

"I'm so sorry," said Meg, offering her a sympathetic look. "You'll have to find some new favourites, that's all."

"You're right. I'm going to try some new recipes out and see what works for me. It's not that bad. I know so many people have it much worse."

"You can complain to us any time," replied Meg. "You've got to have someone to vent to."

They walked in silence for a few minutes before Rebecca blurted. "Can I talk to you guys about something?"

Sarah grinned. "Of course, what's up?"

"I know we haven't spent much time together, but I need a female opinion on something."

"Shoot," replied Meg.

"I haven't been married long, so I'm not sure if this is normal, but I've been keeping something from Franklin, and I don't know what to do about it."

Vicky and Sarah exchanged a look.

"What kind of thing?" asked Vicky.

Rebecca chewed on her lower lip, then inhaled a

deep breath. "I got a call from a solicitor in Sydney yesterday. He reminded me about a trust that I'm going to inherit on my thirtieth birthday, wanted me to sign some paperwork, that kind of thing."

"Sounds exciting," said Meg.

"I guess." Rebecca's nostrils flared. "It's a lot of money, and I've known it was coming for years, but it seemed so far away and now it's taken me by surprise. I haven't told Franklin about it. What'll he think? Anyway, I started worrying about how he'll react. But then I thought—I don't need to tell him. I mean, we don't have to talk about everything, do we?"

Sarah laughed. "I don't know… it seems to me that you should talk about those kinds of things in a marriage. I mean, I'm no expert, but I'd want to know something like that about Mick."

Meg and Vicky nodded, murmuring their agreement.

Rebecca sighed. "So, I should tell him?"

"Do you mind if I ask why you're worried about it?" Meg pushed a curl of red hair behind one ear.

"I don't want it to change things between us. We're so happy…"

"This wouldn't ruin that, would it?" asked Vicky.

Rebecca pushed a smile onto her face. "I suppose you're right. I should tell him. I only have to figure out when and how."

"I would think he'll consider it good news. I know I would," added Meg.

Rebecca didn't reply, only offered a quick nod of the head. Vicky considered their conversation—it was clear there was more to the story since what Rebecca had shared didn't make complete sense on its own. But if Rebecca didn't want to share it with them, they couldn't push her. In fact, Rebecca's cheeks were decidedly flushed—perhaps she should change the subject to make her more comfortable. After all, it'd been brave of her to open up so vulnerably on their first outing as a group of four together. And from what she'd learned of Rebecca so far from their conversations at the gym, she seemed like the kind of woman who kept most things to herself. Although there was something very endearing and sincere about her. Vicky could imagine them becoming long-term friends. She seemed to mesh well with Meg and Sarah too.

"So, Sarah—what's new with you?" asked Vicky. "I feel like I haven't spoken to you in ages."

Sarah hesitated, her cheeks pinking. "I finished my book."

"Wow, that's amazing. Congratulations!" Vicky's heart swelled. She'd watched her friend go through all the ups and downs of moving away from the city, ending a relationship, finding new love, quitting her job, and then facing her fears by writing her book.

"I can't imagine doing that," said Meg. "Well done."

"Thanks," replied Sarah. "It's a weight off my shoulders, but of course now comes the horrible part—putting it out there for people to read and critique."

"I'm sure you'll do really well," replied Vicky. "You're so talented and smart."

"I must be to have chosen friends like you," replied Sarah with a smirk. "And Mick has been so supportive. I don't deserve him. Honestly."

"Yes, you do," replied Meg. "He's a lucky guy."

"Speaking of lucky guys, have you met anyone lately Vicky?" asked Sarah.

Vicky wasn't sure what to say. How would Sarah

feel if she knew Vicky was attracted to her newly discovered half-brother. It was like something off the Oprah Winfrey show.

"Um…maybe."

Both Sarah and Meg jumped on the confession with squeals of glee.

"Oh, now you have to tell us everything," said Sarah, tugging on Oscar's leash. "But first, let's sit. I don't want to miss anything. Here's the dog park, I'll let Oscar have a run and we can sit on this bench."

Sarah and Meg let their dogs run free in the dog park. Sarah shut the gate behind Oscar with a sigh of relief. Then, they joined Vicky on the bench. Vicky peeked into the pram and smiled at the tiny sleeping face of baby Amari; one fist curled by her cheek.

"She's adorable," she said.

Meg's nose wrinkled. "I know, I almost can't take it. I want to bottle her cuteness up so I can keep it on a shelf forever. But of course, they tell me, each phase is cute in its own way and she's already so much bigger than she was when we brought her home two months ago."

"So, she's three months old?" asked Vicky.

Meg nodded. "Yep, and finally starting to sleep for a decent part of each night. Thank heavens!"

"You were going to tell us all about this guy you've met," said Sarah, clapping her hands together in delight. "I've waited patiently, but I can't wait any longer. Come on, spill!"

Vicky laughed, her face flaming with heat. "It's no big deal. He's nice but I don't know if he's interested in me."

"Who is he?" asked Meg.

Vicky glanced at Sarah. "Ben Silver."

Sarah's eyes widened. "My Ben Silver?"

"Who's Ben Silver?" asked Meg.

"My half-brother. Diana's son—do you remember him?"

"Ah yes, of course!" exclaimed Meg.

"Anyway, we've been spending some time together and I really like him."

"That's so great," said Sarah. "I thought the two of you shared a spark when we visited him together."

"You're okay with it?" asked Vicky. "I mean, nothing's happened and it may never happen. But I like him, so I thought I should probably mention it, just in case."

"Of course, I'm okay with it—it's fantastic. I don't know him well yet, but he seems like a great guy." Sarah bit down on her lip. "I'm going to try not to get carried away—but yay!"

They chattered together for a while longer, then Amari woke, and Meg had to feed her. "I really should get home. I'm still not very good at feeding, so I like to be in my own house. I know that sounds really backwards, but it doesn't come so easily as I thought it would," she said.

Sarah and Meg caught their dogs while Vicky jiggled Amari in her arms as the baby complained and chewed on a fist.

Vicky waved goodbye to them both, deciding to finish by jogging along the footpath around the point and back to her car the long way. She needed the exercise and hadn't run in a while. Truthfully, she wasn't much of a runner, but the weather was cool, and rain threatened, so she'd need to move faster than a walk if she wanted to finish the entire loop.

She jogged for about ten minutes before she had to

stop. Puffing hard, she leaned against the railing that lined the footpath around the point and looked out over the crashing waves. She'd been nervous to share her feelings with Sarah but hadn't wanted to spend more time with Ben without telling her friend first. She didn't want Sarah to feel like she'd hidden the relationship from her. Not that there was anything to hide yet, but she hoped that something might develop from the spark of attraction she'd felt between the two of them.

When she'd caught her breath, and was about to set off running again, her phone buzzed in her leggings pocket. She unzipped the pocket and pulled it out. It was Ben. Her heart leapt into her throat.

"Hello, Ben, what a lovely surprise."

They talked about the weather, how his leg was healing, and her plans for the upcoming weekend.

"So, if you're not busy on Saturday night, I'd love to take you out to dinner," he said all of a sudden.

Her breath caught in her throat and a smile spread across her face. "I'd love that."

"Perfect," he said. "I'll pick you up at your unit at seven. Does the Chinese Garden sound okay?"

"Delicious, I'll see you then."

When she hung up the phone, she danced in place for a moment, hands above her head. Then, dismissing the curious stares of other joggers passing by, she shoved her phone back into its pocket and set off in the direction of the car.

* * *

REBECCA

The reel in her hand whirred as the line released, the hook skimming through the air and landing with a plop in the dark creek water. Rebecca reeled the line in a few rounds and settled in for the wait.

"Good cast," said Franklin with a nod in her direction.

She smiled. "Thanks. Let's see who catches the first fish."

He laughed. "Oh, that's definitely going to be me, Proby."

"You're so confident, but it's going to be your downfall. You wait and see."

His eyes flashed. "You have no idea how much I want to tickle you right now, but I'm not going to let go of this rod because I've got to win."

"Oh, poor honey, what a conundrum." She poked out her tongue.

He lunged in her direction, falling well short of where she stood.

She laughed. "You make it far too easy, my love."

They stood on the creek bank in companionable silence for ten minutes before Rebecca spoke again.

"How's your head feeling today?"

"Great," he replied. "I haven't had any more pain. Everything's healing up well, and I spoke to emergency services. They said Andy Flannigan and the other family in the van are all fine too. The bridge, however, is not. It'll be a while before they can replace it, I'm afraid."

She nodded. "I still can't believe no one noticed it was failing before it happened."

"I know, they really need a better system. I

mentioned as much to the engineer I spoke with at the council. He said they'd work on it."

"Good to hear."

"We haven't spoken about our fight," he began.

She nodded. "I know. I'm sorry we fought."

"Me too."

"You know how hard I worked to get this job, all the things I went through."

"I know," he replied, his eyes on the water ahead of him. "I shouldn't have suggested you quit."

"But I heard what you were saying, too. When I had a chance to calm down, I realised you were right about one thing—we can't work together. It isn't fair on either of us, as much as I love it."

He inhaled a sharp breath. "I wish —"

"I know."

"So, what will we do?"

"I think I should try for a transfer to the Tweed Heads station," she said.

"No, I should do that."

"But you're the boss, they'd miss you here in the Cove. No one will miss me."

He grunted. "That's not true, we'd all miss you."

"Okay, well we can talk about it another time. But I'm open to the idea. And I know you only wanted what was best for me. I'm sorry I turned it into something else," she said.

He smiled at her. "I'll admit, it sounded bad. But it came from a good place."

"Another thing I wanted to talk about—you mentioned babies."

He rolled his eyes. "Did I?"

She chuckled. "Yes, you did so there's no backing

out of it now. In all seriousness—what do you think? Should we try for one?"

He grinned. "When we're ready. I'd like to keep you to myself for a little bit longer."

"And when that happens, when we're ready for children, the house we're living in really won't be big enough for us all. Right?"

He frowned. "I don't know about that, it's got three bedrooms."

"Two really—the third is more like an office. It's tiny."

He grumbled beneath his breath.

"What was that?" she asked.

"Nothing—only it seems every single aspect of my life is going to change whether I'd like it to or not, I suppose."

"We should start looking for somewhere bigger, with a nice sized backyard," she continued, ignoring his protest.

He quirked an eyebrow. "Already? But you're not even pregnant yet."

"I know, but it's good to see what's out there—finding the perfect house might take us some time and I want to be prepared before we start a family."

He reeled in his line, then cast it out again before answering. "Fine, if you think it's necessary. Although I think our house is perfect."

"Thanks, honey. I'll start looking next week." Rebecca smiled to herself—he wanted a family. For years she'd believed it would never happen, that she wouldn't be a mother, couldn't be one. She hadn't wanted to bring children into the world if all she was doing was running from trouble. But now she'd found Franklin, she couldn't wait to get started.

CHAPTER 18

BEN

The light outside the glass door shone dull in the twilight gloaming. Ben buzzed Vicky's unit number, waited, then buzzed it again. It was 7 p.m.—perhaps she'd forgotten about their date. Although, if that was true, it didn't bode well for him. He shook his head and was about to press the buzzer again when her voice rang out.

"Sorry Ben, just on the phone, come on in."

He pushed through the glass door and waited for the lift, taking it up to the third-floor unit. He drew a deep breath, then knocked on her door. She flung it open, a mobile phone pressed to one ear and waved a hand.

"Sorry!" she whispered.

He shook his head. "No worries. Take your time."

He wandered into the unit behind her and sat in an armchair by the glass sliding doors that led to a small balcony. A lonely ficus tree squatted in one corner of the balcony, the rest was taken up by a glass-topped table and four chairs.

"No, that's not a good idea," said Vicky, pacing out of the room, head down. "I don't think so."

He couldn't hear what she said next, as she disappeared through a door and shut it behind her. She emerged a few minutes later, her cheeks and neck blotchy and red.

"Everything okay?" he asked.

She offered him a smile. "I'm so sorry. Everything's fine. I'm ready to go if you like."

They walked down to his car, exchanging pleasantries. There was a tension in the air. Things weren't starting well. He shouldn't have called to ask her out—it was clear she didn't want to be there. She could've just turned him down.

In the car, he flicked on the radio to fill the silence as she stared out the passenger window.

"Anything I can help with?" he asked.

She sighed. "No. It's my sister."

"Oh. Then, I definitely can't help because I've only recently met my sisters." He laughed, an attempt to break the tension.

She grinned. "You're lucky."

"Not close to your sister?"

She shook her head. "Not anymore. We used to be —we were inseparable when we were younger. But now…now she's not the person she used to be. She's changed so much and I'm really not sure what to do about it—how to deal with her."

"I'm sorry to hear that."

It wasn't far to the restaurant, and as he pulled into the parking lot, he felt the tension between them ease.

It wasn't a tangible thing, but the atmosphere shifted as she relaxed in the seat next to him.

"Thanks," she said.

He inclined his head. "Sure. I know family can be hard."

"That's an understatement," she replied with a groan.

Outside the car, he reached for her hand and took it in his. A flash of heat raced through his body as she entwined her fingers through his—a simple gesture that almost took his breath away. He'd never felt that kind of chemistry on a first date before. It was unexpected and threw him for a moment.

They walked hand in hand into the restaurant and were taken immediately to their table. He sat across from her and reluctantly released his grip on her hand when the waitress offered him a menu. He ordered Sichuan Chicken and she opted for scallops in oyster sauce. Then, the waitress took their menus and left them alone with a basket of spring rolls, dumplings, and prawn chips.

He reached for a spring roll and took a bite, the pastry crunching and crumbling onto his plate. It was delicious, filled with vegetables and seafood, perfectly seasoned with sauces and spices.

"You grew up an only child?" she asked.

He chewed and swallowed. "Yep, my parents adopted me late in life. They weren't able to have children of their own and didn't have the money to adopt any other children. So, it was just the three of us."

"It must've been quiet. I have a sister and a brother, and our house was always filled with noise and bedlam."

He nodded. "It was quiet at home, but I liked it that

way. I had a wonderful childhood, and plenty of friends at school, soccer, Boy Scouts…"

"You were a Boy Scout?"

"Yep, for ten years."

"I can definitely see that," she replied with a grin.

He laughed. "Oh, can you?"

"You seem like the kind of guy who's always prepared."

"I don't know how to take that," he said with a chuckle. "Thanks?"

"It's a compliment. I'm the opposite—never prepared for anything."

He laughed. "Well, maybe we're a good match then."

"Or a disaster," she agreed. "One or the other."

"I suppose we'll have to wait to find out which."

* * *

THE FOOD WAS delicious and the company delightful. It wasn't long before Ben completely lost track of time as their conversation wandered from cooking to travel, then religions to politics and finally lighted once again on family dynamics.

"You mentioned your sister earlier. Are you close with the rest of your family?" asked Ben as he pushed his plate forward. He couldn't eat another bite; it'd been a long time since he'd enjoyed a meal as much.

"I have a younger brother who travels a lot for work, I think he's currently somewhere in Indonesia. And no, we're not very close these days."

"I'm sorry to hear that," he replied. Family was important to him; it was hard for him to imagine how he'd handle the stress of life without his parents to rely on.

"It's fine—it is what it is. There isn't much I can do about it. My mother died years ago when I was a teenager. That was back when we all lived in the Cove together. When I left for uni, my dad moved to Ballina and didn't look back—I think the memories here were too much for him. He wants me to move to Ballina, to be close by. But I don't know."

"You're considering moving?" The idea that she might move away from the Cove just as he was getting to know her made his heart drop.

"I probably won't do it. I've built a life here, if I go to Ballina there's nothing there for me but Dad. And I don't think that would be enough—although he seems to think I've got no reason to stay here. I think friend-ships and a good job are reason enough."

"I agree," he replied.

She took a bite of dumpling, then sighed. "Wow, I'm so full, you may have to roll me back to the car."

He laughed. "Me too. But I've had a wonderful time. I hope we can do this again soon."

"I'd like that. But I think I should head home. It's getting late."

Ben was taken by surprise. They'd been enjoying each other's company, had barely taken the last bite of food, and he'd hoped they might grab some ice creams and take a walk along the beach in the moonlight.

"Oh, okay. I'll drive you home."

As he drove through the dark streets of Emerald Cove, he glanced at her a few times. She stared out the window, her arms crossed over her abdomen, her expression blank. Had he done or said something wrong? He walked her to her door, and she said goodbye with a smile, but quickly shut it behind her. He stared at the door for a few moments, scratched his head then wandered back to the truck. The evening had begun with such promise, but he doubted she'd want to see him again from the way she'd rushed into her unit and almost slammed the door in his face. With a shake of his head, he climbed into the truck and revved the engine. Then, with a last glance in the direction of her unit, he pulled onto the road and headed for home.

CHAPTER 19

SARAH

*T*he car cruised to a stop in front of the cottage and Sarah climbed out. She hesitated as the blood rushed from her head, making it light. Everything went black for a moment and she steadied herself by placing one hand on the door frame.

"Whoa."

The feeling passed and she went inside. Still, she didn't feel good. Perhaps she should eat something, that might help. She'd spent the morning at Mum's helping to pack boxes. Before she finished up, she and Ethan had attempted to move Mum's piano. But it was too heavy. They'd strained and pushed, pulled and jiggled to no avail. They'd have to leave it to the professionals.

Ever since, though, she'd felt a little off.

"You shouldn't be lifting something so heavy,"

Mum had admonished her when she walked into the living room. "Not right now."

Ethan had quirked an eyebrow. Sarah hadn't told the rest of the family she was pregnant yet. She wanted to wait until the first trimester was over. Still, the baby wasn't any bigger than a grape, how could lifting something heavy impact her pregnancy?

Now, she wasn't so sure.

It'd been stupid. She shouldn't have done it. What was she thinking? She was thinking that nothing had changed—that she was still the strong, athletic woman she'd been, but with a grape-sized baby in her uterus.

Fatigue washed over her. She wandered into the kitchen and poured herself a glass of cold milk, then chugged it. Wiping her mouth dry she padded over to the couch, then lay on it, one arm flung up over her head doing her best to avoid looking at all the half-packed boxes strewn around the living room.

Perhaps all she needed was to lie down for a few minutes and she'd be okay. She'd taken to having naps in the afternoon lately—something she'd never felt the need to do before. But the pregnancy was making her feel as though she hadn't slept in days, even though she was going to bed earlier than ever and sleeping as though she were dead.

She stared at the ceiling. There was so much to do, she didn't have time to lie around for hours on end. As soon as her eyes drifted shut all she could think about was the laundry list of items on her to-do list. Her eyes flicked open again and she rubbed them with a groan.

There was nothing else she could do but work on her list, otherwise she'd never get to sleep. She reached for her phone and held it in her hands, staring at the screen, her heart pounding. She'd been procrastinating over one particular item on the list—calling her former boss to talk about her newly finished book. She dreaded the conversation. No doubt it'd go along the lines of hundreds of phone calls she'd overheard from outside Beverley's office.

It's a lovely book. There's real depth to it. Of course, I'm sure there's a big market for this type of book, but, unfortunately, we don't have room in our stable for it at this stage. But we'll keep you in mind if something opens up.

It was what Bev had said to all the up-and-coming writers whose hopes she didn't want to dash, but whose books weren't up to scratch. If Bev said the same thing to her, she'd know it was over—there would be no way Greenmount publishing would take on her book if Beverley Watson didn't love it.

Of course, the last she'd heard, Bev had been pulling away from her role as Editor in Chief and focusing more on her personal life. She was at the age where retirement loomed, and perhaps she'd handed over some of the decision-making to others in the firm. Which made the chances of Sarah getting published by Greenmount that much slimmer, since at least Bev knew and liked her: the junior editors probably barely remembered her at this point.

She dialled Bev's number and waited as it rang, her breath caught in her throat.

"Greenmount, this is Pauline," sang a high-pitched voice.

"Oh, Pauline—I wasn't expecting you. I thought I'd dialled Beverley's number," stammered Sarah, completely thrown by the switch.

"Who is this?" snipped Pauline.

"I'm sorry, this is Sarah Flannigan, I mean Sarah McIntosh. How are you Pauline."

Pauline's tone immediately shifted to a forced cheerfulness. "Sarah, how are you? It's good to hear from you. Didn't anyone tell you—Bev's retired?"

Sarah inhaled a quick breath. Retired? She hadn't said anything to Sarah, and she'd thought they were friends. Now there was no chance Greenmount would consider her book for publishing. And now Pauline was sitting in the chair that Bev had been grooming Sarah to take for years before she moved to the Cove.

"Wow, no—I didn't realise. How long ago was that?"

"Um, let's see. Maybe four months ago. Not long. She'd had enough, or so she told me." Pauline laughed. "Never mind. She's loving the quiet life—riding horses, swimming, holding dinner parties. Retirement suits her."

"That's wonderful. I'll have to give her a call at home sometime."

"Yes, do that. I know she'd love to hear from you," replied Pauline. "So Sarah, how can I help you? Or is this a purely social call?"

Sarah swallowed. "Actually, I wrote a book."

I wrote a book?

Couldn't she have warmed Pauline up to the subject first with a little more chitchat, or an introductory passage about how her life had changed and she'd had time to think, ponder, pen her imaginings? Ugh.

"Isn't that nice," replied Pauline. "What's it called?"

"Um, well it doesn't have a title yet."

"Oh, what's it about then?"

Sweat beaded on Sarah's forehead. All those years working as an editor and she'd never realised how gut-clenching and nerve-wracking these conversations must've been for the authors she dealt with.

"It's a nostalgic piece of historical fiction set in World War Two. There's romance, adventure, betrayal, and plenty of history thrown in."

"Sounds interesting," said Pauline. "Could you send me a copy of the manuscript to take a look at? You know this business, so I'm sure you've hit all the right notes."

"Wow, thanks Pauline. I'd be happy to do that. I really appreciate it."

"It's not a problem. We're looking for something historical, and I could probably sell the team on a war book. But we'll have to see if it's the type of thing that'd fit our brand. You know how these things go."

"Yes, I do. Thanks again."

When she hung up the phone, Sarah stared at it in disbelief. Pauline, her arch enemy from her Greenmount days, had asked for a manuscript. It might be nothing, or it could be a big step in the right direction —it could mean that everything she'd been working for was about to come true.

She shouldn't get too excited. This was only one step. There were about a hundred more she needed to take after this, but it was a big step.

She pumped a fist in the air, and squeezed her eyes shut. "Yes!"

Just then, her abdomen cramped. The pain sliced through her like a sharp knife.

* * *

CINDY

"I think cream paint would work on the walls. What do you think?" Cindy stood in the middle of the living room at her new chalet and studied the vaulted ceilings through narrowed eyes. Her glasses were perched on the end of her nose and her hands were pressed to her hips.

Athol wandered in from the kitchen. "That would be perfect. Or yellow would work too."

Her nose wrinkled. Definitely not yellow, although she wouldn't say that to Athol. It was lovely he wanted to be involved in decisions about the new house, but she had firm ideas about decorating that he couldn't possibly understand.

She glanced at him. "So, since we're engaged, we're going to have to talk about where we'll live once we're married, I suppose."

He smiled. "I thought we'd live here."

"Really? You're okay with that? I mean, I could move into your place if you'd prefer that." She really didn't mind where she lived, as long as they were together. Now that they'd made the commitment to get married, she was filled with a nervous energy to get things underway. Living together, starting their new life, it was the only thing she could think about—that and the fact that she'd soon be a grandmother.

Everything was changing. But this time it was all for the better and she couldn't be happier.

He shrugged. "Yeah, I like it here. It's closer to the beach, so we can take walks on the sand together. Plus, it's smaller than my place. And there are too many memories tied to every single room there —I want us to start fresh. You're doing that, by moving in here and I've been a little jealous, truth be told. But if we do it together then it'll be *our* fresh start."

She walked to him and wrapped her arms around his neck. "Really? I love that."

"So, are you okay with it? I mean, you bought the place so it's officially yours."

"Of course, I'm okay with it. Does it really matter whose name is on the deed? I'll tell you what, you can pay for all our wonderful, lavish holidays, since I've got our home covered."

He chuckled. "Sounds good to me."

"It's funny isn't it?"

He quirked an eyebrow.

She continued. "Getting married the second time there are so many things I see differently now to the way I did the first time around."

"Ain't that the truth," he replied with a shake of the head. "I'm so glad we're on the same page with everything. It's a relief not to have any tension between us. You make this whole thing so easy and enjoyable, my darling."

She smiled. "It's a shame you're such a bear."

"Am I?"

She kissed his lips. "Absolutely horrible. I don't know how I put up with you—always in a foul mood, stamping around the place...ugh. And you're really unattractive too. It's a miracle we found each other. Can you sense the sarcasm?"

He threw his head back and laughed then found her lips and kissed her gently, pulling her close.

When Cindy's phone rang, she intended to ignore it at first, but then her responsible nature got the better of her and she peeked at the screen. It was Sarah.

She pulled away from Athol. "I'm sorry, love. It's Sarah, I should answer this."

He nodded.

"Hi Sarah, honey. How are you feeling? You worked

too hard this morning at my place, I think you should probably rest this afternoon. Don't go packing up the cottage today, all that can wait."

"Mum." Sarah's voice was soft, pitiful, like when she fell off her bike at ten years of age and scraped the skin from her knees to her hips.

Cindy's heart thudded against her ribcage. "What? What is it, honey?"

"I don't know, I don't feel good. I'm cramping."

Cindy let the words hang between them a moment, her head spinning. "Okay, well it might be nothing, but I think you should get Mick to drive you to the hospital just to be safe."

"He's on his way home now. But Mum, I'm scared. What should I do?"

Sarah's voice tore at Cindy's heart. "Oh honey, you're going to be fine. Lie down and try to relax, wait on Mick, and let me know when you're headed to the hospital. I'm with Athol and we're going to drive your way now."

"Okay. Ahhhh." She cried out in pain and Cindy bit down on her lip, her eyes filling with tears.

"Are you okay, honey?"

"Yeah, I'm fine. It hurts." Sarah's voice was weaker still.

A lump grew in Cindy's throat. If Sarah lost the baby, it'd be devastating.

"Well, hold on, honey. It's all going to be fine."

She hung up the phone, then stood like a statue staring at the floor, as though paralysed. What to do first? Should she pick up some food from home, or grab something from the café? They'd be hungry when they got back from the hospital. Perhaps some soup, fresh bread, maybe there'd even be some apple crumble left over from the lunch service.

"Cindy?" Athol rested a hand on her arm.

She startled. "Huh? Oh, we've got to go. Sarah's cramping and Mick's going to take her to the hospital."

"Okay, let's go then."

"Can we pop by the cafe, I'd like to grab some food to take to the cottage with us?"

He nodded, already headed for the car. Cindy was close behind him. "That's fine."

She reached for him, pulled him to a stop. "Is she going to be okay? You're a doctor, what does it mean?"

He wrapped her in his arms and kissed the top of her head. "It could mean any number of things. It might be that she's overdone it, and her body is telling her to slow down, or it could mean…well, let's not worry about things that haven't happened yet. We'll deal with things as they arise. Okay?"

She inhaled a slow breath, pushing back the tears that threatened to spill down her cheeks. "You're right. I shouldn't get worked up. She needs me to be strong for her."

He traced a line down her cheek with his fingertips, cupped her face in his hand. "Yes, she does. And you're just the person for that—since you're the strongest person I know."

She smiled. "You always know the right thing to say, Athol."

"Come on, we'll go and get that food, then we'll figure out what to do after that."

CHAPTER 20

REBECCA

*T*he entire morning Rebecca couldn't stop thinking about the conversation she'd had with Franklin regarding her position at the Emerald Cove police station. If the two of them couldn't be partners any longer, it meant one of them either had to join the night crew—which meant they'd never see each other—or move to another station.

The only thing was, she didn't want to do either of those things. She could see Franklin's point, now that she'd given herself time to think it through rather than simply reacting out of fear. Working together put them both in danger, not to mention the community they were supposed to protect. But what else could they do? The Emerald Cove station wasn't big enough to warrant another team of officers, and as a proby she couldn't work without a partner.

And what about when they had a family? As much

as she hated to admit it, he had a point there too. It wasn't as though she'd be able to head back to work the next day. She'd have to take maternity leave, then possibly reduce her hours to part-time. Maybe it would be better for everyone if she was transferred to the station at Tweed. It was only a twenty-minute drive from the Cove, and she'd likely find a position there without too much trouble since it was a large station.

Still, she'd miss the cosy camaraderie of the team here.

She glanced around the office. A couple of coast guard officers laughed in one corner. Franklin slapped the side of the photocopier machine, while Steph attempted to give him directions on how to fix it. And Phil Conway chatted on the phone with someone about the local theatrical production of West End, in which he played a main role—he'd been singing beneath his breath for days, rehearsing quietly, and driving the rest of them mad in the process.

She loved it all. Loved them. The whole, crazy lot of them.

With a shake of her head, she switched off her computer and strode into Franklin's office, where he'd retreated with what looked like a successfully copied wad of paperwork.

"Hey, can I talk to you for a minute?" she asked, pulling his door shut behind her.

He nodded, waving a hand at the seat in front of his desk. She took it and crossed one leg over the other.

"I've been thinking about what you said—I think I should put in for a transfer to the Tweed Heads branch."

His lips pursed. "I've been thinking too, and I don't

agree. I'm the one who raised the issue, it's not your problem it's mine—I'm going to transfer."

She shook her head. "No, this is your station. You love it here, it's your whole life."

"Not true," he replied. "You're my whole life now. I raised the issue, so I should be the one to transfer."

Her brow furrowed. "But —"

"It'll be good for me to have a change."

"I don't want you to compromise—" she began.

He interrupted her with a raised palm. "No, that's not what this is. I want to do it."

Her throat tightened and emotion swelled in her gut. She loved this man and he continued to surprise her.

"I love you for saying that, but I've made up my mind." She knew him too well and knew he'd never want to leave the Cove and his position there. He'd do it for her, but it wouldn't be right to ask him to give up his position there. The entire community loved him, relied on him. "Besides, there's one thing you haven't thought about."

He quirked an eyebrow. "Oh?"

"If I do have a baby, I'll have to take maternity leave and a larger station will be able to cope better with that."

He shrugged. "We'd manage fine. I mean… you'd manage, since I wouldn't be there."

"No, I want the transfer, Franklin. It'll be good for me—bigger opportunities, more chance of a promotion."

"So, you're sure?" he asked.

She offered a quick nod. "I'm sure."

He stood and walked around to sit on the front of his desk, took her hands in his and kissed the back of each, one at a time. "Okay, I support you if that's what you want to do. But I'll miss seeing you every day."

"You'll still see me. I'll come home to you after work."

"It'll be the best part of my day," he replied, kissing the tip of her nose.

"And our kids."

"And them too. Although how many are you thinking, because when you say kids, plural, it starts to sound like a lot."

She grinned. "Is seven too many?"

His eyes shot wide and he shifted on the desk. "Uh, what?"

"Just kidding. I don't know, I think we should play it by ear. See what they're like before we commit to a number. But off the top of my head, I'm thinking two or three."

He cleared his throat. "I guess I can live with that."

"Well, now that's settled, I'm going to head home for the day. I've made an appointment with a real estate agent to look at some properties in Edenbrook Acres this evening, so do you mind cooking dinner?"

He stood to his feet. "Edenbrook? Um, are you sure we should look there? I mean, those houses are huge— I'm pretty certain they're completely out of our price range."

"Maybe, but I'll take a look and figure it out. If I see something I like, I'll let you know."

She kissed him and left, smiling at the look on his face — as if the wind had been knocked from his lungs. He was right, the Edenbrook Acres houses would be completely out of their price range if all they had to rely on were the salaries of two police officers, but she hadn't told him about the trust fund yet. With the money coming her way, she'd have more than enough to purchase a large, luxurious home. She wasn't sure if she wanted to raise the subject of her inheritance with him just yet.

There was a time when she didn't believe she'd live to see her thirtieth birthday. When her ex-boyfriend Jake was tracking her down, she'd given up hope that she'd escape him forever. So she hadn't given much thought to the inheritance in years. But she'd be turning thirty next month and the money would be hers. As far as she was concerned, it was perfect timing. She only hoped Franklin would see it the same way. She still wasn't sure how to broach the subject with Franklin —*remember how I was running from my psychotic boyfriend and lied to you about who I was? Surprise! More secrets—now I'm rich.*

Her heart constricted as though a band tightened around it. She missed her Dad. There was that too. Speaking it out loud made it worse. She should've been able to manage the grief by now, but she didn't want to talk about his death, the inheritance, any of it. Especially with Franklin's recent loss of his own father —it could open those wounds further still and she knew he must still be grieving, although he hid it well.

All of it made her heart rate accelerate and sweat bead on her brow. The thing that made it all worse was the way the knowledge of her inheritance had made her Jake's eyes gleam and his hold over her grow stronger when she'd first told him about the trust fund. But Franklin was different, she knew that. It didn't hurt to wait a little longer though, then bring it up with Franklin when the timing was right. Later was better.

* * *

SARAH

The light over the front door of the cottage glowed in the darkness. A light rain misted the windscreen, the wipers screeching across the glass with each pass.

"I'm sorry again," said Sarah.

"Please don't apologise," replied Mick, offering her a warm smile. "I'm happy you and the baby are okay."

"I got everyone all upset."

"No, we were worried, but that doesn't matter—what's important is…"

"I know… we're okay."

He winked. "Bingo."

He parked his truck in front of the house and switched off the headlights. "Wait here a minute, I'll go grab an umbrella."

"I'm not an invalid," she complained to his back as he leapt from the vehicle.

He hurried back with a large blue umbrella and helped her from the truck.

"Really, I'm okay."

"I know, but I like helping you. Is that all right?"

She grinned, holding onto his arm. "I suppose so."

"Good. Now, let's see what your mother is up to—that's Athol's car parked over there, isn't it?"

Sarah slapped her forehead with the palm of her hand. "Oh, that's right—I forgot they came over to the house. They haven't left yet? It's two o'clock in the morning, they must be exhausted."

They walked into the house, wiping their wet feet on the mat. Mick set the umbrella by the door. Sarah saw them immediately—Athol and her mother were both fast asleep, one on each couch in the living room. Mum had a throw rug pulled up over her legs, and Athol held a decorative pillow with a cockatoo printed on it to his chest.

"They're sleeping," she whispered.

Mick came up beside her, wrapped an arm around her shoulders. "Hmmm…should we wake them?"

"I suppose so. They'll both end up with cricks in their necks sleeping like that all night."

She walked over to her mother and squatted beside her. "Mum." She shook her mother's shoulder gently. "Wake up."

Mum's eyes blinked open, then focused on Sarah's face. "Oh, honey, you're home." She reached out and embraced Sarah, then sat up, her grey-blonde bob smushed flat against one side of her face. "Ugh. I don't think I can turn my head; it's stuck in place."

Sarah chuckled. "I'm sorry, you shouldn't have stayed here so late. Everything's okay, like I told you on the phone from my hospital room. It was all for nothing—the baby's fine, I'm fine. I freaked out for no reason."

Mum put a hand on Sarah's shoulder. "Not for no reason, love. You were in pain, that's not something you should ignore. So, what did the doctor say?"

"He said I should take it easy and not push myself so hard. That I have to be more careful."

"Good advice," replied Mum, standing to her feet. "I'd better wake Athol and we'll leave you two in peace. There's pumpkin soup in the fridge, fresh sourdough on the bench, and some to-die-for apple crumble with cream for dessert. That is, if you're hungry."

Before long, Mick and Sarah were alone again. The cottage sat in a kind of quiet stillness, with the sounds of the ocean muffled by the gentle rain falling on the roof.

"Are you hungry?" asked Mick, peering into the fridge.

"I'm famished," replied Sarah. "I couldn't really eat at the hospital. Besides, a muffin from a vending machine hardly counts as dinner. I need sleep, but I'm dying for some food."

He retrieved a large plastic container of soup from the top shelf and held it high. "Pumpkin soup coming up."

The meal was delicious. The most delectable thing Sarah could remember eating. She was so hungry, she couldn't get enough. The sourdough bread pulled apart in large, fluffy pieces and she coated each with butter before stuffing them into her mouth.

"Slow down, or you'll choke," laughed Mick.

"Can't, too hungry," she muttered around a mouthful of bread.

The soup had the slightest hint of chilli and was full of flavour with a creamy texture. It slipped down her throat and warmed her stomach.

"Mmm, this is so good," she said, slurping up another spoonful.

Mick nodded. "Your mum really knows how to cook."

"This is one of her go-to recipes. We ate it a lot as kids, especially when the pumpkin patch in the garden got out of control. I think everyone on our street ate pumpkin soup for weeks one year."

He laughed. "I can imagine that. It sounds like you had a wonderful childhood. I remember riding my bike past your house and wondering about you."

"You did?"

"Yeah, I mean you were younger than me, but I thought about your family sometimes—you all seemed so happy. You liked each other. Anyway, it seemed that way to me. My family—well, there was a lot of yelling. Home wasn't always a pleasant place to be. But your house was a kind of fantasy. That's the only way I can think to describe it."

She smiled. "And now we'll be raising our children there."

"Yeah." He grinned. "They get to live out the fantasy of a happy family in a fairy-tale house." He leaned across the table to kiss her. "And I get to live it too."

CHAPTER 21

VICKY

*T*he pizza was hot. The scent of it wafted up from the front seat and drifted across to where Vicky sat on the driver's side. Her stomach growled in response.

"You okay over there?" asked Sarah.

Vicky giggled. "Sorry, I didn't eat lunch. There was a Clydesdale with an infected hoof, and she gave me such a hard time I didn't get a chance to stop for lunch. Have you ever tried to pick up the hoof of a Clydesdale?"

Sarah's nose wrinkled. "Uh, no I haven't. I imagine it would be pretty hard."

"They're heavy, for one. And add to that an infection that makes the horse determined not to let me touch it. Anyway, suffice it to say—I'm glad that's over, and I'm ready for pizza."

"Pizza, is there anything in the world that smells better," replied Sarah.

Vicky shot her a side-eye. "That's not like you, miss health nut. In fact, I can't believe you let me get a pizza for tonight. I was sure you'd suggest sushi."

"Nope. Not tonight," was all Sarah said in response.

Vicky sighed. "Since we're babysitting tonight, I hope you have some experience with babies. I'm a complete newbie with the whole thing. Give me a litter of puppies to mind, and I'm fine. But a baby? Yikes. What if it cries or something?"

"She," corrected Sarah. "What if *she* cries?"

"Right, *she*. Sorry."

"Then, we pick her up, give her a cuddle, and she'll be fine. I've held a few babies. How hard can it be?"

"Uh oh, we're in trouble. I thought you were the expert." Vicky's stomach twisted into a knot. Babysitting for Brad and Meg was a big responsibility. One she was certain she wasn't ready to meet. But if Sarah wasn't equipped either, they were in for a long night.

"We'll be fine," replied Sarah with a smile. "I'm sure she'll sleep the whole time. Meanwhile, our friends get to have a date-night for the first time in a long time. They really need it, and I know Meg's been looking forward to it all week. So, we can't call them unless it's an emergency—deal?"

Vicky swallowed hard. "Um. Okay, deal."

They pulled up to the curb in front of Meg and Brad's unit and climbed out. Sarah carrying the pizza, Vicky pulling a shopping bag of chocolates, ice cream, and soda out of the boot and hefting it over her shoulder.

"This thing weighs a tonne," she groaned.

"I told you we bought too much junk food." Sarah giggled. "There's no way we can eat it all tonight."

"We'll definitely have leftovers."

"Sounds good to me."

Sarah knocked on the unit door and a few moments later Brad opened it, greeting them with a wide grin, his blond hair falling in strands across his eyes.

He wheeled to one side and motioned them inside. "Come on in," he said. "Amari's still awake, but Meg's trying to put her down. You can meet her and then Meg will put her in her cot. Fingers crossed she sleeps through until we're home."

Vicky pushed a smile onto her face, her heart racing. She hoped Amari slept too, otherwise she wasn't sure what they'd do.

"Where are you two love birds going?" asked Sarah, as they both followed Brad into the living room.

"The Chinese Garden. So, if you need us, we're not far away."

"That's good to know," replied Vicky.

Sarah shot her a warning look. She raised her hands in a mute question. She wasn't suggesting they should call, but it was important to know the baby's parents were close by just in case.

Meg was in the kitchen, baby Amari in her arms. "Hey, you two. Come and see the little miss. She's getting sleepy, but I'm sure she'll give you a smile."

They took turns holding her. She gurgled and grinned at them in bursts. Her little arms waved over her head and her feet pumped.

"She's getting a bit excited, isn't she?" asked Vicky, handing Amari back to Meg.

Meg nodded. "Yep, time for bed little one. Good night everyone."

They all told the baby good night, then Meg carried her into the bedroom. Vicky and Sarah followed on tiptoe behind.

"Here's the change table. Everything you need should be right here. These are the clean nappies, the wipes, and the moisturiser."

Vicky hated to think what the wipes and moisturiser were for, but simply nodded her head.

Meg set Amari down in the cot, sang her a verse, then they all backed out of the room. Meg pulled the door almost shut, then showed them into the kitchen.

"There's a bottle of milk in the fridge. All you have to do is heat it up. Test the temperature on your arm, here, to make sure it's warm but not too hot. She shouldn't need it, she's already been fed, but this is in case she wakes up wanting more."

"Ah, okay," replied Sarah. "Anything else we should know?"

"No, she usually sleeps until about two o'clock in the morning. I'm sure you won't need to do anything but sit and watch tv until we get home. But if anything goes wrong, just give us a call. We won't be far away."

"Got it," said Vicky.

They left quickly, obviously eager to get out of the unit before the baby made a sound. Vicky and Sarah sat on the couch side by side. Sarah looked for the remote, then turned on a movie. Vicky set the pizza on the coffee table and put the ice cream in the freezer, while Sarah poured them both a cup of soda.

They clinked their glasses together.

"Cheers to our first baby sitting session," said Sarah.

Vicky chuckled. "And to many more."

"Hear, hear."

They drank, then each got comfortable on the couch to eat the pizza before it got cold. The movie absorbed Vicky's attention, and she enjoyed a few slices of pizza before a sound caught her ear.

What was that?

"I think the baby's crying," said Sarah.

The sound grew in volume.

"Yep, it's definitely Amari."

"What should we do?" asked Sarah, straightening in her seat.

"Maybe we should wait a minute to see if she stops?" Vicky had no idea if that was the right thing, but it sounded good. If Amari stopped crying on her own, then Vicky couldn't mess anything up.

But she didn't stop crying. In fact, before long she was screaming, and Vicky felt all twitchy inside.

"I'm going to pick her up," she said.

She hurried into the bedroom and found Amari, red-faced, still partially wrapped in a light cotton blanket with teddy bears dotted all over it.

"Hello, Amari, come on now, it's really not so bad is it?"

She picked up the baby and held her upright. Meanwhile, Sarah had followed her into the room and hovered close by.

Amari continued to howl.

"Hmm…why don't you try rocking her?" suggested Sarah.

"Good idea, Auntie Sarah." Vicky lay Amari down in her arms and rocked her gently back and forth. The screams subsided and her eyelids flickered. "Ah, that's better isn't it."

Finally, Amari settled, and they put her back in the cot and crept from the room. But it wasn't long before she was up again and louder than ever.

They changed her nappy, they fed her a bottle of warm milk, they rocked and they rocked her. It was nine o'clock before she drifted off to sleep and stayed that way.

Sarah and Vicky collapsed on the couch.

"That was intense," said Sarah.

Vicky nodded, sighed. "Wow, poor Meg has to do that every night?"

"I don't know, but…" Sarah burst into tears.

Vicky bolted upright, her eyes wide. "What's wrong?"

Sarah lay on her side and cuddled up to a pillow, tears flowing freely down her cheeks. "What if it's always like that? Every. Single. Night!"

Vicky chewed on her lower lip. "Well, I suppose Meg and Brad take shifts and cope with it. I mean, they seem to be doing okay."

"I know they are, but what about me?" She burst into a fresh round of tears.

Vicky scratched her head. "Um, what are you talking about?"

Sarah sat up, wiping her cheeks with her fingertips. "I'm pregnant." Then she howled into the cushion again.

Vicky grinned and leapt up to hug her friend. "That is amazing, congratulations!"

"How can you say that?" sobbed Sarah. "You saw how terrible I am at taking care of a baby. I'm not going to manage. I'm not up for it."

Vicky took Sarah's hand in hers. "Come on,

sweetie, you'll be a great mum. I'm sure no one really knows what they're doing at first, but you'll learn."

"But what if I don't? It's not like I can give the baby back—it's coming, like it or not." She waved frantic arms around in front of her ever blotchier face.

Vicky tried hard not to laugh at the sight of her usually composed friend behaving like a lunatic. It was nice to know she was as imperfect as the rest of them after all.

"I'm so happy for you," she said.

Sarah laughed at that. "You really think I can do it?"

"I know you can. Now, I'm gonna get us some ice cream. Do you want the chocolates on top of yours, or would you like to eat them separately?"

"On top please," replied Sarah with a pout, as she followed Vicky into the kitchen.

Sarah sat at the bench, while Vicky spooned ice cream into two bowls, then dropped chocolates on top. They carried the bowls to the dining table and settled into chairs across from each other.

"This is nice," said Sarah. "We don't do this type of thing often enough."

"Yeah, well you had to go and get married," replied Vicky with a grin.

"Sorry about that."

"I guess I forgive you."

"Thanks." Sarah poked out her tongue and Vicky laughed.

"In all seriousness though, I'm so glad you found Mick. He's a great guy. I only hope I'll be as happy someday."

"Of course you will," replied Sarah, chewing on a chocolate. "You're going to meet someone wonderful."

"It's hard to imagine." Vicky pushed the ice cream

around her bowl. "And sometimes I think—what if I can't have children? I mean, I'm thirty and still don't have a boyfriend. By the time I meet someone, we date, get engaged, and finally get married—I could be too old to fall pregnant. Plus, with the lupus, everything is more complicated. I mean, I went on a date the other night and I had to ask him to take me home suddenly when a flare-up happened out of the blue.

"I saw the look on his face—he wasn't happy about it. And he hasn't called me again. I don't know if lupus makes pregnancy harder, but I can definitely imagine that it'll make motherhood difficult. Sometimes, I'm so tired and feel so unwell that I have to stay in bed— well, that's not going to work if I've got kids to look after. And I'll probably get sick more often because I'm so tired from taking care of them. I mean, I don't see how it could work, but I desperately want it— marriage, kids—I want all of it."

Sarah stared at her, eyes glistening in the dim light of the tv screen, still on pause. "Oh wow, I didn't think about that."

"I think about it all the time," admitted Vicky.

"I'm sorry, sweetie."

"Thanks. I mean, there's not really anything I can do about it. So, I suppose I'll have to deal with it when it happens."

"That's true—worrying about it now won't help. You should talk to your doctor before you get yourself too worked up. I mean, I'm sure there'll be ways to manage it all."

Vicky sighed and took a bite of ice cream as she pondered Sarah's words. There'd have to be a way to make it work. She'd find a way. She couldn't imagine living her life without children. Some people did it and were content, but it wasn't the kind of life she wanted for herself. She'd always known she'd be a mother. Of course, she had to find a husband first. And the search wasn't going well. Ben hadn't called her since their date three days earlier. And he was the first guy she'd been interested in for a very long time.

"And I don't suppose you're going to tell me the date's name? It wasn't Ben, was it?" asked Sarah, with a sniffle.

"I'm not ready to talk about it yet. But you'll be the first to know when I am." Sarah knew Vicky liked Ben, but the pain of him not calling her back was still too raw for her to discuss, even with her best friend.

Sarah nodded. "I can live with that."

If only Vicky knew why Ben hadn't called—was it because of the lupus episode, or did he simply not like her? She could call him, but that would look desperate. Besides, if he didn't want to see her again, that was something she was in no hurry to hear. It made sense to wait a while longer, then she'd go to see him when she was ready to deal with the rejection.

CHAPTER 22

BEN

"Good dog," said Ben.

The dark red pup wagged his tail, offered a few digs at the grass, then trotted off to explore the backyard.

Ben sighed with relief. Finally—he'd gone all morning without soiling the floor once. It seemed the puppy was catching onto the reason Ben took him outside every hour or so. For the last few days, he'd only had the occasional accident. It seemed they were turning a corner. He'd grown a lot in the ten days since Vicky and Diana brought the little guy into his life.

"Come on, Rusty, let's go inside." He whistled and Rusty glanced at him, ears perked, then ran to meet him.

He was a fast learner, just like Vicky said he would be. Ben scooped him up and carried him inside, while the dog lavished his face with kisses.

Laughing, he set him on the ground by his water bowl and Rusty lapped at the water as though it'd been days. The front doorbell rang, pulling him away from Rusty's antics. Ben strode to the front door, pleased with how well his leg was recovering from the shark bite. There wasn't any pain when he walked now, but he'd carry the scar for the rest of his life.

He hurried out to greet his parents and carry their luggage inside.

"It's good to see you," he said, kissing Mum's cheek.

Dad slapped him on the back. "We wanted to make sure you're healing okay. Your mother worries."

"So do you," quipped Mum to her husband, with a wink at Ben.

Dad grunted.

He made a pot of coffee for them all and sliced up the cinnamon tea cake they'd brought with them. Mum made the cake often when he was a teenager; the scent of it would fill the house when he got home from school and he'd rush upstairs to find her slicing it, hot from the oven, in their brown and orange wallpapered 1970s kitchen.

"I love these cakes," he said.

Mum grinned. "I know. That's why I made it. So, how is your leg today?"

He set everything on a tray. "My leg is fine. Same as yesterday. You worry too much."

"I'm a mother," she replied.

"Let's sit outside," he suggested. "It's a beautiful day and Rusty's getting more adventurous."

The little dog trotted into the room and made a beeline for Mum's long skirt.

"That sounds good," she replied.

"Wait there, Mum. I don't want him to trip you over, so I'll get him outside first."

He let Rusty out the back door, then came back for the tray. They settled around the outdoor table he'd bought a few days earlier. He wanted to spend as much time as possible in his backyard—it was one of the best features of the house. A long, sprawling grassy space, dotted by bushes and shrubs. The single tall jacaranda, bursting with purple flowers, stood in the centre of the yard. It attracted birds of every type and colour, and an old concrete bird bath with feeder beneath the tree kept them there.

They discussed his work and his parents' health. They updated him on everything their neighbours were doing: who was getting married, who divorced, and who had died in recent months. He spoke with them over the phone regularly, so heard many of the same stories over again, but he didn't mind. Time with them was something he'd come to cherish. In the past he'd have been aggravated by the little things they did, the way they spoke, or the repetition. But maturity gave him perspective to see that the moments they shared wouldn't last forever.

"Have you met anyone interesting in town?" asked Mum, before taking a sip of coffee.

"Yes, do you remember the vet who helped to look for the shark that bit me?"

"Vicky Hawkins," replied Dad.

Ben's eyebrows arched high. "How did you remember her name?"

"I don't forget the pretty faces." Dad winked, and cake crumbs dropped to his shirt as he took a bite of cake.

"Well, anyway—we went out on a date."

"That's wonderful," exclaimed Mum. "How did it go?"

"It was great. We get along really well. She's beautiful inside and out."

"But…?" asked Mum.

Ben sighed. "I've told you before. She's too young for me."

"How old is she?" asked Dad.

"Thirty," replied Ben. "That's fourteen years difference. And before you say anything, I know it's fine—that people deal with age gaps like that all the time. But for me, I've always preferred to date women my own age."

"Is she immature?" asked Mum.

"No, not at all. She's very mature."

"Then, what's the problem, son?" asked Dad, his bushy grey eyebrows pulled low over blue eyes.

"I suppose there isn't a problem, but I've been thinking about it—that's all. I'm not sure what to do. I don't want to lead her on if I'm not comfortable dating someone so much younger than me. And I don't think she's keen on the age gap either."

"Why does it make you think that?" asked Mum. She leaned over to pet Rusty who sat patiently waiting by her feet.

"I don't know exactly. I suppose…maybe it's my own insecurities. She ended the date early, seemed anxious to get home. Barely waited for me to say goodnight before she shut the door. But even if she hadn't, all I can think is that perhaps if she sees me again, she'll eventually find out I'm really old and boring." He laughed to mask the pain of the revelation. The truth was it was something he'd heard from more than one girlfriend in his lifetime. He was a homebody

—liked to stay home and watch movies or read books. Enjoyed driving through nature in his truck, bush walking, or mountain biking. Going out to clubs or the hottest concerts weren't his cup of tea—he hated the crowds, the noise, the port-a-loos.

Did that make him boring? He supposed it did, although he had no desire to be exciting if it involved being crushed to death in a sweaty, writhing crowd while your eardrums were blasted into oblivion and you held onto your bursting bladder to avoid the line for the toilets. The boring life suited him perfectly. The problem was, he was beginning to suspect it might be the reason he was still single in his forties. And that was something that didn't suit him. Not at all. He'd convinced himself for years that it didn't bother him, that he liked his own company and could manage on his own. But the truth was, since the shark attack he'd begun to long for someone in his life: someone to share things with, to wake up beside, to hold while watching the sunset over the ocean. It ached in a deep part of him he'd pushed down long ago, and because of his injury he didn't have swimming, cycling, or any other of the myriad activities he'd taken on over the years to occupy his time and distract him from the ache.

Mum clucked her tongue. "You are most definitely not old or boring. Yes, you're often on the quiet side. But that doesn't mean anything at all. You love mountain biking and four-wheel driving—that's exciting. You've travelled the world, spent time in countries where you don't speak the language. I've yet to discover a food you won't try. You're the furthest thing from old and boring in the world—you can trust me and your father on that one. Right, Gary?"

Dad grunted, his eyes flashing. "She's right, son."

He laughed. "Thanks Mum and Dad, I can always count on you for some encouragement."

"It's true," she protested.

"So you think I should call her, see her again?"

"If you like her, you shouldn't let anything hold you back. It's not so easy to find someone to connect with in life."

"You're right about that," he admitted, with a shrug. "I'll think about it. Although don't get your hopes up, since she may not want to see me again anyway."

After a while they returned inside. The afternoon breeze picked up as the sun dipped behind a cloud. Ben pulled out a game of Monopoly and the three of them played for an hour before his stomach growled.

"We should think about dinner," he said.

Mum nodded. "We could order something."

"Or I could BBQ?" he offered.

"I'd love some steak," replied Dad.

"I've got some in the fridge."

"Perfect. I'll make the veggies," said Mum.

"No, you sit and relax. I'll take care of it. We'll put the game on hold until after dinner. I'm about to buy a hotel and put the two of you out of business."

Dad chuckled, leaned back in his armchair, and shut his eyes. "Wake me when it's ready."

In the kitchen, Ben got to work marinating the steak. He rubbed seasoning over it, then set it to rest back in the fridge. As he was slicing onions, the doorbell rang. He frowned; he wasn't expecting anyone.

"Can you please see who that is?" he shouted.

Mum called back to him and shuffled to the front door. Then, she returned to the kitchen with Vicky trailing behind her.

"Look who I found?" said Mum, her eyes twinkling. "Vicky's here to see you."

There was a moment of awkward silence. He hadn't called her after their date, hadn't spoken to her in days. Yet, here she was, meeting his parents for the first time.

"Oh wow," he said, going to embrace her. He kissed her cheek. "Hi Vicky, what a pleasure. How are you?"

She swallowed, pressed a smile to her face. "Uh, I'm great thanks. I came to see you but didn't realise you had guests."

"Not guests, just his parents," said Mum. "And his father's fast asleep in the living room so he barely counts."

Mum winked at him, then returned to the living room.

Vicky met his gaze, her lips pursed. "I'm sorry for barging in. I should've realised the car parked outside wasn't yours—I wasn't thinking."

"It's fine," he replied, his mind in overdrive, trying to figure out how to get himself through this uncomfortable situation.

"I should go…"

"Stay for dinner," he said. "If you want to." He shouldn't have said that, and he immediately chastised himself for it. How would that look—they'd had one date and now she'd be eating dinner with his eighty-something parents. If he wanted to sabotage their relationship, he could've come up with a less awkward way to do it. It'd have been simpler to rent a flashing sign to hold over his head that read, 'Look out! I'm old and boring.'

"Um, okay. Can I help?"

He scooted over, his cheeks red. "Sure, you can cut the mushrooms."

They stood side by side in the kitchen, him slicing onions and potatoes, her dicing mushrooms, zucchini, and capsicum. The conversation was stilted at first, but soon drifted back to the same comfortable banter they'd had during their date. He relaxed with relief as they laughed together and chatted about her work.

Ben wondered why he'd ever hesitated about calling her back. Even if their relationship didn't develop into something romantic, at least they could be friends. He didn't have enough friends to risk losing one over something so inconsequential. And maybe he'd been wrong about her feelings for him—after all, she'd come to his house looking for him and had agreed to stay for dinner.

"I'm sorry I didn't call you, after our date," he said.

She glanced up at him, her eyes smiling. "It's okay."

"I was going to."

"Really, it's fine," she replied. "I hope you didn't get the wrong idea about me needing to go home early."

He cocked his head to one side. "I'm sorry?"

She met his gaze. "It wasn't anything to do with you. I had a great time. But I've got lupus."

His eyes narrowed. He'd heard of lupus, but that was about the extent of his knowledge on the subject.

"I'm sorry to hear that."

"It's okay—usually I'm fine. But sometimes when I'm stressed, or eat certain foods, I'll have a reaction. I might get a fever, or pains, or basically just feel horrible all over. On our date, I overdid it, and I ended up with massive stomach pains and a fever. I had to get home and I didn't want to make a fuss. So, I'm sorry about that—I should've told you the truth."

"Wow," he said. "I had no idea. I feel terrible that I didn't realise you were in so much pain."

She smiled. "You couldn't have done anything. All I needed was to get home to bed."

"So, you're okay now?"

"I'm more than okay," she replied. "And I'm happy to see you."

"So, we should go out again soon."

"I'd like that."

As he lifted the cutting board to drop the potato slices onto a tray, his arm brushed against hers. A buzz of adrenaline coursed through his veins and goose-bumps marked the spot where they'd connected.

No matter what else happened between them, he couldn't deny his attraction.

Together they carried the steak and vegetables out to the barbecue. He lit it and closed the lid to wait for it to heat. Rusty played with a stick close to his feet. He watched the dog with amusement, as it tumbled and growled.

"He's a cutie," said Vicky, with a laugh.

She drifted closer to them, squatting down to tickle Rusty's tummy. When she stood, she came face to face with Ben. He was a head taller than she was, towered over her. He leaned closer still, his gaze fixed on her soft, pink lips.

She looked up at him, moved closer. His heart thundered in his chest, his breathing ragged.

Then his mouth was on hers. He felt her jolt with surprise, then she melted into his arms.

* * *

AFTER DINNER, they resumed the game of Monopoly. Vicky started from scratch and had to catch up, but it didn't take her long. She quipped and teased along with the rest of them, fitting into his family dynamic as though she'd always belonged there. And Ben found himself falling.

CHAPTER 23

SARAH

*T*he pavement flashed beneath her feet as she ran. Sarah glanced at it a moment, then looked up to take in the view. The beach was always beautiful in the evenings. The footpath that meandered along the beach front was one of her favourite places to run. It was easy to be motivated with a view like that. Usually, she'd get lost in her own thoughts, but today she'd brought Adele along with her.

She and her sister had been close when they both lived at home, but years spent apart had left her feeling as though she didn't know Adele as well as she should. There was so much about her younger sister that was a mystery to her, and lately she seemed out of sorts all the time. Mum had hinted at some problems before Adele returned to the Cove. But hadn't gone into details. And so far, Adele had been quiet about the reasons for her extended visit home.

She glanced at her sister, running quietly beside her. Her eyes looked huge in the dusk light, her face lit up by the sunset looked golden, her hair like silk.

"Everything okay with you?" asked Sarah between puffs.

Adele didn't respond right away. She met Sarah's gaze and for a moment Sarah saw the pain lingering there, then it was gone as though a door was pushed shut.

"I'm having some relationship problems, but nothing I can't handle."

"You can talk to me about it," offered Sarah.

Adele shrugged, slowing her pace. They both settled back into a walk. "I don't think you'd understand."

"Why do you say that?"

"Because, your relationship is so perfect." Adele forced a smile.

Sarah huffed. "Please. I've had my fair share of difficult relationships. Do you remember Jeremy?"

Adele laughed. "Fair point. Okay, well, I've been seeing this man—a colleague. Anyway, he's married —"

"What?" exclaimed Sarah.

"Yeah, I know. But they're separated, they're getting a divorce. At least, that's what he tells me. I'm not in Darwin right now, so it's hard to know what's going on."

"You're in touch with him now?"

She nodded, but with more hesitation. "Mum doesn't know that we're still talking. She thinks I ended things, so please keep it between us."

Sarah sighed. "Okay, it's your life, but I don't think it's a great idea. Mum isn't going to judge you, but she will give you advice. She only wants what's best for you."

"You're right, but I'm not ready for that conversation. I need to figure some things out for myself first."

"What are you trying to decide? Maybe I can help."

Sarah's heart ached for what her sister was going through, but she wanted to be supportive. Still, she couldn't imagine what Adele was thinking—dating a married man? She never would've thought her sister capable of that.

They stopped by a park bench. "Maybe we should sit?" suggested Adele.

Sarah agreed and sat next to her sister to look out over the beach. Seagulls trotted closer hoping for some chips, then took to the air in disappointment.

"Antoine, that's his name. He's French. Anyway, he wants me to come back to Darwin. He's left his wife because she found out about us, and it all blew up. He wants us to give it another chance, says he loves me and can't live without me. But I don't know—I've been there before. When I lived in Darwin, we tried to make it work, but he never followed through on the promises he made to me. In the end, I had to walk away to save my own sanity. I'm in love with him, I know that, but sometimes that's not enough."

Sarah turned to face Adele, tucking one leg up beneath her. "He says he loves you, but he's married."

"Yes, but they're separated."

"Separated is still married."

"But they're working on getting a divorce," said Adele.

"He's not divorced yet, though. Which means he's still committed to his wife."

"And his kids," added Adele.

"He has children?"

"Two," replied Adele, her eyes filling with tears. "It sounds really bad, but it's not like that. We love each other, and he's stuck in a horrible marriage. They aren't good together, but we are."

"Is that what he says?" asked Sarah.

"Yes, of course."

"And Mum knows about all this?"

Adele sighed. "All except the fact that we're still in touch. He has my mobile number, so what am I supposed to do, ignore his messages? Mum told me to block his number, but I haven't decided what to do yet."

"Well, you're still in Emerald Cove after almost a month, so I'm guessing you've got misgivings about the whole thing," said Sarah, gently.

Adele nodded. "I do—I mean, I know I shouldn't be seeing someone who's married. But I didn't know he was married at first, not until after I'd already fallen for him. And he's so unhappy in the marriage."

Sarah rested a hand on Adele's arm. "Oh sweetie, I'm so sorry. Is this why you came back?"

Tears rolled down Adele's cheek as she nodded. "I have to block him. Don't I?"

Sarah nodded. "I think that's wise. You deserve so much better than this. It's not fair on you, or on his family. I'm not sure he's being entirely truthful with you, and anyway, you're too young to be involved in this much drama. How old is this guy?"

"He's in his thirties." Adele sniffled.

"You should be hanging out with people your own age, going to concerts, swimming at the beach, enjoying your life. Instead, you're miserable, moping around the place and mooning over a man whose life is a complete mess. And he wants to get you involved in that mess? I don't think you should have anything more to do with him."

"He's not like that, you haven't met him," replied Adele.

"Maybe, maybe not. I know he'd have to be pretty special for you to fall in love with him. But at the same time, that life he's blowing up—you don't want to be part of that. You deserve more. You should be happy. But you're not. This thing between you isn't making you happy is it?"

Adele agreed. "No, it's not."

"Then, I think you know the answer."

"So, what should I do?"

"Why don't you stay in the Cove? Don't go back to Darwin, block him from calling you and get on with your life."

Adele wiped the tears from her cheeks. "You're right, I know you are. Thanks Sarah."

She embraced her sister. "You're welcome. And you can talk to me anytime. Whatever you decide to do, I'm here for you. I'll support you, but I'll always be truthful with you. Okay?"

Adele nodded. "I know what I have to do. I'm going to stay in the Cove. I love it here, it's home to me. And the thought of going back to Darwin and facing everyone again—it makes my stomach hurt. I love him, but I have to let him go. It's for the best."

"It is. You're making the right choice, Delly."

Adele laughed. "You haven't called me that in years."

"I've missed you," admitted Sarah, tucking a strand of Adele's hair behind her ear.

"Me too. But now I'm staying in the Cove we'll get to see a whole lot more of each other."

CHAPTER 24

CINDY

*T*he moving truck pulled into the long, curving driveway, then parked in front of the house. Cindy watched from an upstairs window, sighed, and wiped the sweat from her brow with the back of her sleeve. It was moving day.

"The truck's here!" she called.

They'd been up most of the night before, finishing packing belongings, knickknacks, memories, and more into boxes. She'd started the process by setting aside some items to go to the dump, others to be donated, and the rest to be packed. But by midnight last night, she was throwing everything she found into boxes and bags, with the decision made that she'd have to sort through them later. Hoping she'd have more energy at that time than she did now.

She was drained to the core.

It'd been a long month, weeks of packing, panic

inducing anxiety, preparations for the wedding. Everything was coming together at once and if she didn't have a nervous breakdown before it was over, she'd consider the whole thing a smashing success.

Adele poked her head through the door. "I'll let them in."

"Thanks, honey," replied Cindy with a wave of her hand. At least she wouldn't have to go down the stairs and back up again. She'd only traipsed up and down them about a hundred times in the past twenty-four hours.

The movers came in and cleared the house of furniture and boxes in the space of about an hour, then they were gone. Athol was waiting at the chalet to let them in and she'd follow shortly. She wanted to make sure everything was done, each item in the house accounted for and not too much of a mess before the cleaners came in to go over the place more thoroughly than she already had.

She headed for the guest bathroom. Cleaning supplies sat in a bucket next to the sink. She reached for gloves, spray and a cloth and began to clean.

Adele returned, dust in her hair, her blonde pony-tail drooping, and her shirt smeared with some kind of mud.

"You look like you've been in the wars," said Cindy, as she wiped down the bathroom counter.

Adele shrugged. "You had me cleaning out the attic. Man, there was a lot of junk up there. But I can't believe how empty and cavernous it is now. It's amazing. This house really is very beautiful. Sarah and Mick are lucky to have it."

"I think so too," replied Cindy. "I'm sorry I don't have another just like it to sell to you."

Adele laughed. "Oh, I don't want it. I've got plans of my own, don't worry, Mum."

"But I do worry about you, you know," replied Cindy with her head cocked to one side as she studied her youngest child. "You seem to be doing better. Are you?"

As much as she wished it was true, she hadn't had the chance to talk much to Adele about what was going on in her life in recent weeks. Between preparing for the wedding, packing for the move, and the fact that Adele was spending more and more of her time working at the cafe, they'd barely seen each other.

"I'm fine, Mum. Really—it's been good for me to spend some time in the Cove. I feel more like myself."

"You're still too thin," replied Cindy.

Adele rolled her eyes. "I'm going over to the other house to help Athol. Will you be long?"

"Not long," replied Cindy, ignoring the eyeroll. "I want to take one last look around the place."

"If you forget anything, I'm sure Sarah will bring it to you."

"I know. But it's never going to be the same again here, and I want a chance to say goodbye."

Adele left in the small, green hatchback she'd bought soon after she returned to the Cove, and Cindy was alone in the big, empty house. She recalled another time almost two decades earlier when she'd seen it this way. She and Andy had bought it after her parents died and left her the cafe. They also left her a small inheritance that the two of them had used as their deposit.

They'd been so excited, and certain they'd never be able to fill all the rooms. But the history of the place, the intricate detailing, and spacious rooms had won them over. It needed a lot of work at the time, which was the reason they'd gotten it for a price they could afford. And they'd done the work gradually over the years, as bit by bit they saved up to furnish each room and make the house over into a more modern version of itself. They'd done their best to keep the historic feel, but by the time they were finished, the house was one of the most regal and stylish old homes in the area. She'd been so proud of it.

She took off the gloves, slung the bucket handle over her arm and wandered from room to room, picking up a stray piece of paper here, or a towel left behind there. Finally, she made it to the kitchen. As she looked around the bright room, her throat tightened. She'd cooked many family meals in this place. Casseroles, stir fries, curries, barbecues, roasts, desserts, and more. So many memories around the long, dining table that was on its way over to the new house. She only hoped it would fit in the new space.

Petal dashed inside from the garden and trotted over to her, toenails tapping on the hardwood floors.

"It's just us, girl," said Cindy, tears muffling her words. "It's hard to believe this is the end of the road."

She bent down to scruff Petal's white fur. "What have you been up to? One last dig in the garden, huh?"

When she straightened, she wiped her eyes with the back of her hand. Gazing through the window at the deck she surveyed the expansive gardens she'd spent so many hours building and maintaining over the years. She couldn't help thinking about the things they'd been through together. Every room had a memory, every garden bed a story about the family she and Andy had grown, more beautiful and wilder than any flowers she'd ever planted in her garden.

"Goodbye house," she whispered.

Then she tucked Petal under her free arm and walked to her car, stroking the dog's coat, and pushing old memories from her thoughts.

* * *

"Mum, where do you want to put the saucepans?" called Adele from the kitchen,

The chalet was buzzing with activity—the movers had carried everything into the house and were gone soon after Cindy arrived. Since then, Sarah and Mick had shown up, as well as Ethan. Adele had already unpacked the linen closet when Cindy got there and was well underway in the kitchen.

The dread she'd felt about unpacking everything they'd spent months putting into boxes was replaced with an excitement that tingled in the pit of her gut every time she stopped to look around. She was in her new house. Soon she'd be married, and Athol would be living here too. She wanted to squeal with delight but decided it might scare the family and would be a little childish. Still, she felt young again just thinking about it.

She strode into the kitchen. Light natural timber cupboards, white-tiled floors, and white walls combined to give the place a warm contemporary feel. She should look for some beach prints to put on the walls, turn the place into a true beach house.

She found Adele holding a large pot over her head. "Let's put the saucepans in this cupboard. I've got so many of them, so we need a good-sized space to store them all. Thankfully, this kitchen is nice and roomy—although nowhere near as big as the one at the house."

Adele grinned. "I hope you got rid of a lot of kitchen stuff, or we're never going to fit it all."

"I did, and some things I left behind for Mick and Sarah. I also left you my Christmas china, since I know you love it so much—it stayed at the house too, since I've got nowhere else to store it. But Sarah knows it's yours."

Adele put away the saucepan and embraced Cindy. "Thanks Mum, I'm glad you didn't get rid of that. It's my favourite."

"I know, honey." Cindy rested a hand on her daughter's shoulder and met her gaze. "While we're alone, there's something else I want to talk to you about."

Adele's eyes narrowed. "Oh?"

"There's been a lot of change happening, but you know I'm also selling the cafe. I've been talking about it for a while, and have gone back and forth over it. But I've got a firm offer from someone and I'm going to take it. The timing is right, the price is right, so I'll be signing the paper-work on Friday."

Adele spun away from her and continued unpacking pots and pans into the open cupboard. "I understand."

Cindy's lips pursed. "Does that upset you, honey? You can tell me."

Adele faced her again, eyes flashing. "Why would it upset me? I only work there. After all, you moved house without consulting me, even though I was living with you. So, why not sell my workplace out from under me too?"

Cindy sighed, reached out to cup her daughter's cheek. "I didn't realise you would feel that way. I thought you were only visiting and would fly back to Darwin soon."

Adele pressed both hands to her face, took a deep breath. "I'm sorry for snapping, Mum. I've been going through a lot, and I shouldn't take it out on you. If you want to sell the cafe, you should. I'm sure I'll find something else to do."

Cindy frowned. "How long are you going to be in town?"

Adele met her gaze, her eyes red-rimmed. "I'm staying permanently."

Cindy gaped. "You are?"

Adele's lips formed a thin line. "I've been talking to Antoine ever since I left Darwin —"

"What?"

"I know what you're going to say, so you don't have to say anything, Mum. It doesn't matter, anyway, because I finally broke things off and told him I don't want to see him or talk to him again. I even called the phone company and blocked his number."

Cindy's nostrils flared. "Was he trying to get you to come back, even though he and his wife are still legally married?"

"Yes," whispered Adele, pain written on her face.

Cindy held in the things she wanted to say. They wouldn't help, and she'd regret hurting Adele more than she was clearly already hurting. But how she wished she could call Antoine and give him a piece of her mind. "I'm glad you've finally taken that step. You'll see, my darling, it's all for the best."

She wrapped an arm around Adele's shoulders and pulled her close to her side.

"I know it is, but it's hard." Adele forced a half-smile onto her face.

"It's not in the best of circumstances, but I'm happy you're staying in the Cove," said Cindy.

Adele nodded. "I called the airline and quit my job yesterday. Then, I cancelled the lease on my unit—I have two weeks to fly up there and pack my things."

A lump formed in Cindy's throat and she fought back the tears. She'd been wanting Adele to move home for years, hated that she lived so far away from them all. Now she'd get her wish.

"Do you want some help?" she asked, giving Adele another hug.

"No, I think I should go alone. I'll be fine, Mum. And besides, you'll be on your honeymoon."

* * *

THE NEXT DAY was the bridal shower and Cindy could hardly haul herself out of bed. The sound of the waves crashing to shore in the distance brought a smile to her face though and she found herself excited about the days ahead, even if every single muscle in her body ached.

"We've got to get up," she mumbled to Petal, who'd snuck onto the bed sometime in the middle of the night. Neither one of them moved. "Ugh. This is too much—what was I thinking planning a move and a wedding so close together?"

At least their wedding would be a low-key affair. She hadn't had to do much, and they'd only invited fifty people—twenty-five from each side. Once they'd added family to the list there wasn't much space left for friends.

A noisy minor chattered outside her bedroom window and was answered by the warble of a magpie.

Already the sun heated the room since she hadn't had a chance to put up curtains. A swathe of sunshine slanted across the floor, only missing her bed by a few centimetres.

As she padded to the bathroom to take a shower, her mind returned to her conversation with Adele. If Adele was staying and wanted to keep working at the cafe, could she really sell it? She'd only decided to let the cafe go because she'd believed there was no one in the family to pass it on to. Her parents had left it to her, and she'd always hoped one of her children might take it on someday. But none of them had shown any interest in it until now.

Still, Adele was a pilot—she had no training in the restaurant business, food preparation or business management. She loved to fly. Would she really give that up to manage a cafe in Emerald Cove long term?

She took her time in the shower, enjoying the feel of the hot water on her back. Then dressed for the party.

An hour later, Athol arrived to drive her to the cafe.

"This is exciting," he said, opening her door for her.

She climbed into the car, grimacing at the pain in her back. "Yes, it is, although I wish I'd left the move until after our honeymoon. I'm not sure I'm gonna make it through."

He laughed. "I know what you mean. I'm hurting in places I didn't know I had today."

The cafe was decorated in gold and cream—bunting, balloons, and streamers. All the handiwork of Adele and Crystal. She walked in to find them each blowing up more balloons.

"Mum, you're here early," said Adele, letting her balloon shrink back to its original size.

"I thought you might need some help. It's a lot for you to take on, with everything else you've got to manage."

Adele grinned. "I'll sleep after it's all over. Can I talk to you in the office for a few minutes, Mum?"

They walked together to the office and Cindy shut the door behind them. She ushered Adele into a seat, then sat at her desk, steepled her hands. "What can I do for you, sweetheart?"

Adele sat up straight, twisted her fingers together in her lap. "I know you said you're going to sell this place. And I understand wanting to do that—the money would give you a chance to enjoy your retirement and I know you're ready to give up standing on your feet for eight hours a day carrying heavy plates and scrubbing burned pans and all of that. But what if there's an alternative?"

Cindy cocked her head to one side. "I'm all ears."

"Let me have the cafe."

"Really? You want to take it over?"

Adele nodded, smiled. "I'm not ready to go back to flying, and maybe I never will be. What I want is to live here and there aren't any pilot jobs going in Emerald Cove. I've looked, and there's really nothing on the entire Gold Coast. Plus, I love working here. I've enjoyed waiting on people and learning in the kitchen —the entire team have welcomed me in and are showing me how everything's done. I could do this. I know I could."

Cindy shuffled around the desk to where Adele sat and took her daughter's hands. Adele stood and they grinned at each other, hand in hand.

"Are you sure you want the cafe? I mean, it's a big commitment. People will rely on you for their incomes, they'll call in sick, and you'll have to cover for them. There's a lot of work involved."

"I know, and I'm ready for it, Mum. I don't want you to give it to me, because I know you were relying on the money to fund your retirement. I'll buy it, that way it'll be mine, and you won't have to worry about it anymore."

Cindy frowned. "I'd happily give it to you. My parents left it to me, and I'd love to hand it over to you."

"But won't you and Athol need the money?"

"We're going to be fine, honey. I want to make sure you have as much of a head start as possible—the cafe business is a tough one. Besides, I've downsized, and Athol is selling his house to move in with me. We'll have everything we need, and plenty left over. So, if I can help you, I will."

Adele threw her arms around Cindy. "Thanks, Mum, I won't let you down."

"I can't tell you how happy this makes me. I've longed for one of you kids to take an interest in the business, to pass it on, but I never thought it would happen. Now—well, I'm thrilled."

CHAPTER 25

VICKY

*T*he frisbee sailed through the air. Vicky leapt for it, caught it between her fingers and held it in the air in victory.

"Got it!"

She threw it to Sarah, who ran for it but missed.

Behind her, the ocean sparkled and swayed under the heat of the sun. Lazy waves curled to shore, and seagulls flocked above them, gliding on the up-current as they searched for the next easy meal with beady black eyes.

Vicky watched as the rest of the group passed the frisbee around, laughing and running, leaping and tumbling on the grass. Ben had invited her to a Flannigan family picnic. Extended relatives had come to town for the wedding, and they were taking every opportunity to spend time together.

Ben came up to her, wrapped his arms around her

and kissed her. She relaxed into the kiss, still pinching herself that this was real. All of it. Ben—handsome, smart, caring, and sweet. He was everything she'd always wanted and more. It was almost too good to be true. Now that he'd overcome whatever reluctance had held him back, he was warm, affectionate, and fun. She hadn't realised how unhappy she'd been until the darkness was pushed away and she stepped into the sunlight.

"I'm glad you came," he whispered into her hair, his arms firm around her waist.

"Me too," she replied, looking up into his deep, brown eyes.

"Hey, did you see on the news, they found the shark — at least they think they did."

She nodded. "I saw they caught a tiger shark. Let's hope it was the same one that attacked you."

He grinned and ran off to chase after the flyaway frisbee and Vicky wandered back to the picnic tables where the rest of the group was congregated. She sat beside Diana and reached for a chip.

"How are you, love?" asked Diana.

She nodded, still chewing. "I'm very well, thanks Di. And you?"

"I'm making it through one day at a time. My leg's still a bit sore." She pointed at her foot, propped up on a small, canvas stool. "And I miss Rupert of course." Her eyes misted over. She sniffed and shook her head. "Did you change, dear? I thought you were wearing jeans earlier."

Vicky glanced down at her red and orange floral print dress. "Um, no. I've been wearing this the whole time."

Diana's eyes narrowed. "No, I'm sure you were in

jeans and that lovely blue top with one shoulder. We chatted for a few minutes, you were telling me about a trip you were planning or something—I couldn't quite understand what you meant. Sometimes my hearing isn't as good as it used to be. Not your fault of course."

Was Diana getting forgetful? Vicky couldn't recall any conversation between the two of them that day. In fact, this was their first interaction other than a wave when Vicky first arrived with Ben. Since then, she'd spoken to Sarah, Cindy, and Adele. But had waited until Diana was free to spend some time with her—she wanted to get to know Ben's birth mother better. They'd been acquaintances for years, but Vicky hadn't ever spent much time with Diana.

"Oh well, I'm not planning on traveling anytime soon. Although I wouldn't mind it—there are so many places I'd love to go. But I guess I've always been waiting to have someone to travel with. Perhaps I should've just gone after university like everyone else did." She chuckled. "But who knows— things could change." She gazed at Ben as he leapt in the air to catch a wayward throw. He was so athletic and strong.

Diana smiled, but the look on her face was vague. Vicky would have to mention the interaction to Ben. He might want to keep an eye on her. Perhaps the stress of everything that'd happened in recent months was getting to her.

Vicky ate a grape, eying the delicious food on the table. Cheeses of various kinds, crackers, smoked salmon and hummus, along with chicken kebabs, salad, and large bowl of fruit salad. Everything was laid out nicely on two tables covered with red and white checked tablecloths. A third, smaller portable table held a bevy of soft drinks, various types of wine, beer and cups. Ethan stood over a nearby barbecue, a spatula poised in his hand and a black apron encouraging people to *"Kiss the Cook"* tied snug around his waist while Cindy and Athol engaged him in conversation.

"Oh, hey, Vicky," said Sarah, coming to sit beside her on the long bench seat beside the picnic table. "What are you doing here? I thought you were going for a swim?"

Vicky frowned. "Uh, no. I've been here the whole time."

"But I saw you heading down to the beach in a red swimsuit about ten minutes ago."

What was going on? Sarah couldn't be suffering from the same thing as Diana. First, she was wearing jeans, now she was in a swimsuit? Were they all losing their minds?

Something jogged in her memory—countless incidents in the past when the exact same thing had happened. In fact, she'd experienced this feeling so many times throughout most of the years of her life that for a time it'd been a normal, everyday reality. People recalling things she'd done that she had no memory of. Others talking about outfits she'd rocked that Vicky had never worn. Heart-dropping moments in front of authority figures as she was accused of crimes she hadn't committed. It was all so long ago, and she'd left those times behind when she moved away to university. She'd almost forgotten what it was like to have a twin sister.

"Hello there, little sis," said a smooth voice behind her.

Vicky jumped to her feet and spun to face her own reflection. Her twin, Susan, stood before her, dressed in a tiny red bikini with a towel wrapped around her waist. She dripped with water from head to toe, her long hair pulled back from her face, her blue eyes squinting.

"Oooohhh," said Sarah, crunching on a carrot stick. "That makes sense now. Hi Susan."

Vicky tipped her head to one side. "What are you doing here, Susie?"

"That's no welcome for your beloved sister. Is it, Vicky? Nice to see you Sarah."

Vicky kissed her sister's cheek. "Sorry, you're right. Hello, Susie, what a nice surprise. What are you doing here?"

"Much better."

"Thanks, I tried."

Susan chuckled. "I thought I'd come and visit my baby sister. Haven't seen you in an age. You didn't even come home for our birthday this year. So, I figured it was up to me."

"I don't know why I always have to remind you that I'm not your baby sister, since I was only born about three minutes after you. But you're right, it has been a while since we connected. I *was* home for Christmas, although I wouldn't be surprised at all if you don't remember that."

Susan's eyes narrowed. "I remember. No need for the little jabs, sis. I come in peace."

"It's good to see you again, Susie," said Sarah. "Would you like a drink?"

Susan's gaze flitted to Sarah's face and her lips widened into a smile. "Sarah Flannigan, you haven't changed a bit. I'd love a drink. You have anything stronger than lemonade?"

* * *

By the time the light faded, and everyone had eaten dinner, Vicky was ready to go home. Susan had drunk more glasses of wine than Vicky had been able to count—especially since they were all gulped from a red plastic cup and she wasn't able to tell if the cup had been topped up or not.

She'd switched from loud, drunken conversations to dancing around the picnic area in her swimsuit to attempting to pick up random surfers passing through on their way back to their cars. At least by then she'd changed back into her jeans and T-shirt.

Still, Vicky was humiliated.

It was her first outing with the Flannigan family, a family Ben was still getting to know, and her sister had to come along and embarrass her and ruin everyone's meal. She still had no idea how her sister even knew about the picnic.

She grabbed Susan by the arm, right as she was about to launch into a rendition of "This Girl is on Fire" and tugged her away from her audience. Nearby streetlights flickered to life, and a mosquito buzzed in Vicky's ear.

"What's your damage, little sis? Ouch, let go!" cried Susan.

Vicky clenched her teeth. "I'm sorry, I didn't mean to hurt you. I only wanted to tell you that Ben and I are heading home."

"Already?" Susan slurred.

"Yes. It's getting dark and soon we won't be able to see to pack everything into the car. Where are you staying tonight?"

Susan swayed on her feet, and Vicky did her best to prop her sister up with the grip on her arm.

"I thought I'd stay with you. Hope that's okay."

Vicky sighed. "That's fine, I figured you'd want to but I thought I'd ask just in case you had other plans. And how did you get here, did you drive?

Susan glanced around the car park behind them. "Um, no. I caught a ride."

"You mean you hitchhiked?"

Susan nodded.

"I've told you a hundred times not to do that. Do you know how dangerous hitchhiking is?" Vicky was certain a vein in her neck was about to explode. There was something about her sister that always brought her to the brink of utter frustration in about five minutes flat.

"Oh come on, I'm fine. You're such a worrier."

"How did you find out where I was tonight?" She crossed her arms over her chest, eyes flashing.

"I ran into some old lady downtown earlier. We were chatting and she thought I was you—reminded me all about the picnic by the beach. Told me to bring swimmers. So, I did." She flashed Vicky a grin. "I mean, it would've been rude not to."

Ben walked over, carrying an esky in one hand. "Are we ready to go?"

Vicky smiled. "Yes, and Susan is coming with us. I hope that's okay."

"Of course," he replied. "Plenty of room in the truck, we'll just have to get friendly."

"Fine with me," replied Susan, sliding her hand into the crook of Ben's arm and walking off with him.

Vicky bit down on her lip then followed along

behind them, hefting Susan's luggage strap over her shoulder as she went.

She sat in silence on the drive home while Susan regaled Ben with tales from their childhood, that inevitably ended with Vicky looking the fool and Susan coming out on top. She swallowed it all without a word, anxious to get Susan out of the truck and away from Ben before he realised she came from a crazy family that he'd want nothing to do with. She couldn't help admiring the skilled way Ben directed the conversation and kept Susan calm, with his steady stream of questions and warm smile.

By the time they arrived at her unit, her nerves were so frayed they were about to snap. She helped Susan from the truck and tugged her luggage from the back to carry upstairs. With the high platform shoes Susan was wearing and the amount of wine she'd consumed, Vicky was amazed her sister could walk at all.

"Thanks for the lift home," she told Ben. "And thanks for the invite. I had a really nice time with your family."

He tucked a hand beneath her upturned chin and kissed her lips. "You're welcome. It was great. And what a surprise, to meet your sister too. I guess it was a day for meeting family members."

Her teeth clenched again—she'd get a sore jaw before the end of her sister's visit; she was certain of it. "Yes it was. I'm sorry."

He quirked an eyebrow. "For what?"

Vicky dipped her head in her sister's direction. Susan was leaned up against the outside wall of the complex, staring at the stars.

He laughed softly. "Nothing to be sorry for. Do you

want me to help you take the bag upstairs?"

She shook her head. "No, that's okay. I can manage it."

"You feeling all right?"

She loved how attentive he was. Ever since she'd told him about her lupus, he always checked on her, made sure she was okay. "I'm fine. Tired, annoyed, but fine."

He chuckled. "Okay, I'll call you tomorrow."

She waved him goodbye, then turned to face her sister who had her arms crossed over her chest and was grinning at Vicky.

"Well, he's nice. Good on ya sis."

Vicky rolled her eyes. "Yes, he is nice. So please don't mess this up for me."

She marched past Susan and into the foyer.

Susan followed her. "I don't know what you're implying, but that's not the sort of thing I'd ever do."

Vicky huffed, but didn't respond.

"And anyway, I've got a man of my own. He's wonderful, and he's waiting for me back in Ballina."

Vicky gave her a side-eye. "Really?"

"Yes, really. We're in love."

"I'm happy for you."

The lift dinged and the doors swished open. Vicky pressed a hand to the side of the door and motioned for Susan to go in.

"After you."

Upstairs, Susan gave herself a tour of the unit then collapsed on the couch with a grunt.

"Nice unit you've got. Very nice."

"Thanks," replied Vicky, suddenly exhausted.

"Must be all that money you make in your fancy vet job."

"It's hardly fancy. I pulled a calf from a cow with my bare hands this morning."

Vicky switched on the kettle to boil, then leaned against the counter, stretching out the tension in her neck by tipping her head slowly from side to side.

"Ugh." Susan shuddered. "You can keep that job. I'll stick to bartending."

"Probably for the best."

"You seem tense, Vicky. What's going on with you?" asked Susan.

Vicky sat beside her sister on the couch and studied her face. "I suppose I am a little tense. The last time we saw each other it didn't go very well. Actually, it ended up with me calling the police on your boyfriend of the time, and you half naked running down the street with them chasing you."

Susan's eyes clouded over, and she looked away.

"I'm glad to see they didn't lock you up for good."

Susan met Vicky's gaze with eyes full of pain. "Don't you ever talk to Dad?"

Vicky sighed. "I do, and he told me you got out, but we don't talk about you often. We only end up arguing if we do."

"Oh."

"I'll get you a mattress and sleeping bag." Vicky stood and turned to go. "I use the second bedroom as an office."

"Hey, thanks for letting me stay," said Susan.

The tone of her voice surprised Vicky. Susan was usually cocky, snide, sneering, or any number of similar descriptions, but very rarely was she sincerely grateful.

"You're welcome." Vicky reached out to squeeze Susan's arm. "It's nice to see you."

CHAPTER 26

BEN

*T*he buzz of the office was a welcome change from the quiet of his home. Ben strode along the corridor, waving in response to greetings from various colleagues he'd gotten to know since he'd started working for *Benchmere Technology*. Two walls of the office structure were made of glass windows with a view over the Brisbane cityscape. Skyscrapers towered on one side, and a long, muddy river curved around the building on the other side, like a thick, brown snake. Ferries and boats zigzagged across it and on the opposite bank, a giant Ferris wheel turned slowly.

"So, as you can see, we've added about a dozen more desks to the web development team. We're growing faster than we can keep up with at the moment."

His supervisor, Brendan Olsen waved a hand in the direction of a set of cubicles pushed up against a long glass wall of windows that looked out across the city from the fourteenth-floor office.

"That's good," replied Ben, blowing on the top of his takeaway coffee cup.

"Come and meet the rest of the programming team. They're in the conference room, we're discussing a new project."

Ben followed him into the conference room, where a dozen programmers sat around a long table, tapping away at laptops as the project manager, a young woman with long blonde hair, spoke from the front. He'd worked with Rita on several projects and found her both competent and friendly.

"…so, we'll have to keep on top of scope creep. Ah, Ben Silver is here. Hi Ben, I hope you've met everyone on the team already. If not, please feel free to introduce yourself to Ben after the meeting, I know he's keen to get to know you all."

Ben waved at the group. "Hi all, good to see you again."

"Are you with us for long this time?" asked Rita.

"Just the day," replied Ben.

Brendan interrupted. "I hate to dash, but I've got to run through some things with Ben. He'll be back to join you shortly."

Rita nodded.

Ben followed Brendan from the room. "I'm not staying? I probably should sit in on that meeting if I'm going to be on the project team."

Brendan smiled. "Let's talk first."

He didn't like the sound of that. He'd had these kinds of conversations before—they usually went along the lines of how he didn't quite fit in the team, or they were heading in a different direction. This job was one of the better ones he'd had in recent years—he liked what the company did, what it stood for, and enjoyed his colleagues. Although he still missed the office environment and often regretted the choice to work from home and the solitude it brought.

In Brendan's office, they sat around a small round table. Brendan crossed one lanky leg over the other then unbuttoned his black suit coat.

He leaned forward. "How are you liking Benchmere?"

"It's great—I'm enjoying the team, the work is challenging. I don't have any complaints."

Brendan grinned. "I'm glad to hear it. Listen, I wanted to talk to you about an opportunity that's come up. We're looking for a project lead in our Melbourne office. Now, I know you only recently moved to…where is it again?"

"Emerald Cove."

"Right, Emerald Cove—Melbourne's a long way from there, and it's a big step to take. So, if you don't want to jump at this opportunity I will understand. But here's the thing—this job would involve leading an entire development team on a massive project we've signed on for with one of the biggest manufacturing firms in the country. I can't say much more about it right now, but it's big. There are a lot of people who want this job but I'm offering it to you. I like what I've seen so far, and from what I can tell, you've never fully tapped into your potential. You've got the skills, the experience, the temperament for management, but you haven't stepped up."

Ben inhaled a deep breath. "Wow. I'm not sure

what to say."

"Don't say anything yet, you should think about it. But can I ask, is there a reason you haven't taken the leap into a management position before now?"

"I don't know exactly. I think I wanted flexibility for a more balanced lifestyle at first."

"And now?"

"Now, I think I'm ready for a new challenge. I'd be open to pursuing a management position, but I'm not sure about the move to Melbourne. I have family here in Brisbane and in Emerald Cove to consider."

Brendan dipped his head in acknowledgement. "Sure, of course. But I have to tell you, we're discontinuing your current role."

Ben blinked. "You're making me redundant?"

"Your role, yes. We're almost finished the current project, and we don't have funding to continue your role into the next."

"Well, thank you for letting me know." He hadn't seen it coming, wasn't expecting to have to be thrown back into the job seeking scene again so soon.

"Of course, if you take the job in Melbourne, we'd get to keep you on board. We don't have any openings in our Brisbane office, and when I found out your role was being made redundant, I looked into the Melbourne opportunity for you. They said I could offer it to you myself, based on my recommendation."

"You really went out on a limb for me, Brendan. I appreciate it."

Brendan leaned back in his chair, linked his fingers together behind his head. "Don't mention it. I didn't want to see you lose your job so soon after starting with us, but I also didn't want to let your talent walk out that door. I wouldn't have recommended you if I didn't believe in you. This is your chance to take your career to the next level, Ben. I suggest you take it."

CHAPTER 27

SARAH

*I*t felt like dust bunnies were residing in her hair. Sarah's nose wrinkled as she braced for a sneeze. No, she could hold it in. She'd spent the morning traipsing through her new home—empty rooms, cavernous ceilings, and plenty of dust in the attic. The cleaners had arrived a few minutes earlier, and she'd let them in since Mum gave her the keys on the day she moved out.

The excitement she felt about her own upcoming move was tempered by a healthy dose of anxiety. In the end, both came together with the same symptoms really—racing heart, adrenal overload, and a light head.

She inhaled a long, slow breath, in an attempt to calm her nerves.

The house was enormous without all her mother's furniture to fill it. Although thankfully, Mum left some pieces behind in the formal lounge, the morning room, and two of the upstairs guest rooms. She didn't have space for the pieces in her new downsized house and Sarah had asked to keep them, since her mother had exquisite taste and the pieces suited the historical feel of the structure perfectly.

Besides, Mick and Sarah barely had enough furniture between them to fill three of the rooms in their new home. The cottage had been a cosy place for them to live as newlyweds, but it was hardly spacious. With two bedrooms—one of which they'd used as an office—a living room, kitchen, and deck, their furniture was modern and minimal. She imagined when they moved their things into the new house, it'd look tragically under-furnished and completely the wrong style. But with the mortgage they'd taken on to purchase the place, it'd be a while before they could redecorate. For now, what they had would have to do.

"Are you coming?" called Mick from the front door.

She glanced around one more time. Then, with another flutter of nerves in her stomach, headed for the door.

"I asked the cleaners to lock up when they leave," she said.

He nodded. "I'll come and check on it later. So, are you happy?" He curled his arms around her waist.

She leaned into him, taking in his manly scent—cut timber and cologne—with a deep sigh. "Very happy. Although I'm going to miss the cottage desperately. I've loved it there so much, I never imagined I'd be moving so soon after we finished the renovation. But still, we can't stay there forever, and I couldn't pass up the opportunity to buy this house. Who knows when or if it'd come up for sale again?"

"We're doing the right thing, my love. This is going to be a great house to raise our family."

"I know. You're right." She kissed him. "It'll be perfect."

* * *

LATER IN THE DAY, back at the cottage, Sarah sat on the floor, her legs crossed, packing photo albums into boxes. Beside her, Oscar lay with his head on the floor, legs outstretched. His nose rested against her thigh. She pressed a hand to his side, and he picked up his head to sniff her hand then returned to his nap.

"Are you gonna be okay moving into town, buddy?"

His tail thumped on the floor with his eyes still shut.

She giggled. "I'm going to take that as a yes. Look, I know this place is your home, and that you lived here long before I arrived. But I really think you should give the new place a chance. It'll grow on you, I promise. There's an enormous garden and plenty of birds, butterflies and even neighbourhood cats to keep you entertained. It's true, you won't be able to wander down to the beach on your own for a walk anymore, but you're getting a bit old for that anyway. Don't you agree?"

Another tail thump.

She scratched gently beneath his chin, his black coat twitching, then shifted to rest her back against the base of an armchair. She was tired. So tired that it physically hurt—like she'd been asleep and had woken mid-dream. Pregnancy was taking its toll on her body in ways she hadn't expected. Her stomach felt constantly as though she'd caught some kind of virus, and she'd pulled a tendon in her leg the last time she went for a run. But the fatigue was the thing that most surprised her—she hadn't expected that in her first trimester. A nap should do the trick. With a grunt, she got to her feet, disturbing Oscar who also lurched to a stand, and padded to the bedroom.

The curtains were pulled wide, so she crossed to the window. One look outside revealed Mick in the yard, fixing a broken paling on the side of the deck. Beyond him, tall sea grasses waved in the breeze. White fluffy clouds hung overhead like balls of cotton. The brilliant blue of the sky made her squint.

Mick was spending his one day off work fixing up everything that needed mending around the cottage in preparation for an open house happening the following weekend. Her heart swelled at the sight of him, bent over, stripped to the waist, his tanned chest and back glistening with sweat in the harsh sunshine.

With a smile, she tugged the curtains shut, blocking out the brilliant light and throwing the room into shadow.

"He's a good man, that Mick. Right, Oscar?"

Oscar's tail wagged in response and he threw himself onto his own bed against the wall with a small sigh.

"You know when it's nap time. You're loving the new schedule, huh, bud?"

She sat on the bed then shuffled beneath the covers and let her eyes drift shut. The phone on the bedside table rang, the jangle jolting her back to wakefulness.

"Hello?"

"Hi, Sarah it's Pauline. How are you? I hope I haven't caught you at a bad time."

Sarah jerked back up to a seated position, her heart pounding. "Oh, hi, Pauline, I'm fine thank you. It's good to hear from you."

"I wanted to talk to you about your manuscript. I've read the draft you sent me, and I love it. It's heartfelt, evocative, and everything we look for in a story. Let's talk about a contract."

Sarah blinked. "Really? Wow. That's great, thanks, Pauline."

"Of course," crooned Pauline. "Look, I know we haven't always seen eye to eye on everything, but I hope you'll understand this is purely about the piece—it's a wonderful story and I don't want to pass it up. This is a great opportunity for you, and as your former employer, Greenmount Publishing would love to partner with you."

A grin turned up the corners of Sarah's mouth, her heart thundering now. "I'd love to see your proposal."

"I'll email it to you and we can talk more then. Okay?"

A lump built in Sarah's throat and she blinked back happy tears. "Thank you. I look forward to it."

"Oh, and one more thing. We're hoping to get the book out before next summer, so we'll want you to do a book tour over the summer months. It'll be a nationwide tour, possibly with some international stops along the way depending on how things work out."

"Ah, okay."

"Great, talk later."

As she hung up the phone, Sarah's elation turned to dread, pooling in the pit of her gut like molten lead. The baby was due in October. If she was to do a book tour over the summer, that mean she'd be traveling when the baby was only two months old. Traveling all over Australia, possibly internationally too, staying in hotel rooms and eating takeaway and sitting for hours on end to smile, answer questions, and sign books. A book tour was no place for a baby. But what could she do? She knew how these things worked—if they wanted to do a book tour, it wouldn't be optional. If she turned down the tour, she could well be turning down the publishing contract and everything that would mean for her family.

She slumped back down on the bed and stared up at the ceiling, her stomach in knots. There was no way she'd be able to get to sleep now.

THE SLAM of a door woke Sarah from her nap. She bolted upright in bed, her heart pounding. After lying awake riddled with anxiety for several minutes, she must've fallen to sleep after all. Footsteps echoed in the hallway, then Mick peered into the bedroom with wide green eyes.

"Oh, sorry—I didn't realise you were sleeping."

She glanced at her watch. It was five o'clock. She'd slept for two hours. She shook her head in an attempt to clear her muddled thoughts. "It's fine, I should get up anyway."

"The railing is fixed," he said, sitting on a chair to remove his socks.

She smiled. "That's great—thanks honey. You're amazing."

"I'm gonna grab a shower. Are you okay? You look a little pale."

"I'm fine," she replied. "Actually, I have some news."

He stood, stretching one arm over his head with a grimace. "Ugh, my arms hurt after all that hammering. What's your news?"

She set her feet on the ground beside the bed. "Pauline called; she wants to buy my book."

He hesitated mid-stretch and grinned. Then, took two steps forward and scooped her up into his arms and squeezing her tight. "That's amazing! I'm so proud of you."

He kissed her and Sarah's anxiety faded, her swirling thoughts stilled under the power of his touch.

"Thanks," she replied.

"I have one thing to say." His eyes sparkled. "I told you so."

She laughed. "You did. But there's one thing I'm a little nervous about. A lot, actually."

He frowned. "What is it?"

"They want me to start a book tour in December and travel around for three months. Possibly even internationally."

His eyes narrowed. "But what about the baby?"

She shrugged. "I don't know. That's what I'm worried about—how would that work? I mean, he or she will be only two months old, I'm not sure the road and crusty hotel rooms are the best place for a newborn."

"What did Pauline say when you told her that?"

Her cheeks flushed with warmth. "I didn't say anything."

"Why not?" he asked.

"I know how these things work. I say, I'm not sure I can do the book tour. They say, I'm not sure we want the book after all."

He shook his head. "Are you certain about that?"

"It's not always set in stone, I mean it's possible they'd let me postpone. But I suppose I didn't want to rock the boat."

Mick kissed her forehead before heading into the bathroom. He called back to her over his shoulder as he shed clothes. "You've got to talk to her about it, honey. The baby is coming, there's no getting around that. Besides, I'd miss you too much if you were both gone for that long."

CHAPTER 28

REBECCA

Cathedral ceilings, a lap pool and a jacuzzi tub, along with ducted air-conditioning and a home gym—the house was everything Rebecca had been hunting for since she first called the real estate agent. With another glance at the grey and natural timber kitchen, she strode to the front door then stood on the front porch waiting. One foot tapped a steady rhythm, she chewed on a fingernail, and finally Franklin's cruiser pulled into the long driveway.

He climbed out, stared up at the imposing house and shut the door with a bang. As he walked to meet her, he emanated the grouchy-mc-grumpface vibe she was used to seeing on him before they got engaged.

With a sigh, she pressed her hands to her hips. He kissed her lightly, then shook his head.

"What's this?"

She shrugged. "This is the one. Don't you think?"

His nostrils flared. "Really? Okay, let's look around."

She showed him the formal living room, the media room, games room and upstairs to the five bedrooms and three bathrooms, along with a rumpus room and study. By the time they'd made it back downstairs to look outside at the sprawling gardens and sparkling pool, his face was red, and she was jittery with nerves.

What was the problem? The house was stunning. If he didn't like it, he could simply say so. But from the dozens of places she'd seen over the past couple of weeks, it was by far the most beautiful and sumptuous. Probably the best luxury house in the Cove—at least the best on the market.

"So, what do you think?" she asked, biting down on another nail. She'd have none left by the end of this if he didn't change his attitude.

He grunted. "It's not really us."

"I love it."

"I don't."

"Okay, what don't you like about it?"

He sighed. "How much is this place, Bec?"

She raised her chin. "I don't want to talk about the price yet. I want to know what you think of it."

"It doesn't matter what I think of it, because I can tell you right now without even knowing how much it costs that we can't afford it."

He spun on his heel and stormed back through the house. She trotted after him, frustration making her bite down on her tongue to keep from saying something she'd regret.

Why did things always have to be on his terms? Why couldn't he listen to her before jumping to conclusions. They could afford it. It was true, he didn't know how much money was coming her way.

The truth was, she wasn't sure exactly what to do with the money she was about to inherit, but a house seemed like a worthy investment. Neither one of them was materialistic—as long as she had a car, gym membership and food on the table she was happy. But they did need a bigger house and one that was truly their own, rather than Franklin's childhood home. This house would be an amazing place to live—a bit like residing in a resort.

She pulled the door shut behind her and flashed an apologetic look at the agent who was waiting at a discrete distance on her request.

"Wait, Franklin, let's talk about it before you storm off."

He faced her, crossing his arms over his chest. His brows were low over his eyes, like thunderclouds. "It's a no from me."

"You can't just say no, and that's that. We're married, which means we're partners. We should make decisions together."

"I'm vetoing this one."

"You can't."

"I can."

She stamped a foot in anger. "Franklin!"

He shook his head. "I'm sorry, Bec. I had no idea you'd want something this grand. I can't give it to you." The anger melted from his features and his hands fell to his sides, curling into fists. "It's not who I am. I thought you knew that."

She stepped forward, raised a hand to cup his cheek. "You're right. I'm sorry. I know this isn't really you. It's not me either, but I thought maybe it could be."

"We made choices in our lives to live a certain way —we gave up the idea of wealth for something more noble: serving the community. I don't regret it. But I'm starting to wonder if you do."

She shook her head, her throat constricting with tears. "No, I don't regret it. It's one of the things I love about you. I feel the same way you do. But there's something about me I've never told you."

Everything inside her fought against revealing her secret to him now. It wasn't right to blindside him in public, but he was angry with her and she couldn't think of another way to explain herself. She hadn't talked to him about her inheritance earlier because she'd been putting off their conversation—she didn't want to talk about her father's death or remind him of his own recent loss. Besides, when she'd shared the news of her inheritance with Jake, it'd changed everything between them. He'd always been controlling, but the idea of her money took his manipulation to another level. She'd seen it in his eyes—he'd decided that he'd never let her go, not with so much at stake. What if the money changed the way Franklin saw her too?

She was uncomfortable with how much she was inheriting—money she'd done nothing to earn, other than through losing someone she'd loved more than anything else in the world. She'd give it all back in a heartbeat if it meant another moment with her Dad.

She knew she had to tell him about it sometime— but she'd been putting it off, hoping to ignore it for a few more weeks to give her a little more time in their honeymoon bubble. They were so happy, so in love. What if this changed everything?

Eaten up with anxiety over the whole thing, she'd convinced herself it would be a fun idea to surprise him by showing him their dream home before revealing that she could buy it for them. So far, her big revelation wasn't exactly going to plan.

He stepped back, eyes wary. "What do you mean? What are you talking about? More secrets, Bec? We discussed this—we were going to be completely honest with each other."

She swallowed. "I know, I should've told you this before, but it's been a bit of a burden. The last person I told was Jake, and it didn't go well for me after that. I've kept it to myself ever since."

His eyes softened. "Go on."

"When my Dad died, he was a bit of a stock whiz. He'd spent a decade or so building up a portfolio of stocks. He bought them all under a family trust that has my sister and me as the beneficiaries. But we couldn't access the funds until we turned thirty. In the time since his death, the stocks have increased in value so much that—well, I'm about to become a millionaire."

His gaped at her. "Are you being serious?"

She nodded, her eyes filling with tears. "Yes, and I'm sorry."

"Sorry that you're going to be rich, or that you didn't tell me."

"Both."

He chuckled and wrapped his arms around her, pulling her close. "You don't have to be sorry for being rich. But I don't know why you wouldn't tell me something like that before you drag me out here to look at an overpriced mansion."

She wiped her eyes with the back of her hand. "It's not overpriced."

"Well, I thought calling it ostentatious would be a bit too harsh, given the fact that you're crying."

She sniffled then blurted. "You're right, it's completely ostentatious."

He laughed and tightened his hold on her. "It's okay, honey. Everything's gonna be fine. But please don't make me live here."

She laughed, play slapping him on the shoulder. "You're such a grouch."

He stepped back, still laughing. "Ouch! Come on, you know I'm right. This place doesn't suit us. I've come around to the idea of buying something bigger, but not this."

She wiped away her tears, mostly from the laughter welling up inside at the thought of her grouchy husband sulking around the gleaming modern mansion behind them and drew a deep breath. "Really? You're happy to move?"

"I'm not sure happy is the right descriptor for what I'm feeling."

She slapped him again.

"Ouch!" he chuckled. "But I'll do it, if you'll stop hitting me."

She sat down on the front steps and patted the space beside her. He sat too, folding his lanky frame to fit on the step.

"Well, if this isn't the type of thing you're interested in, I did see a farmhouse a few days ago that might suit you. It's on five acres, it's an old timber house but has been completely renovated with modern fixtures and decor. And it's got a chook pen, a couple of paddocks where we could put cows or horses, or even goats if that's what we wanted. Would that be more to your taste?"

"How far is it from the station?" he asked.

"About ten minutes."

He nodded slowly. "That sounds pretty good."

"Well, the agent can take us over there now, if you like."

He stood, reached out to take her hand and pulled her to her feet. "Perfect, let's go."

She could tell he loved the place from the moment they pulled into the gravel driveway. The white, two-story house sat in the centre of a green field and was surrounded on one side by a range of tree covered hills and on the other by rolling green pastureland.

Franklin climbed out of his car and beckoned to her as she parked hers beside his. She walked to him with a smile on her face.

"This is beautiful," he said, grinning.

He took her hand and together they walked through the farmhouse. He loved the spacious kitchen overlooking the back garden and chook pen. Raved about the stone fireplace and cosy living room. And the large master bedroom with modern en suite sealed the deal.

He pulled her into his arms and kissed her passionately, then gazed into her eyes, his own sparkling with contentment.

"*This* is the one," he stated.

She grinned with her heart full. "I agree. Let's make an offer."

CHAPTER 29

VICKY

*T*he clock on the wall ticked loudly in the silence. Vicky glanced up at it again and tapped her fingernails on the side table in beat with the clock's hands. She was fuming.

It was half past twelve and she had an appointment at the dentist at that exact time. She reached for her phone, dialled the dentist, and cancelled her appointment. Then, set down the phone and resumed her tapping.

Susan had borrowed her car earlier that morning, with the promise that she'd return it before lunch so that Vicky could make her appointment. But so far there'd been no sign of her, and Vicky's calls had gone directly to voicemail.

With a huff, she stood to her feet, smoothed her pants, and got to work cleaning up the unit. She might as well use her nervous energy for something other than shouting at her sister whenever she deigned to reappear.

There was something about her twin that always brought out her inner schoolmarm. She'd hated it as a teenager, and she hated it even more now that she was an adult. It wasn't who she was, but it reared its ugly head every time Susan was around. Her sister was so irresponsible, she'd taken on the role of being the responsible one for their entire childhood. She couldn't stand the person she became around her sister—always irritated, angry, yelling at Susan over what she'd done wrong or hadn't done right.

This time, she wouldn't do it. She wasn't going to allow her sister's behaviour to turn her into someone she despised. She'd be bigger than that and show Susan how much she'd changed. By the time she'd finished cleaning the unit, the door clicked open and there was Susan, smiling brightly in her ripped cut-off shorts and crop top, her pierced belly button protruding beneath the neon pink fabric.

"Oh, you're back," said Vicky, holding the rest of what she wanted to say inside.

Susan threw her purse on the floor and headed to the refrigerator. She pulled out a soda and chugged it for a few moments before answering.

"Wow, I needed that. I had the craziest day."

"Did you forget my appointment?" asked Vicky.

Susan's eyes narrowed. "Um. Appointment? Oh yeah, that's right. Sorry about that, sis. Time got away from me. We can go now if you like."

"No, it was two hours ago—we've missed it, I'm afraid."

"Okay, never mind. I suppose these things happen."

Vicky tugged her purse from the coat rack by the door. "I'm going to pick up some groceries. Is there anything you need while I'm out?"

Susan took another swig of soda, wiped her mouth with the back of her hand. "I'll come with you. I'd like to get a few things, but it's easier if I tag along. Besides, I haven't seen you all day."

Vicky pushed a smile onto her face. "Of course, that's fine."

Susan reached into the fridge and grabbed a chocolate bar. "Great, let's go."

* * *

VICKY PULLED her car into the car park at the Foodstore. She felt bad about the way she'd been treating her sister, or at least for the things she'd thought about saying but hadn't. Susan was her sister—her twin. They had so many things in common, it was difficult to remember them at times given their many differences, but they did. They both loved to sing, they shared the same laugh. Susan was as much of a softhearted nature lover as she was herself, although she hadn't followed the same career path, choosing instead to become a bar tender after high school and forgo university entirely.

Instead of always judging Susan, she should recall the things that'd drawn them together as children. They'd played together every waking moment of the day back in their youth. They'd been inseparable. It wasn't until they were teenagers that the cracks appeared in their relationship. Susan had been drawn to boys and Vicky wasn't. Susan took up smoking, but Vicky couldn't stand the smell. Susan hated school; Vicky felt challenged to do her best.

But was any of that worth losing a relationship over?

With a deep sigh, Vicky spun in her seat to face Susan. "I'm sorry if I've been a bit testy with you."

Susan's lips pursed. "Thanks, sis. I appreciate it. I'm never sure exactly why you hate me so much."

"I don't hate you."

"It seems like it at times."

"I'm sorry for that too."

Susan nodded. "Okay, I accept your apology."

"Can we start over?" asked Vicky.

"Fine with me."

"Great, let's get some groceries." Vicky felt better already.

She and Susan walked into the shop, chatting together about days past, life in Ballina, what Susan was doing now.

"I'm between jobs," she said. "Stupid manager fired me for drinking on the job. Turns out, that's not allowed even if you're tending bar."

Vicky quirked an eyebrow. "You didn't know that?"

Susan laughed. "Well, I've been doing it for years. No one ever complained until now. That'd be like your boss saying you can't sell animal drugs on the side for a bit of extra cash."

"That's illegal!" cried Vicky.

"Seems unfair to me," muttered Susan. "But what do I know? Hey, look watermelon. Let's get some."

The rest of the shopping trip was fairly uneventful, apart from Susan trying to buy everything she laid eyes on. Vicky began to wonder how long it'd been since her sister ate a decent meal. She stocked up on everything Susan asked for, only objecting when her sister snuck mascara and lipsticks of various colours into the trolley.

"We're not here to shop for makeup. It's past dinner time and I'm tired. It's been a long day. Can we please stay focused?"

Susan pouted, but agreed to put the items back and they headed for the register. When they got there, they found Marg Cook at the only open register. The store was quiet, they were the last customers, most of the doors had been pulled shut and it seemed the staff was waiting for them to finish shopping before closing up for the day.

"I'm sorry we took so long," said Vicky, looking pointedly at her sister.

Marg nodded. "No worries, love. You find everything you need?"

She smiled. "Yes, thanks, Marg."

"This must be your sister I've been hearing so much about."

"That's me," said Susan. "Although I'm fairly certain she'd never admit it if we weren't identical."

All three of them laughed a little awkwardly as Marg continued checking out their groceries. One of the other staff came over to Marg and whispered something in her ear. She nodded, her face growing grim.

"It's so nice to meet you, Susan—just wondering if you put anything in your pockets you want to add to the belt so I can scan it? Maybe something you've forgotten all about?" asked Marg.

Vicky's heart fell into her stomach. This couldn't be happening. Not again. "Susie?"

Susan rolled her eyes. "Oh yeah, that's right. I did forget."

She pulled the mascara and lipsticks from her shorts pockets and tipped them one by one onto the belt. Marg scanned them with a little nod, her lips tight.

"Thanks, love."

Marg packed their purchases into the cloth bags Vicky had brought in with her. Then, Vicky pushed the trolley out to the car, Susan trailing after her. She didn't say a word, simply unloaded the groceries, rage fuelling her silence.

Susan climbed into the car and lit up a cigarette to smoke while she waited. After finishing loading up, Vicky flicked on the radio and turned up the music. The last thing she wanted right now was conversation. She'd vowed not to say something she'd regret while her sister was visiting, and if she spoke now that vow would go right out the window, along with the smoke from Susan's cigarette.

Susan took a drag, as Vicky turned out of the parking lot and headed for home. She glanced at Vicky, then reached for the radio's volume knob, turning it down.

"It was a misunderstanding, Vicky. Don't get all...ragey."

Vicky's nostrils flared. She clenched the steering wheel so hard her knuckles whitened. "I'm not ragey."

"Yes, you are. You're doing that thing where your neck gets covered in red blotches and you hold your breath."

"I am not."

"I know you too well, sis. Come on, it was a mistake. Don't you ever make mistakes?"

Vicky shook her head slowly. "A mistake? You took that makeup. I asked you to put it back, and like a child you shoved it into your pockets. I can't even...I don't know what to say. I'm so angry. Those people are my friends, my community, my neighbours. I have to look them in the eye every day. And you tried to steal from them."

"You should've just bought me the makeup," muttered Susan. "I don't know why it's such a big deal. You're the one pulling in the big bucks."

Vicky turned into her parking garage and pulled the car to a stop before facing her sister. "I'm sorry I make more money than you. I didn't set out to make you feel bad—I only wanted to take care of animals. You could've done anything you wanted to do. You were smart enough, but you chose to be a bartender. That's not my fault. I'm happy to buy you makeup, but all I asked was that it wasn't tonight, as I was tired, hungry, and the shop was trying to close. But you couldn't take no for an answer, could you? You've never been able to take no for an answer."

She ran her fingers through her hair and drew a deep breath. No more, it was too much. She could see her barbs had landed, her sister had that injured look she got when she'd pushed Vicky too far and they argued.

Vicky climbed out of the car and loaded up as many bags as she could in her arms. She headed for the lift, with Susan coming behind her, carrying a few bags too. They rode the lift together in silence then put away the groceries in Vicky's kitchen.

She pulled a ready-made lasagne from one bag and

set it in the oven to heat, while she found a home for the rest of the groceries.

"I'm sorry, okay?" said Susan, suddenly. She leaned against the bench with her arms crossed over her chest.

Vicky folded the empty bags and put them by the door to take back to the car. She slumped onto the couch with a sigh. "I'm sorry too. I shouldn't have said those things."

Susan sat beside her, pressed her hands to her face. "I don't know why I do stuff like that."

Vicky hadn't heard a confession like that from Susan before. "I don't either."

"It's easy for you—everything goes your way. You're good at so many things, people like you, you're successful at whatever you try. It's not like that for me."

Vicky's brow furrowed. "What are you talking about?"

"I don't know how to tell you. Ah, it doesn't matter. The past is the past, there's no point talking about it. Let's get a drink. Shall we?"

Vicky reached for her arm and stopped her before she stood up. "What do you mean? What happened that you don't want to talk about?"

Susan's eyes glistened with unshed tears. "Nothing. Forget it."

"No, I can't forget it. Look, I don't want to upset you but if there's something you want to tell me, I'm here for you okay. I've always wondered, I suppose I knew something was up. When we were kids, you and I were so close. Then suddenly you changed—turned into someone I didn't recognise. Did something happen to you, Susie?"

Susan's head dropped into her hands. She groaned. "Ugh. Yes, of course something happened." She glared at Vicky. "I didn't think you even noticed. The perfect little Miss Vicky."

Vicky ignored the jab. "Susie, tell me."

Susan stood to her feet and paced the length of the living room just as the oven timer dinged. Vicky's heart was racing, her thoughts a whirlwind in her head. There was something on the edge of her consciousness, just out of reach, and even without knowing what it was, she knew that understanding it would change everything between them. But if she pushed Susan too hard, her sister would never say a thing. She had to give her the space to speak.

Vicky found two plates and dished up servings of lasagne onto each. She poured two glasses of mineral water and carried everything to the small, round kitchen table.

"Let's eat," she said.

Susan nodded mutely, sat down with one leg bent up on the chair beside her. She ate great bites of lasagne, staring at the plate with red-rimmed eyes.

Finally, she spoke. "Do you remember when Uncle Des used to come and visit on the weekends?"

Vicky dipped her head. "Of course."

"Didn't you ever wonder why he came over so often?"

Vicky's eyes widened. "Well, no. I guess I thought he was there to see Dad."

Susan's hollow laugh rang out. "Not exactly. He wasn't a good man. I'm glad he's gone."

"Did Uncle Des abuse you, Susie?"

Susan nodded, still staring at her plate, her face a deathly pale hue.

In that moment, Vicky's entire world, and everything she thought was true about her childhood, her sister, and her family, shattered into a million tiny pieces.

CHAPTER 30

BEN

*M*elbourne was a bustling metropolis. Not what Ben was accustomed to, but he found he liked the liveliness and the look of the place. People rushed here and there. There was a cold chill in the air, and he pulled his coat more tightly around his body. He should've packed a scarf and some gloves, although he was fairly certain he didn't own either these days—his old ski clothes were shoved away in some corner of his parents' garage.

With a coffee cup in hand, he caught the lift up to the twentieth floor and stepped out into the modern and very stylish office suite owned by Benchmere Technology. It was all very impressive. Ever since he'd arrived in Melbourne that morning on the breakfast flight from the Gold Coast, he'd been treated like royalty by the Melbourne team.

They'd sent a town car to pick him up at the

airport, provided a fresh breakfast on arrival at the offices, and had an intern squire him from meeting to meeting all morning long. After a lunch at a nearby Mediterranean style restaurant with the team, he'd grabbed a coffee to help him stay awake—his full stomach and the early morning making him blink with sleep.

"Ready for our two-thirty?" asked Richard, the Operations Manager.

Ben offered a quick nod. "Yep, I'm ready. Let's go."

Richard would be his boss if he accepted the Team Leader job in the Melbourne office. And so far, he liked the man. He could imagine working for him. Already he could tell that Richard was a high energy, enthusiastic manager who seemed to be treated with genuine affection by his staff.

They walked down a long hallway together, past teams of software developers and into a small meeting room. Ben sat across from Richard, and they were soon joined by a Project Manager Ben had worked with remotely in the past. Catherine set a large coffee cup on the table, along with a black folder, and crossed one long leg over the other.

"Good to see you, Ben."

He smiled. "You too, Catherine."

"Didn't think we'd ever manage to lure you to the big city and away from that beach lifestyle," she said with a chuckle.

He arched an eyebrow. "I suppose we'll see."

Richard and Catherine laid out for him what the job would entail. He'd already met the teams of developers he'd be working with and had sat in on some of their project meetings that morning. Now, the choice was laid out before him. Move forward with the company in the new role, a promotion, or move on to something else. The decision was his to make.

"So, what do you think?" asked Richard.

Ben drew in a deep breath. "I'd love to take the job."

"Great, welcome to the team." Richard slapped him on the back.

Now he had to tell Vicky and his parents what he'd done. And that included Andy and Diana. He had no idea how any of them would react. He was excited about new beginnings and a chance to finally push himself to reach his potential. The job in Melbourne piqued an interest in him, a passion, he'd not felt in many years. After the shark attack he felt a drive to reach for things in life he'd been too afraid to reach for before. This job was one, and someone to share his life was the other. Still, the idea of leaving the Cove so soon after he'd moved there laced the excitement with a layer of sadness he couldn't shake.

* * *

CINDY

The garden was decorated with twinkle lights, chiffon streamers, and bouquets of fresh flowers. Cindy glanced out of the bedroom window to take it all in. She barely remembered her first wedding. It'd rained that day and she'd been beside herself over it. It had to be perfect, but of course like anything in life, it wasn't. She'd been so nervous she'd believed she might throw up walking down the aisle, and the rest of the day was a blur of hazy memories, anxiety, nausea, and irritation at everything that'd gone wrong.

This time she planned on enjoying every single moment.

It wouldn't be perfect, but it would be filled with love and laughter if she and Athol had their way. And that was more than enough for her.

Athol.

A smile warmed her face as her gaze found him waiting, hands clenched together in front of fifty white folding chairs centred around a lavender carpeted aisle. Behind him, an archway was covered with vines and climbing white flowers—she'd bought the archway and planted the vine a year earlier, and it was perfect for the backdrop to their ceremony.

It was Sarah's house now, her garden too. But Cindy was grateful they could get married there—it meant a lot to her to marry Athol in the gardens she'd dug, planted, weeded, and fertilised with her own bare hands. So much blood, sweat, and plenty of tears had gone into creating the colourful wonderland below.

She stepped away from the window as Sarah walked into the room.

"Oh, wow, Mum, you look beautiful."

Sarah wore a strapless lavender dress that swished around her slender frame as she walked. The look was completed with a simple string of white pearls—a gift Cindy had given both her girls when she asked them to be her bridesmaids.

Adele followed Sarah into the room. Her blonde hair and blue eyes contrasted with Sarah's brown hair and deep brown eyes. But apart from their colouring, the two looked so similar in their lavender dresses it took Cindy's breath away.

"Thanks, honey. The two of you are stunning."

Adele smiled and walked over to kiss Cindy's cheek. "I love that dress on you, Mum."

Cindy wore a fitted dress with matching jacket, both in a shade of cream and tastefully decorated with pearls. She'd skipped the necklace, instead opting for pearl earrings. Her hair was piled on top of her head in a mass of curls, and her fingernails were painted with the same lavender her girls wore.

Adele took Cindy's hand. "So, Mum—are you sure you want to go through with this? Because you know, you don't have to."

Cindy's brow furrowed. "Adele, what?"

Adele laughed. "I'm only kidding, Mum. Athol's great. I wish both of you many years of happiness together."

Cindy chuckled, a hand on her heart. "You gave me a scare. Thanks, honey—I appreciate your kind words."

Sarah sat beside the two of them. "Everything's changing."

Cindy nodded. "True."

"But having Dr Miller—I mean Athol—as part of our family doesn't feel like so much of a change. I've always thought of him that way, to some extent. So, as Adele already said, much happiness to both of you."

Sarah kissed Cindy's cheek too, and the three of them regarded each other wordlessly and with tears in their eyes.

Sarah walked to the window and looked out with her arms folded across her chest. "Well, I suppose we should get going. The seats are full, the string quartet is playing. And it's time."

Cindy swallowed, stood, and smoothed out her dress. She reached for her bouquet of lavender and baby's breath and studied her reflection in Sarah's bedroom mirror. She didn't often take much time to really look at herself these days. When she did, she was always shocked by what she saw—who was the old woman in the mirror? When did those lines appear? Why were her hips so wide? But not today—today she was pleased with her reflection. She looked happy, pretty even. And whose opinion mattered more than her own? So, she should be kinder to herself. She'd learned that the words she spoke to and over herself mattered more than what anyone else said.

You look amazing. You're going to be so happy. This time it will be different.

With a lump in her throat, she offered her reflection a wink.

"Let's go girls."

The ceremony was light-hearted, fun, and full of love and beauty. Sarah and Adele recited poetry. Ethan sang a hymn and accompanied himself on the guitar. Diana conducted the ceremony, with her brand-new license downloaded from the internet. She told jokes, shared stories about the bride and groom, and laughter echoed through the garden.

When Athol and Cindy recited the vows they'd written for each other, the laughter faded, and eyes glistened with tears. Then their friends and family cheered as they were pronounced husband and wife and Athol dipped Cindy to kiss her passionately in front of them all.

She grinned and pumped her bouquet in the air in victory when she was upright again. Together they marched with the rest of the group, chattering and laughing, to another part of the garden where a large, white tent had been set up and filled with tables, chairs and even a dance floor. Wait staff dressed in white, handed around glasses of champagne and hors d'oeuvres and the DJ pumped rock and roll classics through a set of black speakers set strategically around the walls. The sun set behind the house, throwing the garden into darkness, and leaving the twinkle lights sparkling like stars.

They headed for the dance floor, and Andy stopped them. He and Keisha had been invited to the wedding, but Cindy wasn't sure they'd come. Still, she was glad to see them there. Keisha hung back, standing awkwardly on her own by the drinks table, arms crossed over her chest.

"I wanted to congratulate the two of you," said Andy, a warm smile lighting up his face.

Athol grunted in response.

Cindy held out a hand to squeeze Andy's. "Thank you. I'm glad you came."

Andy met Athol's gaze. "Look mate, I'm sorry for the things I said. We were friends for a long time, so it hurt when you cut me off. But I get it—that was my fault. I don't blame you. I lashed out, and I regret it."

Athol sighed. "I was upset, I didn't understand how you could do what you did to your family."

"I hope you can forgive me," replied Andy.

Athol's face relaxed. "I can and I do. Thanks for the apology, Andy. I hope we can put it all behind us."

The two of them shook hands and Andy wandered back to Keisha.

"That was very nice of the two of you," said Cindy. "Maybe someday you can even grow to like each other again."

"Don't push it," said Athol with a wink.

As they danced their first dance to Eric Clapton's

Wonderful Tonight, with Athol's arms around her, Cindy couldn't stop beaming. This was the first day of her new life. No more loneliness or solitude. No more fretting over how she'd pay the bills. No more sitting at home alone wondering where her husband might be or when he'd come home and hiding her worries from her children. No more shame, feeling as though she wasn't good enough or was somehow unlovable. Athol loved her, he was a good man, and together they'd build a life she'd only dreamed of during those long years of pain.

CHAPTER 31

VICKY

*A*s they danced together, Vicky wondered whether Ben had taken lessons. His grip on her was firm, confident. He moved smoothly and easily around the dance floor, taking her with him in a way that left her breathless.

"You're very good at this," she said.

He smiled down at her. "Thanks. My mum was a dancing instructor, so she made sure I learned a few moves. Although, she found me a bit of a disappointing student I'm afraid. I was more interested in riding my bike, swimming, and running than I was dancing."

"Well, you certainly picked up enough to impress me."

He chuckled. "Exactly what I was going for."

They danced another few songs, then, dripping with sweat, Vicky led Ben by the hand back to their table. His name card next to hers made her heart flutter in her chest. She'd never taken a boyfriend to a wedding as her date before. Anytime she'd been invited to a wedding in the past, she'd found herself single and alone by some strange and painful coincidence. But not this time—she was amazed at how much satisfaction it brought her to have his name next to hers above their place settings.

She sat with a huff, her long, black dress too tight to lean forward—instead, she propped herself against the back of the chair and pushed out her legs. It was so hot and since they were outdoors, there was no air conditioning. Humidity sat in the air as though a storm might be headed their way. She took off her silver silk scarf and wrapped it around the top of the chair, giving her neck some respite. Then, she fanned herself with both hands. "Ah, that's better." She drained her glass of water and poured another. "Dancing is tiring."

He laughed. "Wait until I take you mountain climbing."

"Really? I'm up for it. Although, give me a bit of warning so I can get fit before we go."

"You'll need at least six months to prepare for the one I have in mind," he said. "So take this was your warning."

She grinned. "Fine—challenge accepted." He was planning their future six months in advance. Perhaps he felt the same way she did.

The last few times they'd been together, there'd been a simple, but powerful truth that'd attached itself to her thoughts. Her heart felt full. Her emotions were calm. Everything inside her at peace. She was in love.

It'd come on strong, but so stealthily she hadn't

realised it at first. She loved him. It was too soon for her to tell him about this revelation she'd had, of course. Although, she wasn't exactly sure about the rules of dating when it came to declarations of love—since she'd never told a man she loved him before. Truthfully, she'd never been in love until now. It was the first time she'd felt this strong, calm assurance—the confidence of knowing, without any doubt, that she and he were meant to be together for the rest of their lives.

And the knowledge didn't scare her, didn't roil in her gut, didn't make her want to push him away. The truth of her feelings felt strangely alien, yet completely normal, all at the same time.

"It sounds fun but fair warning, I'm not sure how much lupus will impact the likelihood of me climbing mountains with you."

He scratched his chin. "Oh, Good point. I didn't think of that. I've still got a lot to learn about it, I guess. You seem so capable and strong most of the time, I forget that it can limit you."

She shrugged. "It can at times, if it gets out of control. So far, for me, it hasn't been too bad. But it does mean that sometimes I feel under the weather. I may not have the strength or energy to do strenuous activities like climbing mountains. And I really don't know ahead of time if or when the flare-ups will happen."

He smiled. "So, it just means we'll do something else together instead. Something a little easier."

"I don't know, honestly. I haven't really pushed myself since I got my diagnosis. But I'm managing it well at the moment."

"Let's play it by ear then. We don't have to climb

mountains if you'd rather not. I'm happy doing anything with you at all, honestly. Even sitting together watching a movie is fun if you're there with me." He held her hand up to his lips, kissed the back of it.

His lips sent a spark of heat up her arm that set her heart racing. "I feel the same way."

"We haven't talked much about what's happening here, between us," he said, his voice soft, his brown eyes dark with desire.

"Then, let's talk."

He hesitated. "I'm falling for you."

She smiled. "Me too."

He let out a quick breath. "I haven't felt this way before. I can see a future for us, together. In fact, I can't imagine my future without you."

"I can see it too, can imagine it—it's the strangest thing because it doesn't feel strange at all."

He laughed. "Yes! I'm so glad you're on the same page."

"I am. And I'm sorry that I've been a bit crazy lately, with my sister visiting. Susan's been through a lot in her life and she acts out to get attention. I'm only now discovering just how much she's suffered. Anyway, I know she's taken up a lot of my time, and I've been irritable—she brings that out in me."

"I understand—and you've been perfectly fine. At least with me, anyway. I don't have siblings, but I've heard they can really push your buttons if you let them." He combed his hair with his fingers, before leaning back in his chair. "So, how long do you think she'll stay?"

She sighed. "I'm not sure. I haven't broached that particular subject yet. But one thing I've learned about

Susan, is she never stays anywhere very long. She gets itchy feet and moves on pretty quickly. And usually I'm thrilled about that, but this time it's different. She told me something. I can't talk about it yet because it's not my story to tell, but it changes things."

"Well, that's progress."

She nodded. "We stayed up until about two o'clock in the morning talking it through and for the first time in years, I got to see the real person beneath the facade she shows everyone else. The sister I remember from when we were young showed up and had a real discussion with me about her life, everything she's been through, how she feels. It was kind of amazing."

"I'm glad for you—maybe things will be different now."

"I hope so," she said. And she meant it. She hoped, longed for, believed with everything she could muster that things would change. That her sister would be different, their relationship forever altered. That they'd go back to being close and sharing everything the way they used to. It was what she'd wanted for so long, and until now hadn't even realised how much of her heart was holding out for that connection with her twin sibling, but it felt like a vacuum in her soul sucking out the light. She needed her sister in her life —the revelation smacked her in the gut like a mallet.

"Do you think we could go?" she asked, reaching beneath the table for her silver clutch.

He nodded. "Of course."

"I want to see Susan." She tugged her silk scarf from the top of the chair and wound it back in place on her neck. "We need to talk some more. Maybe she could move closer, or we could set up a time to visit each other again. I don't know—it feels urgent for some reason. Like if we don't talk now, she may snap back to wearing that mask again—the obnoxious, irritating, party girl mask that's been such a destructive force in our relationship for so long."

He stood to his feet, reached for her hand. "Then, let's get you home."

* * *

THE UNIT WAS QUIET. The kitchen light was on, but everything else was dark when Vicky walked through the front door. The sheets were still neatly folded in a pile on the spare mattress where she'd left them that morning. Ben followed her inside and shut the door.

"Is Susan sleeping?" he whispered.

She shook her head and walked over to the sofa, sitting down with a grunt. Where was her sister? A quick glance over the side of the couch revealed the empty space where Susan's backpack had been, the carpet still mussed in its shape.

"She's gone."

He arched an eyebrow, sat down beside her. "Oh."

"Her bag isn't here, and she usually sleeps on this couch."

It wasn't unusual, she'd done this kind of thing before. It was her calling card. She hated goodbyes, she'd said whenever Vicky asked her about it. Didn't like the intimacy of a farewell, looking into a person's eyes, knowing that you cared for one another, that you'd miss each other. It was too much for her. But Vicky had hoped she'd changed—that the conversations of the previous evening had opened up the space between them as a kind of safe zone. But apparently, she'd misread the situation, or overestimated her sister —it wouldn't be the first time.

"Back to Ballina, do you think?"

She shrugged. "Who knows."

With a sigh, she stood to her feet then carried her clutch to her bedroom as anger rose up from her gut and travelled through her veins. She opened the clutch, took out her phone and credit cards, along with the twenty she'd stuffed inside it, just in case. In the closet, she pulled down her purse to find her wallet to put everything away.

This was just like Susan, to run away when things got difficult. Don't bother to say goodbye, or thanks for having me, feeding me, caring for me. No, she couldn't spare the energy to do that.

Ben leaned against the closet door. "Wanna talk about it?"

"It's typical, that's all. I don't know why I'm surprised."

It was then the warning bells in her head began to ring.

Something was off. The wallet was already open, the clasp unlatched. She tugged it wider, looked inside and saw it was empty. The five hundred dollars she'd stowed there to pay for her horse-riding lessons was gone.

She slumped onto the bed, heavy-hearted. Nothing had changed. Susan was still the same as she'd always been—underhanded, unreliable, sneaky and a million other awful things Vicky didn't want to allow herself to think because it made her feel dark inside and gave her a pain in her gut.

"She stole my horse-riding money," she said, resignation tinging her voice.

Ben's lips tightened. "I'm sorry. That's horrible."

"She's done it before. But for some reason I thought we'd connected last night and maybe—oh it doesn't matter what I thought. Clearly, I was wrong. Would you like a cup of tea?"

"Tea would be nice. But why don't you sit, and I'll make it?"

She let him lead her back out to the couch and sat while he boiled the kettle. He brought two cups of tea over and set them on the coffee table, then sat beside her and took her hand in his.

"Everything's going to be okay."

"I know," she agreed. "But is Susie?" Her throat clogged with tears. She'd wanted this for her sister—wanted to see her turn her life around, become someone different, someone better, than she had been.

He simply pulled her to him, wrapped her in his arms and kissed the top of her head.

"Dad's been wanting me to move back to Ballina to be closer to him and Susie. But clearly that'd be a mistake. And anyway, now I have you—I don't want to move. In fact, with the way things are, it'd be best for me to live as far away from them as I possibly can."

Ben cleared his throat. "Funny you should mention that."

She straightened, peering at him with narrowed eyes. "Yes?"

His cheeks flushed pink. "I have something I need to talk to you about."

CHAPTER 32

REBECCA

The Tweed Heads police station was bigger than she'd expected it to be. The office space was divided in two sections. She sat in the first—the largest part of the office. Uniformed cops were her colleagues, she was surrounded by them. No one called her Proby, but there was a definite vibe about her being new. No matter, she'd wear them down eventually, it was only a matter of time.

She grinned to herself as she flicked off the computer screen. Then she stood, put her cap on her head, and turned to go, coming face to face with her new partner, Don Allen.

"Oh hey, Don. I'm heading out. I'll see you tomorrow."

He grinned, his long brown moustache twitching. "Sure thing, Bec. Hey, I wanted to tell you—you've been great this week. I can see a lot of potential for you in this office. Keep doing what you're doing. Okay?"

"Thanks, Don. I really appreciate it. There's a lot to learn, but I'm loving it so far."

"Have a good night."

As she walked away, she felt good about her new role. She had a new partner, worked at a new police station, two things she'd dreaded, but in the end, it'd happened quickly. The Tweed Station had been desperate for new staff. They'd asked Franklin if he had anyone who might be interested in a job there and he'd asked her if he should apply. She'd quickly told him she wanted the job, and she'd moved to the new station in less than a week. So far, she was loving it.

Firstly, there were other female officers whom she'd already befriended. There was a gym, with boxing equipment, attached to the station. And there was the opportunity for a promotion if she kept her head down and did what was right.

At first Franklin had objected to the idea of her moving stations—said that he should do it, since he'd been the one to raise the idea in the first place. But she knew he didn't want to move, that he loved being in charge of the station in Emerald Cove. Besides, working in an office fifteen minutes from home wasn't the worst thing in the world.

As she drove home, she found herself looking forward to seeing Franklin. She missed him now that she was working in Tweed Heads, and he seemed to miss her too. And he'd already begun complaining about the man corporate had assigned to him as a proby. A boy really, according to Franklin. She grinned at the memory of his irritated expression when he'd come home and told her about the new recruit that first day. No doubt his reaction was similar to the way he'd felt when she'd waltzed into his office for the first time.

There was a chill in the air when she pulled the car into the carport outside the farmhouse and climbed out. It was dark already, the days were growing shorter, and a cow lowed in the distance. Lights in the farmhouse glowed in the darkness, drawing her in. When she stepped inside, music greeted her, blasting from a speaker in the kitchen. She followed the sound, her brow furrowed. Why would he need to listen to anything so loud?

She found the kitchen deserted, then remembered he didn't know how to turn on the upstairs stereo system. With a laugh, she climbed the stairs and found him getting dressed in their spacious walk-in closet.

She leaned against the door frame with a smile. "Well, hello, husband. Don't you look handsome? What are you getting all dressed up for?"

He spun to face her, a smile lighting up his countenance. Then, he kissed her long and hard, before taking a step back to hold up competing ties.

"Red or blue?"

She nodded at the blue, and he slipped it around his neck. "Tomorrow is your thirtieth birthday, so I'm taking you out tonight to celebrate."

"Oh?"

"Yes, and don't think that's all that I'm doing. Because it's not. But I thought we should celebrate for more than one day, since this is such a big birthday—and really, you're worth celebrating all year long."

She grinned. "Sounds good to me. Where are we going?"

"Surfer's Paradise," he replied. "We're going to eat seafood at Lure Restaurant and Grill."

"Ooooh, I've always wanted to try that place. It's supposed to be divine."

"I know, that's why I booked it a month ago. So, come on—put on something gorgeous and let's get going, because I'm already hungry."

She slipped into an emerald green dress that she knew brought out the brown in her eyes, along with some strappy silver stilettos and a silver jacket. Then, they drove to Surfer's Paradise. It was a long way, but they passed the time by discussing their workdays and laughing together over the rookie mistakes the proby had made in his first week on the job. By the time they got there, Rebecca's stomach was growling, and her head was light.

"Food. Must have food," she muttered, as they sat down in their reserved seats. "I'm so hungry I could eat this menu."

Franklin laughed and waved the waitress over. "Let's start with some bread and dip, plus a bottle of champagne," he said.

"Thank you!" She exclaimed. "My stomach is turning on me."

"You're welcome. I don't want you to eat the menu because it looks a bit chewy and has probably been handled by at least a dozen other people tonight."

She laughed. "Good point."

They ordered the seafood platter with lobster and it came on a three-tiered tray for them to share.

Before they ate, Franklin raised his glass high.

"To my darling wife—thirty years old tomorrow. I'm proud of the police officer you're becoming, but I'm even more impressed with the woman you already are. I love you more than I can ever express and thank God every day that you're in my life."

Her vision blurred with tears as she clinked her glass to his and took a sip of champagne. The bubbles tickled her nose, and his words warmed her heart.

* * *

VICKY

The horse plodded beneath her as Vicky, lost in thought, let the reins fall loose alongside Mindy's long neck. She was riding alone today and was grateful for it. There were things on her mind—things she had to think about, consider, weigh up and figure out. Her thoughts flitted from one subject to the next, unable to land on any one thing in particular for very long.

The only thing that kept repeating as background noise in her mind was a single, heart-stopping sentence.

Ben is moving to Melbourne.

It didn't seem fair. No, that was an understatement —it was completely and utterly unfair. She'd finally found someone she cared about, was in love for the first time in her life, and he was moving away before she'd even had the chance to tell him how she felt. And he'd broken the news with a smile on his face—he was happy about it. He'd been considerate, of course, in the way he'd said it. Had answered her questions and kissed her goodnight—the kiss itself had been mind-blowing. But that only made things all the worse.

What now?

Should she let him walk away without saying a thing? It was a big opportunity for him. A chance to take his career to the next level, and he'd expressed to her openly how much that would mean to him. He'd been more animated about that than he had anything else she'd seen him discuss, perhaps other than his feelings for her. At least she could content herself those were genuine—but if he truly felt for her the way she did for him, how could he leave?

With a sigh, she slumped in the saddle and urged the horse back to the stables. She didn't have the heart to ride any longer. Sadness seeped through her veins, rendering her devoid of energy.

A truck crept along the road to the stables, parked next to hers. It was Ben's.

She frowned—what was he doing here?

With a click of the tongue, she urged the horse into a canter, gathering up the reins as she went. Before long, she was beside Ben's car. He climbed out as she slid down from the horse's back, her feet tingling when they hit the ground.

"Hey," she said, offering him a kiss.

"Hi, I wanted to come and check on you after our conversation." He waited for her to say more.

She shrugged. "Thanks. I'm okay."

"You don't sound okay."

"I'm gonna miss you. That's all."

He pressed his hands to his hips. "Come on, there's somewhere I've been wanting to take you."

* * *

WATER CASCADED down the falls in a steady stream that roared. It pummelled the deep, dark pool below, a haze of droplets peppering the air around her head. She paddled forward, slowly stroking as she gazed up at the falls. It was spectacular. Set against black rocks, with a cave behind the falling water and surrounded by brilliantly green foliage that crept up the rocky cliff faces on either side and disappeared into a dense rainforest at the top.

"This is amazing," she said, her teeth chattering from the cold.

Ben smiled, swam over to her, and wrapped an arm around her. "I thought you'd like it. I stumbled across it when I was four wheeling out here a couple of weeks ago. Doesn't seem like many people visit."

"It's freezing though," she admitted, as goosebumps travelled rapidly across her entire body.

He laughed. "It's a bit cold for swimming. But with a pool like this, who can resist?"

They swam beneath the waterfall, ducking under the hardest hitting part of it, to find themselves facing the cave beyond it. Ben climbed out, bending low to walk into the small space, then sat, wrapping his arms around his legs. Vicky followed, sat beside him, and he shifted to hold her to his side.

They sat that way, watching the back of the waterfall and listening to its roar. Then, when they were too cold to stay any longer, they dove into the water again and swam to shore. Wrapped in towels, they sat on two small folding chairs Ben had in his truck and ate Vegemite and cheese sandwiches. Vicky couldn't remember anything tasting so good. Her lips were numb, her entire body shivered, and yet she was completely content.

The future was unknown, but the present was perfect.

When they'd eaten an apple each, Vicky's shivering finally stopped. She dressed in her jeans and jumper again, then lay with Ben on a picnic rug. She stared at the sky, so blue behind the clouds drifting by. Birds twittered and sang, ducked and dived in the rainforest that crept up to them on all sides. One sounded like a bell, repeating over and over.

"I don't want you to move," she said suddenly.

Ben lifted himself to rest on an elbow and met her gaze. "Okay."

She sat up, hugged her legs close. "I know that's selfish. I'm sorry—but you're not giving us a chance. We could be —" She sighed. How could she explain the way she felt inside? Words failed her.

"I know we could," he said. "Why don't you come with me?"

"What?"

"I'm not saying that as a response—I've been thinking about this and I brought you here to talk about it. Come to Melbourne with me."

She issued an incredulous laugh. "I can't! I have a practice here. We haven't been dating for very long. How can I move to another state, leave everyone I know and care about, leave my business behind, in the hopes that we'll keep seeing each other?"

He rubbed his chin. "Look Vicky, I'm too old to play games."

"You're not that much older than me, Ben. And what games are you talking about?" Irritation laced her words with venom.

He shook his head. "Let me finish—I don't want to play games with you. I want to be honest. I'm not dating you because it's fun, and I enjoy your company, well not only because of that. I'm looking for something serious, someone to spend my life with."

She swallowed and the retort she'd been planning to say stuck in her craw.

"For me, you're it. You're the woman I've been waiting for. I don't want to go to Melbourne without you. I want you to come with me."

"But I'm not going to live with you," she countered. "I'm thirty years old, I want a family."

He nodded. "I want a family too."

"So, what are we saying?" She shifted in place, tucking her legs up beneath her.

He rose on his knees took her face between his hands and met her gaze, his own unwavering. "I'm saying I want to marry you, Vicky Hawkins. I think we should spend the rest of our lives together. I never do anything this quickly — I always think things through, procrastinate and miss the moment. But I almost died. I thought I was going to die when I was swimming back to shore, blood everywhere. And something inside me changed. I realised that life isn't guaranteed — things can change in a single moment. You've got to speak up, to say the things you want to say, to reach for the things you want. And I want you in my life. I want to spend my days with you by my side. Will you marry me?"

Joy rushed into her heart, and a grin tickled her mouth. This was crazy. They'd only known each other a few months and had been dating for an even shorter time. It didn't make any sense. No one got engaged after such a brief period of time together. She'd never come close to being engaged before, even though she'd dated a few men for two or three years each. But she'd never felt for them the way she did for Ben. Panic rushed up her throat and she pushed it back down again—he was the man she would marry, whether now or in a year. Why should they wait when they both knew it was true?

She nodded. "Yes."

He kissed her, his lips exploring hers as the emotion of the moment overwhelmed her, pounding in her head, and pulsating through her body. When he pulled away, they both laughed—unbelieving but elated.

"We're really doing this?" she asked, with a shake of her head.

"No looking back," he said, and kissed her again.

CHAPTER 33

SARAH

*O*scar trotted down the beach, his black coat wet halfway up as he searched for the tennis ball. He wasn't as fast as he had been; arthritis seemed to be sneaking into his bones. Sarah sat down on the beach towel and reached for the sunscreen. She slathered it over her face and neck, then pulled her half-shucked wetsuit up over her arms and zipped it in place.

Mick trotted over to her, dripping wet, with his surfboard tucked beneath one arm. "Going for a surf?"

She nodded. "It looks good out there."

"Bit of a rip on the north end of the beach," he replied, pushing the end of his board into the wet sand and dropping down beside her.

"Okay, I'll keep that in mind."

"Hey, when do you think you should stop?" he asked.

She frowned. "Stop what?"

"Surfing. Are you supposed to keep surfing when you're pregnant?"

She bit back a retort. Why was it that everything she loved was suddenly off limits now she was carrying a child? No more soft cheeses, or sushi, no more scuba diving, and now surfing too?

"Um, I hadn't thought about it. I suppose I'll probably have to stop sometime."

"Because we had that scare, so I'm concerned. That's all."

She sighed. "You're right—I've been winded plenty of times while surfing, taken a few tumbles and hit the reef more than once. I'm sure it's too risky for the baby."

"And for you," he added.

She nodded. "Okay, I'll stop. But maybe after today."

He chuckled. "After today, then."

She stood to her feet, picked up her board. "See you after."

The water was cold, but not as cold as the air around her. She duck-dived beneath a set of waves and paddled out beyond the break. Then she sat on the board to watch the waves roll in with Emerald Cove as a backdrop. The town looked quaint and inviting from where she sat—she couldn't believe she'd ever found it stifling and antiquated.

They'd moved into the new house. It was big, and as she'd expected, their furniture barely warmed the place up—still, they'd decided to live only in a few rooms for now until they could afford to buy more furniture. She'd even suggested trawling through weekend garage sales to see what she could find—

something she'd never done before since she wasn't the shopping type. But desperate times and all that.

The cottage still hadn't sold. In fairness, it hadn't been listed on the market long either, and the agent had warned them that a small cottage so far outside the town limits might take a while to move. That'd sent her into a minor panic attack since they'd already overextended themselves on the mortgage for the new place. But Mick had assured her they'd be fine, they'd figure it out.

So, when her advance for the book arrived the day before, she'd danced around the house with her hands in the air, squealing with delight. They'd decided that morning, instead of putting it right onto the mortgage, that they'd keep it to help with living expenses while the baby was small. Otherwise, she'd have to find a job and it was slim pickings in the Cove. Besides, she already had an idea for her second book, and this would give her the opportunity to write it.

She'd also had a conversation with Pauline, who'd agreed to postpone the book tour without too much pleading. So, today Sarah was feeling good—all her anxiety had turned out to be baseless, which Mick had taken great delight in pointing out. And now she could relax, write, and shop at garage sales while she waited for the baby to arrive. Today was a good day, and she planned on enjoying every moment of her last surf for many months. She leaned forward on the board and paddled.

CHAPTER 34

VICKY

The courthouse steps were lined with friends and family. The only ones who'd come inside to witness the wedding ceremony were Ben's parents, Vicky's dad, and Susan. She'd been disappointed not to have a big church wedding so that Sarah and Meg could be bridesmaids too, but her disappointment faded as soon as she and Ben recited their vows to one another.

They were driving straight to the airport to leave for Melbourne. Their things had already been packed in a moving truck the day before and were well on their way. The engagement had been a whirlwind of preparations, packing, phone calls, and goodbyes.

Vicky had found another vet who willingly purchased her practice from her, so she'd had nothing else to do other than prepare for the wedding and the move.

She and Ben walked slowly along the line of well-wishers. She hugged, kissed cheeks, cried, and said farewell to each and every person who was important in her life.

"Goodbye, honey," said Sarah, her eyes gleaming.

Vicky embraced her, feeling emotion welling up from within. "I'm gonna miss you."

"Me too."

"I'll call you the moment I get there," said Vicky.

Sarah dabbed at her eyes with a handkerchief. "You'd better."

Meg was next. She held up Amari for Vicky to kiss, then embraced Vicky herself. "Take care, okay?"

Vicky nodded. "I will."

"This is very romantic," whispered Meg with a wink. "Good for you."

Vicky chuckled. "I think so too."

They both hugged Diana goodbye. The older woman shook her head. "I'd hoped you'd stay longer."

Ben smiled. "I'll visit, I promise."

"Good," replied Diana.

She cupped his cheek with her hand, then patted it gently. "Call me when you get there."

Ben's parents were next, and he spent several minutes telling them farewell. Vicky waited patiently, kissed their cheeks too when he was done. She knew how much they meant to him, and how he'd dreaded telling them goodbye. She squeezed his arm as they moved on.

Her father stood, hat in hand, his comb-over floating in the breeze above his balding pate. "Safe travels," he said brusquely as she hugged him goodbye.

Finally, she stopped in front of Susan, who met her gaze with glistening eyes. "Hey, sis, congratulations."

Vicky nodded. "Thanks Susie."

"Listen, I'm sorry," she began.

"I know."

"No, let me finish—I'm sorry for all the ways I've mistreated you over the years. You've been nothing but a good sister to me. I wanted to be different, truly I did. And after our conversation—well, I couldn't stand the way you'd looked at me. You pitied me, and I'd always fancied myself the strong sister, the one you looked up to. But then—well, I ran. Which isn't new, I know that. But I'm apologising because I've made a decision—I'm not running anymore. And I've been sober for a week. It's not much, but it's a start."

Vicky's eyes filled with tears and she hugged Susie hard. "I'm so proud of you. Thank you for trusting me enough to share those parts of yourself with me. I know it must've been difficult. And we'll talk more, I promise. All the time if you want."

"I only wish I'd figured this out before you moved halfway across the country," sniffled Susan.

Vicky laughed. "You'll just have to visit. And I will too."

They climbed into a waiting town car, and as it pulled away from the curb, Vicky turned in her seat to wave goodbye through the back window. Tears fell down her cheeks, dripping from her chin as she sobbed openly.

Ben sat quietly, reached for her hand, and squeezed it as she returned to her seat.

"I can't believe we're leaving, just like that."

He nodded. "I know. It feels very odd."

"But I'm glad you're with me."

"Always and forever," he said with a smile, before he kissed her.

CHAPTER 34

She sank into his arms, her heart full, tear stains on her dress.

THE END

ALSO BY LILLY MIRREN

THE WARATAH INN SERIES

The Waratah Inn

Wrested back to Cabarita Beach by her grandmother's sudden death, Kate Summer discovers a mystery buried in the past that changes everything.

One Summer in Italy

Reeda leaves the Waratah Inn and returns to Sydney, her husband, and her thriving interior design business, only to find her marriage in tatters. She's lost sight of what she wants in life and can't recognise the person she's become.

The Summer Sisters

Set against the golden sands and crystal clear waters of Cabarita Beach three sisters inherit an inn and discover a mystery about their grandmother's past that changes everything they thought they knew about their family...

Christmas at The Waratah Inn

Liz Cranwell is divorced and alone at Christmas. When her friends convince her to holiday at The Waratah Inn, she's dreading her first Christmas on her own. Instead she discovers that strangers can be the balm to heal the wounds of a lonely heart in this heart-warming Christmas story.

EMERALD COVE SERIES

Cottage on Oceanview Lane

When a renowned book editor returns to her roots, she rediscovers her strength & her passion in this heartwarming novel.

Seaside Manor Bed & Breakfast

The Seaside Manor Bed and Breakfast has been an institution in Emerald Cove for as long as anyone can remember. But things are changing and Diana is nervous about what the future might hold for her and her husband, not to mention the historic business.

Bungalow on Pelican Way

Moving to the Cove gave Rebecca De Vries a place to hide from her abusive ex. Now that he's in jail, she can get back to living her life as a police officer in her adopted hometown working alongside her intractable but very attractive boss, Franklin.

Chalet on Cliffside Drive

At forty-four years of age, Ben Silver thought he'd never find love. When he moves to Emerald Cove, he does it to support his birth mother, Diana, after her husband's sudden death. But then he meets Vicky.

Christmas in Emerald Cove

The Flannigan family has been through a lot together. They've grown and changed over the years and now have a blended and extended family that doesn't always see eye to eye. But this Christmas they'll learn that love can overcome all of the pain and differences of the past in this inspiring Christmas tale.

HOME SWEET HOME SERIES

Home Sweet Home

Trina is starting over after a painful separation from her husband of almost twenty years. Grief and loss force her to return to her hometown where she has to deal with all of the things she left behind to rebuild her life, piece by piece; a hometown she hasn't visited since high school graduation.

No Place Like Home

Lisa never thought she'd leave her high-profile finance job in the city to work in a small-town bakery. She also never expected to still be single in her forties.

GLOSSARY OF TERMS

Dear reader,

Since this book is set in Australia there may be some terms you're not familiar with. I've included them below to help you out! I hope they didn't trip you up too much.

Cheers, Lilly xo

Terms

Boot - trunk of a car.

Capsicum - bell pepper.

Chook pen - chicken coop.

Fella - slang for fellow.

"Good onya" - A term used to express a job well done. Slang for "Thanks" or any other gratitude. Can also be used sarcastically to mean, 'you idiot'.

"In the wars" - when someone is hurt or injured repeatedly. Used mostly to describe a series of minor injuries.

Kelpie - The Australian Kelpie, or simply Kelpie, is

an Australian sheep dog successful at mustering and droving with little or no guidance. Some say it is part dingo.

Lift - elevator

Unit - apartment

Loo - toilet.

Moisturiser - lotion.

Nappies - diapers.

Panadol - also known as acetaminophen, is a medication used to treat pain and fever.

Prawn chips - shrimp crackers that are served with Chinese food.

Pressie - slang for present or gift.

Schoolmarm - a person who exhibits characteristics attributed to schoolteachers (such as strict adherence to arbitrary rules)

Sunscreen - sun cream.

Zucchini - green squash.

ABOUT THE AUTHOR

Lilly Mirren is a USA Today Bestselling author. She lives in Brisbane, Australia with her husband and three children.

She always dreamed of being a writer and is now living that dream. When she's not writing, she's taxiing her children to various after school activities, visiting her parents at the beach, or drinking coffee with friends.

Her books combine heartwarming storylines with achingly realistic characters readers can't get enough of. Her debut series, The Waratah Inn, set in the delightful Cabarita Beach, hit the USA Today Bestseller list and since then, has touched the hearts of hundreds of thousands of readers across the globe.

Follow Lilly:

Website: www.lillymirren.com
Facebook: https://www.
facebook.com/authorlillymirren/
Twitter: https://twitter.com/lilly_mirren

BookBub: https://www.bookbub.com/authors/lilly-mirren

Instagram: https://www.instagram.com/lilly_mirren/

Binge Books: https://bingebooks.com/author/lilly-mirren